"Joe M

my all-time favorites of the genre. It hits the ground running and never lets up. *Apocalypse of the Dead* proves that Joe is far from being a one-hit wonder. This book is meatier, juicier, bloodier, and even more compelling . . . and it also NEVER LETS UP. From page one to the stunning climax this book is a rollercoaster ride of action, violence, and zombie horror. McKinney understands the genre and relies on its strongest conventions while at the sarne time adding new twists that make this book a thoroughly enjoyable read. That's a defining characteristic of Joe's work: the pace is so relentless that you feel like it's you, and not the character, who is running for his life from a horde of flesh-hungry monsters.

"And, even with that lightning-fast pace, McKinney manages to flesh the characters out so that they're real, and infuse the book with compassion and heartbreak over this vast, shared catastrophe.

"This book earns its place in any serious library of living-dead fiction."

—Jonathan Maberry, *New York Times* best-selling author of *The Wolfman*

"*Dead City* is much more than just another zombie novel. It's got heart and humanity—a merciless, fast-paced, and genuinely scary read that will leave you absolutely breathless. Highly recommended!"

—Brian Keene

"The pace never lets up as McKinney takes us through the zombie apocalypse in real time—every second of terror is explored in depth as the world goes to hell."
—David Wellington, author of *Monster Island*

"*Dead City* is an absolute must-read for zombie lovers, but McKinney's excellent storytelling makes it a great read for anyone who loves the thrill of a gruesomely delicious page-turner."
—Fran Friel, Bram Stoker Award–nominated author of *Mama's Boy and Other Dark Tales*

"*Dead City* is a zombie tour de force—the story moves along at breakneck speed and never lets up. Joe McKinney knows how to toy with readers' emotions, masterfully capturing the essence of humanity in the face of unspeakable horror."
—Amy Grech, author of *Apple of My Eye* and *Blanket of White*

"Joe McKinney's *Dead City* is a tense, thrill-a-page nightmare, written with great passion and authority. Surely one of the best zombie novels ever set down in blood."
—Lisa Morton, two-time Bram Stoker Award–winner

"*Dead City* wastes no time jumping straight into mile-a-minute thrills and gruesome action. This seminal zombie novel culminates in a heart-wrenching finale, and I found that as the undead hordes multiplied, so too did my respect and admiration for author Joe McKinney. If you like your thrillers served with an extra helping of intensity, you're going to love *Dead City*!"
—Joel A. Sutherland, Bram Stoker Award–nominated author of *Frozen Blood*

"*Dead City* is an action packed, pedal-to-the-metal zombie novel that never loses sight of its humanity. McKinney uses his background as a homicide detective to bring a level of realism to his vision of the apocalypse that is both urgent and frightening. A timely nightmare that you will not put down. I can't wait to see where this series leads."
—Gregory Lamberson, author of *Personal Demons* and *Johnny Gruesome*

"McKinney writes zombies like he's been gunning them down all of his life."
—Weston Ochse, Author of *Empire of Salt*

"*Dead City* is a full-throttle page burner that torques up the terror and does not let up. You'll want the shotgun seat for this wild ride. Bring a crash helmet."
—J. L. Comeau, Countgore.com

"Welcome to Joe McKinney's *Dead City* universe, a relentless thrill ride where real characters do bloody things on nightmare streets. Break out the popcorn, you're in for a real treat."
—Harry Shannon, author of *Dead and Gone*

"*Dead City* is a well-written and compelling first novel. A scary, fast-paced ride, full of hair-raising twists and turns that keep the reader spellbound. Do yourself a favor and snag a copy . . . thank me later."
—Gene O'Neill, author of *Taste of Tenderloin* and *Deathflash*

"Fast-paced, entertaining . . . five headshots out of five."
—D. L. Snell, coauthor of *Demon Days*

"A fantastic tale of survival horror that starts with a bang and never lets up."
—Zombiehub.com

"McKinney continues to lead the genre of zombie fiction."
—Craig DiLouie, author of *The Infection*

"*Mutated* delivers pulse-pounding action with precision, intelligence, and most importantly, heart. McKinney proves once again that he understands the power of the zombie subgenre better than any other writer."
—Peter Giglio, author of *Anon* and co-author of *The Dark*

THE DEAD WON'T DIE

A DEADLANDS NOVEL

JOE McKINNEY

PINNACLE BOOKS
Kensington Publishing Corp.
www.kensingtonbooks.com

PINNACLE BOOKS are published by

Kensington Publishing Corp.
119 West 40th Street
New York, NY 10018

ISBN-13: 978-0-7860-3399-7
ISBN-10: 0-7860-3399-1

First printing: October 2015

10 9 8 7 6 5 4 3 2 1

Printed in the United States of America

First electronic edition: October 2015

ISBN-13: 978-0-7860-3400-0
ISBN-10: 0-7860-3400-9

THE DEAD WON'T DIE

Prologue

Chelsea leaned over the side of the building and watched as the dead fell on her brother. They started to feed immediately, tearing him to pieces, fighting like dogs over every scrap of flesh they pulled from him.

Jacob stood next to her. He was exhausted. So many people had died, and he just couldn't watch anymore. He turned away, and focused instead on the young girl's back. Her chest was hitching with sobs. Part of him wanted to tell her that her brother wasn't worth the tears, but he held the words back. Chris Walker had betrayed them, tried to kill them, but he was still Chelsea's blood brother, and that counted for something. Even out here, surrounded by the dead, blood was blood.

Even bad blood.

"Jacob," said Kelly, from behind.

From her tone he knew something was wrong even before he turned around.

Casey was standing there by the ladder.

His face was blackened and blistered from the burn

he'd taken when the aerofluyt exploded, and most of his hair was missing. He'd been shot in the leg and twice in the left arm, and yet it didn't seem to slow him down. He had Sheriff Taylor's gun pointed at Kelly's ear. He took the weapon from her hand and pushed her toward Jacob and Chelsea.

"Get on your knees," he said.

"Kiss my ass," Jacob said.

Casey tossed Kelly's gun behind him, then quickly stripped the magazine from the M4 and slammed in a new one. Jacob could see the white smiley face on the bottom of the magazine as Casey charged the bolt and brought up the rifle to center it on Jacob's head.

Taylor's little surprise, Jacob thought, remembering what he'd said about the magazine with the smiley face. Good God, please work. Please, please, please.

"Get on your knees," Casey repeated.

"No way," Jacob told him. "Shoot, if you're gonna do it. But I won't die on my knees."

"You'll go to your knees one way or the other," Casey said. He lowered the muzzle so that it was pointed at Jacob's legs and pulled the trigger.

The weapon exploded in his face.

Screaming in rage and pain, Casey threw the gun to the ground. He lurched to one side, holding his bleeding face in his hands.

Jacob saw the gun Casey had taken from Kelly and ran toward it. He almost had it when Casey tackled him.

Both men went over the side of the building, and Jacob landed hard on his left arm. He felt it break. The pain was so intense he nearly blacked out. Casey was already on his feet. The man was a tank. He roared and lashed out, half-blind, but still managed to land a crushing haymaker across Jacob's chin. Jacob's legs wobbled beneath him, but he didn't fall. He took a few steps back and turned his hurt arm away from Casey.

Still bellowing in rage, Casey charged him again, wrapping his arms around Jacob as he dragged him to the ground. Attracted by the noise, more zombies closed in around them. Casey got on top of Jacob and twisted his broken arm. Jacob screamed and his vision went purple. When he opened his eyes again, Casey had flipped him over. He was holding Jacob by the hair and he had his legs pinned so he couldn't move. There were three zombies coming toward them, and Casey was holding him still for them.

"Which one of them do you think will take the first bite?" Casey whispered in Jacob's ear.

Jacob thrashed, but couldn't break Casey's hold. He tried to lash out with his right arm, but Casey was just out of reach.

"I listened to all that bullshit you said about your Code, and you know what? For a little bit there, I was impressed. But it's all bullshit, isn't it? Every word. What kind of code allows you to let a pregnant woman die? Can you answer me that?"

The zombies were just a few feet away, closing fast. Jacob struggled, but couldn't get free.

"You ain't got an answer? You gonna go to your death without an answer?"

Jacob lashed out. He tried to push his way to his feet, but Casey leaned forward and held him down.

"I'm gonna watch you die, Jacob. And I'm gonna enjoy watching every step your dead hypocrite ass takes as you walk this earth. Get ready to die, asshole."

A gun went off somewhere to Jacob's right. Casey lurched to one side with a loud grunt. Jacob jumped to his feet, ducked his shoulder, and ran into the zombies that were closing on him. Before any of them could react, he knocked them to the ground, then wheeled around and found Casey climbing to his feet.

Jacob swung at his chin. Casey's snapped back. Jacob swung again and again. Casey tried to raise his arms to block the hail of punches Jacob threw at him, but Jacob overpowered him, and eventually Casey sank to his knees.

"Look who's on their knees now, motherfucker," he roared.

Casey looked up at him. His face was a ruined mess, his eyes nearly swollen shut. Jacob glanced up at Kelly and nodded.

She fired twice, hitting Casey in the chest.

The man shook with the impact, and then collapsed to the ground. Jacob stared down at the dead man, and he could feel the anger and the hate and all the rest of it draining away, leaving only emptiness in its place.

"Jacob," Kelly shouted. "Behind you!"

The zombies had regrouped. They circled around him, fifty of them at least. "Throw me the gun," he said.

She tossed it at his feet.

With his left arm useless, Jacob scooped it and started firing one-handed. He needed to clear a hole to the ladder so he could get back on the roof, but every time he hit one, three more took its place. Firing one-handed wasn't working very well, and he was only landing headshots every third or fourth shot.

And he was almost out of ammunition.

"Behind you!" Kelly shouted.

Jacob wheeled around just in time to see a zombie's

head get blasted into a red mist. When the body fell to the ground, Jacob saw three of the gray space suits he'd seen back in the aerofluyt's cargo bay. The three figures made the same hydraulic sound as they moved, yet they were far more coordinated than the one he'd faced on the aerofluyt. These moved with purpose, their movements powerful but precisely controlled.

The figures spread out, their suits clanking and sighing as they brought up strange-looking weapons. They fired at the zombies, but their weapons made no noise. They pointed, shot, and another head would explode. In a few quick seconds they'd cleared most of the field, leaving dozens of headless corpses on the ground at Jacob's feet.

One of the figures advanced on Jacob, and he raised his rifle.

"Jacob, no!" he heard Chelsea shout.

The suited figure caught the rifle and turned it away. There was so much power in his grip. The figure pulled the gun out of Jacob's hand as easily as if Jacob had given it to him.

The figure seemed to study Jacob's clothes. He examined the shirt and shoes Jacob had gotten from Chelsea's father's closet, and then raised what looked like a white microphone with two small wings up near the head. He ran the device up and down Jacob's right arm. A little green light blinked on it, but it didn't make a sound.

"Wait!" Chelsea yelled.

Jacob glanced over his shoulder and saw Chelsea and Kelly climbing down from the ladder. They ran toward Jacob.

The figure released him and turned to face the girls.

Kelly stopped short, but Chelsea walked right up to the figure in the space suit. "I'm Chelsea Walker," she said. "Are you Templenauts?"

The helmets and high protective collars of the space suits made it hard to see the men inside the suits, but Jacob could recognize their surprise. The three suited figures glanced at one another. Chelsea stuck out her right arm. The figure with the microphone-type device ran it over Chelsea's arm, and right away the thing beeped and the light began flashing faster.

The figures glanced at each other again, and the one with the microphone twisted his helmet off. He was an older black man with a gray beard and a dense network of lines at the corners of his eyes. He had earphones in his ears and some kind of flat black electronic device secured to the side of his throat.

"You're from the *Darwin*, aren't you?" the man asked.

"Yes," Chelsea said. "Yes, that's right."

"Are there any other survivors?' the man asked.

"No," Chelsea said, after what seemed to Jacob to be a thoughtful, measured pause. "No, I'm the only one."

"I'm Lester Brooks, from the *Faraday*. We saw the explosion. We've been surveying this area ever since, trying to determine the degree of environmental impact. It's lucky for you the wind was blowing south during the explosion. If it had been blowing north, we'd be up in Jacksonville instead of down here. We'd have never found you."

"I'm glad you did," she said.

"I bet. It's been a long time, Chelsea. Are you ready to go home?"

"Yes," she said. "More than you could ever imagine."

"Who are your friends?"

Again that thoughtful, measured pause before she answered. "That's Kelly Banis, and that's Jacob Carlton. They're from Arbella."

"Arbella?" Brooks asked. He looked to Kelly, and then to Jacob.

Jacob was in so much pain he could barely stand. He tried to speak, but managed only to mutter.

Kelly said, "It's on the maps as New Madrid."

"Ah," Brooks said. "Yes. Yours is a very successful community. We've been watching you."

"You have?"

"Yes, for several years now. Yours is one of about twenty successful outposts east of the Rocky Mountains, and one of the largest."

"Twenty others?" Kelly asked, stunned.

"Twenty-two, actually," Brooks said. "Most are smaller than Arbella."

"You say you've been watching us? Why haven't you made contact with us? With all the things you can do, we could have learned so much from you."

"You still can, now that you've contacted us. That's our way, Kelly. Our law. We don't force ourselves on others, but once another society reaches out to us, we offer what we know freely. If you and your friend want to come with us, we will share all we know with you."

For Jacob, it was too much. His head had become a soupy mess, and the world around him started to swirl. He grew dizzy and fell over. He woke with his head in Kelly's lap. Chelsea was next to her. Lester Brooks was pressing a series of white tabs onto his face and arms and chest. Jacob could feel electricity move over his skin, prickling at his hair.

Brooks was looking at a flat black device that looked like a small TV. "Left arm is broken in four places. Two broken ribs. Internal bleeding. Brain swelling. Massive infection from the injuries on his arms." He put the device down. "Your friend is in some serious pain. We'll need to get his fever down right away."

"You can help him?" Kelly asked.

"Oh yes. He'll be in bed for a while, but we can patch him, no problem." He touched the device on his throat. "Brooks three-ninety, requesting extraction. We have three packages. Have a medic standing by for our arrival."

A few moments later a dust cloud appeared on the road. Jacob rallied enough to sit up and stare in amazement at the gigantic ten-wheeled armored vehicle that rolled through the ruins, crushing zombies in its path before finally pulling up next to them.

Brooks opened the back door to the vehicle and helped them inside one after another. When Jacob was seated and buckled in, Brooks said, "We'll get that arm fixed up for you in a bit."

Jacob nodded. "Thanks."

"Hang on," Brooks told them. "It gets a little bumpy out here."

He closed the door and the vehicle took off.

Jacob leaned his head against the window and watched the ruins of Little Rock slip into the distance. The armored vehicle trundled through the abandoned city, causing Jacob to sway in his seat. In places the streets were black rivers seething with bodies. In others, ivy climbed the sides of buildings, creating green canyons through the past glory of man.

And what of glory?

It made him think of Sheriff Taylor, the man who had meant so much to him, and so much to Arbella, gone now, dead and rotting in the sun on some nameless street in a small town a million miles away.

He thought, too, of Bree. She'd been so young and so devastatingly gorgeous, yet the only image of her he could hold in his mind was of her slipping to the grass under a hail of bullets. She had, in his memory at least, seemed almost grateful to receive them.

But mostly he thought of Nick.

He watched a solitary zombie lumber down the road, reaching for their vehicle even though it was much too far away to put its hands on them, and he thought of the time he'd had with his dearest friend. He felt heartsick at all that had happened. He had loved Nick as a brother. For all the tension that had run under the surface of their friendship since that fight twenty years earlier, they had been the best of friends, and Jacob couldn't shake the memory of the tears running down Nick's face right before he pulled the trigger. What had he cried for? Was it out of remorse? Or for what had happened to their friendship? Or was it simply for his own life?

Jacob looked across the darkened cabin of the armored transport. Chelsea had her eyes closed, a blanket pulled up under her chin. It didn't look to Jacob like she was sleeping, more like she was trying to wipe the last seven years from her mind.

Next to him, Kelly was looking out the window, tears rolling down her cheeks.

Jacob looked away. Though this journey of theirs was really just beginning, in so many ways, it was the end of the man he'd thought himself to be.

Chapter 1

Jacob woke to a pretty girl dressed in white standing over him.

"Bree?" he said, his voice sounding weak and raspy, like he hadn't used it in a very long time.

He coughed, and the pain that shot down his left side was so blindingly intense he cried out.

"Easy," the girl said. "Don't try to move. You're hurt pretty bad."

She held up some kind of device that clicked and beeped as she passed it over his body. She circled around him, moving the device over his chest and his arms and his legs. Sometimes, when she moved, the harsh glare of the overhead lights flooded into Jacob's eyes and blinded him. Everything hurt. He turned his head and saw a bank of monitors and medical equipment, a lot of fluctuating numbers and rhythmic beeps.

"Bree, my chest hurts."

"Who's Bree?" the girl said, putting down the device she'd been checking him with.

Jacob blinked at her.

After a moment his vision cleared enough that he could see the girl standing over him wasn't Bree Carlton.

She wasn't even blond.

Jacob couldn't quite marshal his thoughts. He felt utterly lost and confused, unable, even, to separate the physical pain in his chest from the ceaseless roar of white noise sounding in his ears. But he did remember Bree, so pretty and smart. So young. The girl every able-bodied man back in Arbella fantasized about having.

And yet, now, as he struggled to bring his thoughts into focus, all he could think of was the cruelty that had marked her final minutes back in the Slaver caravan run by Casey and his mother, Jane. Bree had been beaten and raped. She'd been driven mad with pain and shame. And in the end, she'd chosen to die in a hail of bullets rather than suffer another night of depravation. Had he been in her shoes, he only hoped he would have had enough backbone to die as she died.

"Who's Bree?" the pretty girl said again. "You've said her name just about every time you've woken up."

"Just a friend," he said, his voice a whisper.

"My name is Megan," the girl said. "I'm a nurse. I've been taking care of you these last few weeks."

"Weeks?"

"Yes," she said. "Almost a month now, actually. You were hurt pretty badly. Two broken ribs—that's the pain in your chest, by the way—a broken left arm, two broken fingers, and a pretty serious staph infection. Also, does your left knee still hurt?"

"What?"

"Your left knee. You were shot in the leg." Her brow furrowed a little, accentuating the little upturn at the tip of her nose. "You didn't know that?"

"No," Jacob said. He groaned and tried to roll over.

"Easy," Megan said. "Don't move too fast. I imagine you have a pretty bad headache."

"Yeah."

"That's the fever and the infected wounds. You're lucky Dr. Brooks found you when he did. Too much longer and the infection would have killed you. As it is, we'll have you up and running in no time."

Jacob collapsed back on the bed, realizing for the first time that his hair was wet with sweat.

"Really," said Megan. "You're safe now. We can fix all this."

"Where am I?" he said.

"You're in Temple," she said. "In a hospital. Do you know about Temple?"

Jacob groaned again. "That's where Chelsea's from. It's Galveston on my maps."

"That's right," Megan said. "Do you remember your friends you were with?"

"Kelly Banis and Chelsea Walker. Where are they?"

"Well, Chelsea, I don't know about. But Kelly Banis has been in here to see you almost every day for the past few weeks."

"Where is she?"

"I don't know. She'll probably be back sometime this afternoon. She usually comes in after lunch."

Another wave of pain hit him, and Jacob closed his eyes and braced against it.

"Still hurting?" Megan said.

"Yeah."

"I'll up the painkillers. But you should expect more of that over the next week. After that, we should have you pretty much patched up."

Jacob nodded toward the device she'd been using on him. "Is that what that is?"

"No," she said. "I was measuring your CDHLs."

"Ah," he said, and tried to smile. "I'm going to be a zombie, aren't I?"

"Afraid so, yeah." She touched her hand to his forehead and smiled. "Your fever's better. That's good."

Back in school he'd learned about the origins of the First Days, the near Great Extinction of the Human Race. The zombies weren't the product of terrorism or a rogue virus or junk DNA. They came, instead, from the entrepreneurial desire to make vegetables last longer on the shelves.

In the late 2080s, China began experimenting with advanced pesticides and preservatives, looking for a way to make their domestically grown foodstuffs stay fresher longer. Their efforts culminated in a family of chemical compounds known as carbon dioxide–blocking hydrolyzed lignin, or CDHLs. The Chinese tested it, claimed it was safe, and spread it over everything that grew.

The compounds were tested around the world, and eventually vetted, first in Europe, and then in the United States by the FDA. Once the Food and Drug Administration declared CDHLs safe for human consumption in August 2098, they spread across the globe. Suddenly plums could stay purple and juicy for months at a time. Roses never wilted. Celery, carrots, even lettuce could sit on a grocery store shelf for weeks and still look as fresh as the day they were harvested. Even bananas could stay traffic light yellow for three months.

The blood banks were the first to report signs of trouble. CDHLs didn't appear to break down in the human bloodstream the way they did in plants. There was no cause for immediate worry, except that blood supersaturated with CDHLs seemed to stay unnaturally healthy and vital well beyond any sort of conventional measure.

In hindsight, Jacob's teachers had said, it should have been obvious.

There were clues something was wrong. Lots of clues.

CDHLs were linked through study after study to hyperactive behavior in children.

Unfocused aggression was a common symptom of adults of middle age. Housewives killing their children and waiting at the kitchen table with a butcher's knife for their husbands' return from work shouldn't have seemed like business as usual.

And yet it was.

Clues were missed.

The First Days had crept up on them like a thief in the night, even though it should have been obvious what the CDHLs were doing to them.

The trouble started in China. The central cities of Weishan and Qinghai were the first to erupt in anarchy. The Chinese, much to their credit, made no attempt to cover up what was going on. Video streamed out to every news service and website, and those first glimpses of the dead crowding the streets were terrifying beyond all reckoning.

From central China the zombie hordes spread to the

more densely populated coastal cities, and by that point there was no saving mainland Asia. Everyone who could evacuate did. They fled to Japan and Australia, some even to the United States, but many millions were left behind to be devoured. There were simply too many to save.

The rest of the world watched it happen, believing that their quarantine efforts had worked. But of course the quarantine effort was merely shutting the barn door after the cow was already out. The culprit, the CDHLs, were already in the ground, already in the food, already in the bodies of everyone who had ever eaten something bought from the grocery store. All that was needed was for the body to reach a point of supersaturation. Once that happened, zombification spread.

Eight months after the first incidents in China, more were reported in Japan, and Mexico, and the United States. Living through the First Days was like being caught up in a wildfire, Jacob's teachers had told him. No sooner had you smelled smoke than the flames erupted all around you. Every night the televisions had shown maps, and on those maps, red circles spread like bloodstains.

But the real terror, and it was a terror that every man, woman, and child still lived with, was the fact that the CDHLs were already in their bodies. You didn't become a zombie by being bit, or scratched, or accidentally ingesting any of their bodily fluids. You didn't have to, because you were already a zombie waiting to happen. They were all, to a body, carriers of the zombie plague.

And once they died, they came back.

He'd come back.

They all did.

Jacob sighed, then nodded at the device in the nurse's hand. "So what's my count?"

"Your count? You mean your CDHLs?"

"Yeah."

"Environmentally consistent. You're at nearly six hundred parts per million. About the same as you'd find in any wild animal or fruit tree out in the Zone. We can reduce that count a little, maybe eighteen to twenty percent, but anything greater than thirty parts per million pretty much guarantees you a zombie afterlife. Unfortunately, we can't come anywhere close to that for you. I'm sorry."

"Grrr," he said. He tried to raise his hands, zombie fashion, but a pain pierced his shoulders and made him forget any more joking. He collapsed with another groan.

"Well, I'm glad your humor's still intact."

He settled into the pillow, waiting for the pain to ebb away. When it became bearable again, he said, "What's your count?"

"Mine?"

"Yeah. You look about, what, twenty-five?"

He couldn't be sure, but she might have blushed.

"I'm thirty-two," she said.

"Ah, so you were born after the First Days. But you were raised here, weren't you? They started trying to lower your CDHLs from the start, right?"

"Yes."

"So what's your count?"

The smile drained from her face. She hesitated for a long time, but eventually said: "I'm at three-oh-six."

"Ah. So we'll be doing the zombie walk together, eh?"

"Apparently."

He picked up on the drop in her tone and automatically, clumsily, came back with a crack that she'd be one of the finest-looking zombies around.

Almost, anyway. Thankfully, his inner filter turned on, and the comment died before he had a chance to put his foot in his mouth.

Instead of embarrassing both of them, he went for empathy.

"I'm sorry," he said. "It sucks knowing we're all going to end up that way. I just hope there's somebody I love there to put me down when it's my time."

"Me, too," she said.

The silence grew between them, until Megan looked up suddenly. "Oh, looks like you have a visitor."

Jacob tried to sit up, but couldn't quite manage it.

He collapsed back onto the bed. He turned just enough to look at the tall, slender black man standing in the doorway. He had closely cut gray hair; a wide, intelligent-looking forehead; a strong chin; and an unblinking gaze that was somehow possessed of both a grandfatherly kindness and the unwavering confidence of command. He remembered seeing a similar look, back in Arbella, from his old boss, Sheriff Taylor.

But Taylor was gone now. He'd taken a bullet in the mouth from the Slaver caravan that had wrecked their expedition. Now Sheriff Taylor, the hero of Arbella, the George Washington of his community, was dead in some weed-choked side street in a forgotten town.

"Jacob, how are you feeling?" the man said.

Jacob sighed again. So many friends gone. "Like death warmed over," he said.

"I can only imagine. You've been through a lot. Do you remember me?"

"Vaguely," Jacob said, though in truth he didn't.

"I'm Dr. Lester Brooks. I was part of the expedition

that brought you here. Do you remember being in a gunfight?"

"That I remember," Jacob said. "Sorry, my mind is still a little hazy."

"Probably the painkillers. I triaged you the day we found you. You were a mess."

"That's what everybody keeps saying."

"Well, you're on the mend now. That's all that counts." Brooks motioned to a chair and said, "Mind if I sit and chat with you for a moment?"

"Sure."

Jacob wasn't sure, but he thought a little of the grandfatherly kindness slid away from the man's face.

"I'm a member of the Executive Council of Temple," Brooks said.

"Never heard of it."

"No, of course you wouldn't have. We are the leaders of Temple. We are the ones tasked with long-term urban planning, foreign policy, scientific development; basically, we make sure the trains run on time."

"Trains?" Jacob said.

"A joke from before your time, son. Don't worry about it. Basically, the Executive Council is responsible for safeguarding Temple's best interests, and, within that scope, we'll be the ones overseeing your hearing."

"My what?"

"It's just a formality," Brooks said. "Temple has a very strict policy of leaving isolated communities alone until such time as they reach out to us. We are very careful, for example, to never fly our aerofluyts over your town. It's a policy not everyone here in Temple agrees with, but one we've come to rely on."

"Why?" Jacob said. "You're so much more advanced than us. Those aerofluyts alone . . . you're decades ahead of any technology I've ever seen. And fixing me up like this. Where I come from, people die every day from simple infections and minor injuries. Our medical care . . . we don't have antibiotics or vaccines. And yet, you people have got stuff I didn't even know existed. If you were to contact us, lives would be saved."

"Yes, that's true."

"Then why stay hidden?"

Brooks took a deep breath and tugged at his sleeves. He took on the tired, patient expression of a man who has explained this many times before, but knows full well he'll have to explain it countless more before he's understood.

"As I understand it from your friend Kelly Banis, your expedition was taken captive by a Slaver caravan."

"That's right. They killed almost everybody."

"Tragic," Brooks said. "I'm sorry for your loss."

"Yeah," Jacob said stiffly. "It sucks."

"But it is not a unique experience, I'm afraid. The world has changed. And I'm not just talking about zombies. North America used to be a land of riches, and a land of law. Now, well, it seems that not every community out there is interested in living according to laws. That's why we wait. We wait for those communities who have not only survived, but thrived, to come to us. And when they do, if they are of a like mind with us, we share everything. No one need to die anymore from a minor injury or an infected wound."

Jacob, who, while growing up, had seen more than a few friends die long before their time, merely huffed at Brooks's words.

Finally, he said, "Arbella is a land of laws."

"Yes," Brooks said, perking up. "I've talked to Ms. Banis about that. You have a code. The Arbella Code, she called it. I'm eager to hear more of that."

He patted Jacob on the arm and stood up.

"You get to feeling better," Brooks said. "And when you do, the Executive Council looks forward to hearing from you."

He didn't wait for Jacob to respond. He spun on his heel and headed for the door.

Jacob coughed again, and the pain that had plagued him earlier lanced once again through his rib cage. When he finally recovered, Brooks was at the door.

"Wait," he said, his voice barely audible. "Please."

Brooks stopped in the doorway and raised an eyebrow. "Yes?"

"Where's Kelly? I want to see her."

"I'll see what I can do," Brooks said.

Jacob fell back on the bed, winded from the pain. For a second, he thought he might pass out. But then he caught Brooks's voice from the hallway.

"Nurse," Brooks said, "come here."

Jacob heard a voice that sounded like Megan's answer, "Yes, sir, Dr. Brooks?"

Brooks said something, but his voice had dropped a note, and Jacob couldn't hear what was said.

"But she's outside, Dr. Brooks. She always comes in the afternoon."

Again Brooks said something Jacob couldn't hear.

"Okay," Megan said. "Yes, sir. I'll tell her."

CHAPTER 2

The setting sun streamed in through the windows, filling Jacob's room with shafts of light. Fifteen stories below him, and out beyond the beach, the waters of the Gulf of Mexico were a dancing red and golden sheet of molten brass. He looked for the beautiful clipper ships, with their enormous solar sails, he had seen cruising the waters earlier that morning, but the ocean was empty. Only the seagulls wheeled in the fading light.

Frustrated, he turned away.

The bed was there, but he didn't feel like resting. He'd been resting for weeks, and he was going stir-crazy. This damn place, beautiful as it was, had become a sort of holding cell for him. Everybody was so nice. They smiled and they chatted pleasantries with him, but he knew what they were really thinking. They were treating him like a slow child, like someone they had to coddle just so he could make it through his day.

And, in fact, it had taken a child, a young girl of

about nine, to help him work the elevator the first time he'd braved a trip outside his room. Megan, his nurse, had noticed he was gone and quickly located him. She'd shepherded him back to his room with an outward smile, but Jacob picked up on her anxiety just the same. It was then that he began to feel less like a patient, and more like a prisoner.

He went to the sink and poured himself a glass of water from the tap.

Which was another thing he was still getting used to.

Tap water.

He held the glass up and shook his head in admiration. Just turn a handle and you got clean, drinkable water. So much these people could share. So much.

And, almost in answer to his thoughts, there was a knock at the door.

"Who is it?"

"Jacob, it's Dr. Brooks. Can we talk please?"

Jacob set the glass down next to the sink. Brooks, huh? He'd been asking and asking for the man for days, and getting nowhere, and then out of the blue—

Jacob went to the door and opened it. He left it open without saying a word to Brooks as he walked back to the window.

"You're feeling better, I see. No more limping. How are the ribs?"

Jacob turned away from the window and faced the older man. Darkness had set in over the water anyway, and the beauty of the ocean at dusk had become just a void of empty space. There weren't even any stars.

Brooks was dressed in a light gray suit with a white, stiff-collared shirt that hugged the base of his neck like a clerical collar. His close-cropped hair was a smoky gray, almost white, and as he smiled, that winning grin of his deepened the wrinkles at the corners of his mouth.

"I'm fine," Jacob said, and turned toward the window. "Been fine for a couple of days."

"I know you've been asking to see me, and I'm sorry to keep you waiting as I have. Press of business, unfortunately. And, also, I had to wait on the official release from your attending physician before I could come to see you. They wanted you good and rested, I guess, before I started in on you with official business." Brooks favored him with his kind, grandfatherly smile. Then he cleared his throat. "I was hoping we could go over your statement for tomorrow's hearing. Do you feel up for that, Jacob? I think it'd be a big help."

"Where are Kelly Banis and Chelsea Walker?" he asked. "Why can't I see them?"

"Jacob, we don't need to worry about that right now. Our big concern is the hearing. A lot is riding on this. The future relationship of both our communities, in fact. So, please, let's get you prepared. Now, as I understand it, you were a sort of police officer in your community. Is that right?"

"I was the chief deputy of the constabulary, yes."

Brooks nodded. "Yes, that's right. Would you prefer if, during the hearing, I addressed you as Chief Deputy Carlton?"

"I go by Jacob."

"Fair enough. Well, Jacob, the Executive Council will no doubt start with that as we try to get an understanding of your people and your values. And, just to give you fair warning, you should probably expect some rather direct questions on that from certain members of the council. We don't have police officers here in Temple. We never have. Our community broke away from a brutal police state during the initial outbreak back in the 2090s. I know you're too young to remember that time, but it was awful. Our community was, and still is, a peaceful one. Research has always been one of our core values, and the authorities back then forced us to direct that research into finding a cure and finding ways to kill the zombies. We were doctors and chemists and physicists and biologists, and yet we found ourselves forced to create weapons of devastating violence. I'm sorry. I get emotional about it, just thinking of those days. I don't mean to philosophize, but it was a rough and difficult time. It cost us dearly to break away from that control, and when we finally did, and we came here, we promised ourselves that never again would we be yoked to the burden of police authority. You should know that many on the council still harbor strong emotions on the subject. I want you to prepare yourself for that. That will, almost certainly, be the main point of contention in bringing our people together."

"Why won't you tell me where Kelly Banis and Chelsea Walker are?"

Brooks let out a long sigh. "Jacob, nobody is trying to keep anything from you. They are safe. They'll be speaking at the hearing tomorrow, in fact. I think Chelsea is scheduled to go before you, and Kelly Banis immediately after you. Once her testimony is complete, you will all be reunited. You'll be given free range of Temple. You can go to the beach if you want. You can even ride on one of those clipper ships I hear you like watching so much. Our doors will be open to you."

Jacob's eyes narrowed. "As soon as the hearing's done?"

"As soon as the hearing's done, yes."

"And until then, I'm to stay sequestered like a prisoner."

"You're not a prisoner, Jacob."

"Really? Is that a fact? I can't leave my room without causing an alarm. I'm not allowed to see my friends. I'm told I have some mysterious hearing to go to and I'm not even told the charges against me. And now you're telling me that your Executive Council will be prejudiced against me simply because I'm a cop. Sure sounds like I'm a prisoner."

Brooks took a deep breath. He crossed the floor to where Jacob stood and put a hand on his shoulder.

"You're not a prisoner," he said. "And you have friends here, Jacob. I need you to understand that. I want our people to come together."

"Yeah, is that a fact?"

"It is, Jacob. You told me, not ten days ago, that lives could have been saved if only our two communities had come together sooner. I couldn't have said it better myself. We are in this together. When you die, you will become a zombie. Somebody will have to put you down. When I die, same thing. The same poison runs in both our veins. We are truly in this together."

With that, Dr. Brooks turned and went to the door. He waited for Jacob to speak, but when he didn't, he opened the door and stepped out.

Before he closed it he said, "You will remember that, won't you, Jacob? I'm on your side."

"Yeah," Jacob said, turning back to the window. "Yeah, I got it."

CHAPTER 3

"What is it you people don't understand?" Jacob said. "Haven't we been through this already? Why do you keep asking me the same thing over and over?"

He was sitting at one end of a long, oval conference table, surrounded by old men who wore expensive-looking gray suits and dour expressions. This was the Executive Council of the Community of Temple, nearly every one of them a senior scientist in his field.

Introductions alone had taken forty-five minutes.

The hearing started out with all the dignity and fanfare of some sort of state function. Jacob sat through the introductions and the pleasantries, ever mindful of what Lester Brooks, who sat three seats down from him on the right, had said about this meeting deciding the terms of friendship between their two communities.

Jacob had gone into the meeting with high hopes.

In the few jaunts he'd taken outside the hospital, he'd seen solar-powered clipper ships out on the ocean and airships bigger than skyscrapers gliding across the sky and electric cars and dozens more wonders he didn't even have words for yet. This community's medical knowledge alone could save dozens of lives every year back in Arbella. Jacob himself had been brought back from the brink of death twice now by their medical knowledge.

But, of course, he was young and strong.

Back home, there was an entire generation of aging heroes of the First Days, of which his mother was a member. They looked on a broken hip as a death sentence. To them, flu season was a killing field. In recent years, his mother's main social function had been to attend the funerals of people she'd learned to call brothers and sisters. The idea of bringing Temple's medical knowledge back to Arbella, and using it to restore the lives of his community's aging heroes and the dozens of people who died from curable diseases and minor injuries every year, was absolutely critical, he realized.

And so he'd settled into the high-backed leather chair they'd offered him and readied himself for their questions.

That had been four hours ago.

Now, he was exhausted. Mad; irritable; so frustrated he wanted to knock the hat off a random stranger's head; but above all, exhausted.

Jacob looked around the table, hoping to find at least one encouraging face, but found none. Not even Lester Brooks, who had pointedly refused to meet his gaze even once during the hearing.

"I think you need to look at this in a more pragmatic sense," said a man on Jacob's left. His name was Steve Welch, a thin, tall man with a crane-like neck who spoke like a man accustomed to spending most of his life in front of classroom. He'd been steering the questioning for the last forty-five minutes. "Please. See this our way. Now, you freely admit to shooting a man. A Mr. Nicolas Carroll, I believe you said."

"Nick, yes," Jacob said.

The older councilman nodded. "You and Ms. Chelsea Walker tell similar stories, up to a point, Mr. Carlton. Apparently this Mr. Carroll was involved in some petty theft back in your community of New Madrid, and you, acting as the town's first deputy, murdered him for it. That's it in a nutshell, as I understand your testimony?"

"I did not murder him," Jacob said, his voice rising. He had to stop himself, take a mental step back. He took a deep breath, and went on. "I told you. He invaded the homes of at least four young girls and drew pictures of them while they were sleeping. He also took mementos of each break-in. That's called burglary, Mr. Welch. Burglary is very different from petty theft."

Welch reached forward and tapped the surface of his computer tablet. He read the message that popped up there, nodded in agreement, and tapped the tablet again, shutting it down. Then he sat back in his chair, steepled his fingers, and directed his attention once again on Jacob.

"Continue, please, Mr. Carlton."

Jacob's mouth fell open. He looked from Welch to the others, all of whom sat staring at him, still as vultures studying a dying animal. "Continue with what?" he said. "We've been over this already."

"You've admitted to murdering a man, Mr. Carlton. I want to know why."

"I didn't murder—" Jacob bit off the words before

he could finish the sentence. It wouldn't do any good anyway. They weren't listening. "Look," he said, after another deep breath, "I've told you. Nick Carroll violated one of Arbella's most fundamental laws. He stole from another person. I don't know how you people look on theft, but we see it as one of the worst things a person can do to another person. And even if that wasn't enough for you, Nick stood back and did nothing while another man was put on trial for the crime. He just stood by while that man was executed for a crime he did not commit."

"Yes," said Welch. "Now, as I understand it, you murdered that man, too."

"I didn't murder him!" Jacob said. "Good God, what is wrong with you people? I told you. Jerry Greider was executed according to our laws."

"For a crime he didn't commit?"

Jacob started to respond, but the words failed him. He sank back into his chair and stared around the room. Dr. Brooks still wouldn't meet his gaze. The rest of them were grim, expressionless. They seemed to look on him like he was a member of a different species, like he was something nasty they were going to have to scrape off their shoes.

How could he make them understand?

Indeed, how could he make himself understand? That was the real question. He'd killed an innocent man. He'd carried out the order of execution, handed down from the elders of Arbella, based largely on evidence he himself had gathered. He'd been sick to his stomach before and after the execution, but he'd never questioned the rightness of it.

Until now.

Now he couldn't stop thinking of how Jerry Greider

must have suffered. Not just at the moment when the bullet punched its way through his skull and into his brain, but during the trial, listening to evidence that spoke so soundly and confidently of his guilt, knowing all the while that the evidence was meant to damn some other man.

And that man, Jacob had discovered later—too late—was Nick Carroll, his best friend since childhood. Jacob had presented the evidence in the kitchen of a ruined suburban house in North Little Rock. Kelly heard the evidence, and turned to Nick, begging him to deny it.

Nick hadn't.

He couldn't.

Jacob and Kelly had exchanged looks, and in that moment they both knew their duty according to the Arbella Code. She'd given him a nod, a death sentence, and Jacob had raised his weapon to Nick's forehead and pulled the trigger.

But the funny thing—and not funny as in ha-ha, but funny as in so fucking tragic it was tearing his soul to pieces—was that Jacob felt absolutely no guilt at all about executing Jerry Greider, an innocent man, and absolute horror at the knowledge that he'd killed a guilty man.

How could he make these men, these vultures, understand that?

Indeed, how could he make himself understand that?

There were so many hard questions. It made his head spin.

"I still don't understand this code of yours," Welch said. "Perhaps you could elucidate that for us."

Jacob sat up straight in his chair. Nobody had bothered to ask him about the Arbella Code. Maybe they were finally about to make some headway. "It's the body of laws that govern the way we conduct our lives," he said. "There are ten guiding principles. The first five define an individual's relationship to the community, and the second five define an individual's relationship to his fellow citizens."

"Is yours a religious community, Mr. Carlton?"

The question caught him by surprise. "Uh, no," said Jacob. "Why do you ask?"

"That's the same way the Ten Commandments are laid out," Welch said with a wry grin. "Replace 'community' with 'God' and you've got a pretty good description of how the Ten Commandments are structured."

"Oh," said Jacob. He'd been studying the Code his entire life, and he'd never heard that.

"Can you list these guiding principles for us?" Welch looked around the table and traded smiles with the rest of the council. "I'm sure we'd all love to hear them."

"I can list them," Jacob said. "Every schoolkid in Arbella learns them by heart."

Welch shared a chuckle with the man next to him, then extended a hand toward Jacob as an invitation. "Please," he said.

"Precept one: Arbella is a community of laws, and the law is equally binding on us all. Precept two: Arbella is your home. You shall do it no harm, or through inaction, allow it to come to harm. Arbella is—"

Jacob broke off before finishing the third law. Right after he recited the second law, most of the table started laughing. Everybody was smiling. Confused, Jacob looked around the table. There was a young blond man, perhaps thirty years old, sitting next to Lester Brooks.

He hadn't been introduced during the initial roll call, and he hadn't spoken at all during the questioning. He had a tablet in front of him, and he'd spent most of the meeting typing out messages. He was laughing the hardest.

"Sounds like your town was founded by Isaac Asimov," the young man said.

That brought a fresh round of laughter from everybody.

Even Lester Brooks.

"I'm sorry," Jacob said. "I don't understand."

"Let me guess," the young man said. "Is the next law that a citizen of Arbella cannot injure a human being, or through inaction, allow a human being to come to harm?"

"No," said Jacob, thoroughly confused. "It's that Arbella is—"

"Oh wait," the young man interrupted, "you've already violated that one. I guess we can safely say that Arbella is not a community of robots."

"Robots?" Jacob said. "Mister, what are you talking about?"

The young man's smile suddenly dried up. He turned away from Jacob and made a hurry-it-up gesture to Welch.

"I think we've heard enough," said Welch, taking the younger man's cue. "Thank you for your time this morning, Mr. Carlton. You may go now."

"What do you mean? I thought we were going to talk about establishing a relationship between our two communities. Your medical knowledge could save—"

"Thank you, Mr. Carlton." He rapped his knuckles lightly on the desk. "I declare this session of the Executive Council concluded. We will resume with the next witness after lunch. Mr. Secretary, please record the time for the minutes."

"Noted," said a man at the end of the table.

"Very good," said Welch. "See you all back here in two hours."

Jacob hardly knew what was happening. He started to protest, but before he could get the words out, the others rose from their chairs and started to file out toward the door.

"Wait," he said. "Goddammit, wait!"

But no one was listening. They walked right by him without so much as a glance. Jacob tried to get Welch's attention, but the man hustled right by him.

He turned around and saw Lester Brooks trying to sneak away.

"Hey, wait a minute," he said, grabbing hold of the older man's shoulder. "What was that? I thought you said you were on my side."

Brooks never even met his gaze. The younger man who had made fun of the Arbella Code stepped between them, grabbed Jacob's wrist, and pulled it away from Brooks's shoulder.

Jacob tried to push his way around the younger man, but he wouldn't let go.

"You'd better let go of my hand," said Jacob.

"Not going to happen, Mr. Carlton."

"Dr. Brooks," Jacob called out. "Hey, what is this? Talk to me."

"You're done here, Mr. Carlton."

"I'm telling you," Jacob said, "you'd best take your hand away. I'll put a boot up your ass."

"Security!" the man said. "Somebody get Security over here, please."

Behind him, Lester Brooks slipped through the crowd and out the door, leaving Jacob alone with a few older men and the blond man, who still kept hold of Jacob's wrist.

Jacob wrenched his hand away.

"Security," the man said again.

A team of three large men hustled through the far door and ran straight for Jacob. The blond man stepped back and motioned for the team to advance on Jacob. Jacob started to raise his fists, but he could see at a glance that he wasn't going to get anywhere with the three security toughs. They were on him right away.

He put up a halfhearted struggle, but that ended when one of the toughs wrenched his arm behind his back in a brutal arm bar.

Jacob hardly had a chance to cry out. They pushed him through the door, shoved him down a darkened flight of stairs, and threw him down the sun-washed steps of the old City Hall building before he even knew what was happening.

When he finally regained his feet, he found himself facing a wall of locked doors.

There was no one around.

Only the smell of the ocean and the sound of seagulls wheeling in the sky above him.

Just like that, he'd been kicked to the curb.

CHAPTER 4

Jacob stood in the street, staring up at the front doors of City Hall, not at all sure what to do. After the way they'd treated him, he wanted to go back up there and bang on the doors. Give them a piece of his mind. Maybe throw rocks at the windows. Kick somebody in the crotch. Like maybe Lester Brooks, or that smug bastard Welch. But that wouldn't do any good. He knew that. They'd just have him arrested.

He thought about just leaving, going back to the hospital, which was about the closest thing he had to a home at the moment. The trouble was, he didn't think he could find his way back there from here. He hadn't paid much attention to the twists and turns they'd made through town. He was too distracted by the electric cars and the people in their strange clothes and the ocean crashing in his ears. Everywhere he turned, there was something new, something he'd never seen before. And now, after that fiasco up in the council chambers, he had no idea what they had planned for him. He wasn't sure if he was supposed to wait or if they were going to send a car for him or what.

Maybe he was expected to just leave, go back to Arbella with his tail tucked between his legs like a scalded dog.

An electric car beeped its horn at him and he jumped in surprise.

The driver motioned him toward the curb impatiently, then drove around him.

Still feeling stunned, Jacob stepped back onto the sidewalk.

And the longer he stood there the angrier he got. It was finally starting to sink in that he and the entire community of Arbella had been put on trial for doing nothing wrong and made to look ridiculous. The values that Jacob held dear, his core beliefs, had been nothing but a joke to the Executive Council.

They'd actually laughed at him.

Even Lester Brooks, who had taken the time to come see him in the hospital, who had tried to coach him on how to handle the hearing, had laughed at him.

The bastards, Jacob thought. Fuck those guys.

Except that, really, he and the people of Arbella were the ones who were truly fucked. Back home, his community was busting at the seams. His mother's generation had managed to live through the First Days, thirty years ago, and in the time since, that initial ragtag band of eight hundred survivors had turned what had once been a little backwater burg along the banks of the Mississippi River into a successful community more than ten thousand strong.

But resources were tight. The town of New Madrid, which they took over and transformed into Arbella—named for the ship upon which John Winthrop delivered his famous City Upon a Hill sermon so many centuries ago—had housed only a few thousand people before the First Days. Now, though, they were having to get increasingly creative to feed and care for their growing numbers. Every lawn was a vegetable garden, and every man, woman, and child worked. Most did multiple jobs. Jacob himself was chief deputy of the constabulary, but also a carpenter, and a vegetable picker in the winters, and a former salvage expert. There were no freeloaders in Arbella. No one got to suck off the community teat. Regardless of age, or physical condition, or any sort of infirmity, everybody worked, everybody pulled his or her weight.

But the town was at a crossroads, and there was an ongoing debate about what direction Arbella should take. The older folks, like Jacob's mother and most of the town's leaders, remembered the horrors of the First Days. They'd built the walls that hemmed in the town and kept the zombie hordes at bay. They'd developed Arbella's Code and taught their children how to survive as a community. The older generation preached a policy of *hold what you got*. They were survivors, and they were winning. They had carved out a life for themselves and saw no need to change things.

Others, though, like Jacob and his friends, had grown up in the shadow of the walls that separated the town from the outside world. Many of them, including Jacob, while working on the salvage teams, had seen the world outside the walls.

And it wasn't that scary.

Or at least he thought it wasn't.

He'd convinced the town elders to let him organize an expedition to explore the Zone around Arbella. They'd planned and planned, picked the best and brightest of

Arbella's younger generation, even armed themselves to the teeth.

But in the end, Jacob's great plan had been a bust.

They'd barely made it a week in the Zone before they encountered a sadistic caravan of Slavers and more zombies than they'd ever imagined, and the only thing that hurt more than knowing he'd been so terribly, terribly wrong, was the knowledge that the best and brightest of Arbella's coming generation had died while in his charge.

Remembering the dead blunted his anger.

He turned to the beach and started walking away, thinking that the warm summer sun might clear his head, when one of the doors opened behind him and Kelly Banis stepped outside. She flinched from the bright sunshine, but then she saw him, and relief flashed across her face.

"Jacob!" she said, and ran to him. She threw her arms around his neck and squeezed him tightly.

He hugged her back. Pain shot up his left side from his still-healing ribs, but he didn't care. He just kept hugging her.

"Oh God, Jacob, I was so worried about you."

"They wouldn't let me see you. I asked, but . . ."

"I know. Are you okay? How do you feel?"

"My ribs still hurt, but I think I'll live."

She pushed back at arm's length. "Oh my God, I'm so sorry. Did I hurt you?"

"No," he said. "No. It's good to see you again."

"You, too." She stared at him for a long moment, her eyes glassy with tears she fought back. She sniffled. "I thought I was going to be all alone here."

"You're not alone," he said. "We're here. You and me."

Jacob was thirty-four years old. Kelly was a year

younger. They'd known each other since they were kids in grade school, and there had been a summer, back when she was sixteen, that the two of them had thought the world was a wonderland made just for the two of them. He'd said those very words to her during that summer, and he could tell by the look behind her insipient tears that she remembered them. He wondered, though, if she sensed, as he did, how the meaning was altogether different now.

"These people," she said at last. "What are they doing with us?"

"I don't know," Jacob said. "I don't know."

"This hearing, they've been talking about it for almost a month now. Then they came and got me this morning and kept me in that waiting room for hours just to tell me that they didn't need to talk to me after all. Did you talk to them?"

"Yeah," Jacob said. "It didn't go well."

"What happened?"

He took a deep breath, glanced back at the doors to City Hall, and motioned her toward the beach. "You mind if we walk for a bit?"

"Sure."

They headed south, toward the seawall. When they were out of sight of City Hall, Jacob said, "All they wanted to talk about was Nick."

"Oh God. What did you tell them?"

"Well, they knew about it already. Most of it, anyway. I guess Chelsea told them most of it."

"But you told them about the Code, right? Jacob, what happened . . . we did the right thing. I hate myself for saying that. And I have to admit it, but for a long time, I hated you for doing it. I think, part of me anyway, maybe still does. But we did the right thing, Jacob. He was a thief."

"I know. And anyone who steals from his neighbor steals from all of us. I know."

"So, what did they . . . I don't understand. You told them about the Code. What did they say?"

"They laughed at me."

"What?"

"And then they called Security to throw me out. I just don't get it, Kelly. Why waste four hours out of their day if all they wanted was to laugh at us?"

"Did they say anything? What about sharing their medical knowledge? Dr. Brooks promised that—"

"I don't think we can count on him for anything. He was laughing right along with the rest of them."

"But he . . ." Kelly trailed off.

The look of distress on her face was heartbreaking. Jacob felt the same way. Or at least he thought he did. He wanted to reach out for her, take her in his arms again, as much for his own comfort as for hers. But he knew that would be the wrong thing to do. Like him, she'd watched lifelong friends gunned down and left to bleed out in the weeds of forgotten places. And if anyone could be said to have lost more than he had on this expedition, it was she. She'd watched her husband, Barry, murdered by the Slavers, his body tied to a clothesline so that all the slaves could watch him change. And ultimately, she was forced to watch his zombified corpse get stripped down to the bones by ravens.

And still, she was a rock. He was, once again, both startled and amazed at her strength. He'd been beaten and shot, trampled by horses, and pummeled by evil men, and he was still on his feet, but when he looked at her and thought of all the love that she had lost, and saw that she, too, was still on her feet, he realized that hers was the deeper strength.

They walked on in silence. Jacob was still thinking about the expedition and what had gone wrong when they reached the seawall.

Suddenly, the sea, unknowable in its vastness, stretched out before him.

Seeing it, smelling it, took his breath away.

"What is it?" Kelly asked.

"I've never been this close before," he said.

The breath hitched in her throat. She nodded. Maybe, he thought, she understood how truly beautiful, and how truly frightening, he found that vastness, that endless carpet of green. He'd seen countless wonders in Temple, but none equaled this. None equaled the sea.

He stood staring across the water, watching the white lines of the breakers coming toward the beach. There were groups of teenagers down there, pretty young girls in tiny bathing suits splashing in the waves, kicking water at their boyfriends. They didn't seem to have a care in the world. Certainly very little idea of the world pressing against the backs of their elders. It was a nightmare out there. Even if it was a dream world here, on this beach.

He turned to Kelly and almost asked her if she remembered the Hollow. Back in Arbella, along the banks of the Mississippi, the teenagers of his town had found a little spot just like this one. A place to play with another, to learn about one another, to try out one another.

It was on the banks of the Hollow that Jacob had taken Kelly's virginity.

And where she had taken his.

He wondered if this made her think of that long-ago time.

"Which way do we go?" he said.

She pointed to his right, westward. "That way. We're about a mile that way."

He nodded, and again they fell into silence.

Jacob turned his attention seaward, watching the distant clouds huddled along the horizon, listening to the steady break of the sea against the beach dotted with seaweed. The water called to something timeless within him, some void where memory and emotion came together and were one single, intense need.

It was almost enough to overwhelm him.

He turned to Kelly, the emotion so heavy in his chest it felt like a balloon swelling against the inside of his rib cage, choking away his breath.

But she was watching the island, its glistening buildings and the silent electric cars, all the wonders of a future a woman like her should have had. It was always the way with them, always of two different worlds: Kelly, with her intellect and curiosity, and Jacob, with his simple tastes and rough ways.

How, he wondered, had they ever come together?

But as he wondered about their past, he saw a blue, bubble-shaped electric car come around the corner. It was just like all the others he'd seen, and he wouldn't have paid it any mind if it hadn't suddenly veered toward them, like the driver was struggling to keep it under control.

Jacob put a hand on Kelly's shoulder.

He felt her go stiff with fright.

And then the back door of the car opened and Chelsea Walker rolled out of the backseat.

She landed face-first in the street, lay there for a second, stunned, and then jumped to her feet.

"Kelly!" she yelled. "Help me! Please!"

Behind her, three men climbed out of the car. All three were armed with slender black pistols.

They didn't bother to check for witnesses.

They ran after Chelsea, and closed in on her before she could make it halfway across the street.

"Jacob," Kelly said.

"On it!"

He rushed the men. They'd knocked Chelsea to the ground and were swarming her, forcing her hands behind her back so that they could handcuff her. Jacob slammed into one of the men shoulder-first and sent him sprawling into the street. A second man was still wrestling with Chelsea, caught off-guard. He looked up just as Jacob drove the heel of his hand into the man's face, catching him under the nose with the sickening crunch of shattered cartilage.

The man fell backward, his face a blooming flower of blood.

The third man was faster, though. He backed away and raised his pistol.

Jacob didn't give him a chance to pull the trigger. He lunged for the man, came up under the gun. He curled his right arm over the man's wrist and twisted, wrenching the pistol back on its owner.

The man's eyes went wide in alarm and pain, but he never had a chance to utter a sound. Jacob got his finger inside the trigger guard and squeezed.

The gun lurched, and the next instant the guard's head swelled to three times its normal size and exploded.

But there'd been no sound.

Jacob stared at the weapon, the man who'd held it just moments before nothing but a headless corpse.

But there were two more.

One of them reached inside his coat and pulled out a pistol exactly like the one Jacob held. Jacob didn't give him the chance to shoot it. He leveled the weapon he'd just taken and fired it right at the man's chest.

The explosion caught Jacob by surprise. The man grunted in pain, and then his chest swelled and burst open. He fell onto his back, dead, his chest a hollowed-out crater rapidly filling with blood.

The third man, the man with the bloody face, scrambled toward the car.

Jacob leveled his weapon and fired.

The round hit the man just below the elbow of his left arm. It exploded and the man screamed in pain as his severed hand dropped to the pavement.

He fell to the ground and tried to use his missing hand to crawl away.

All he ended up doing was smearing a long line of blood on the ground.

Jacob followed, coming around the back of the car with his gun raised. The man was panting, whimpering out of shock. But before Jacob could fire, the man scrambled to his feet and somehow managed to get the car door open and crawl inside.

Jacob didn't hurry. He came around the side of the car, leveled his weapon at the window, and fired.

A normal bullet would have punched through and killed the man, but this gun, this round, it hit the window and exploded. It didn't penetrate. The man let out a cry and ducked below the steering wheel.

The car lurched forward, knocking Jacob to the ground.

He rolled away from it to keep from getting run over, then jumped back to his feet and ran after the car. As the car moved forward, Jacob fired. The back windshield shattered, but several of the shots bounced off the car's metal frame and exploded harmlessly in the air.

The next instant, the car was speeding away.

Jacob turned back to the girls. Kelly was trying to hold Chelsea in her arms, but the younger woman was fighting to break loose.

"Let go of me!" she screamed. "We have to run."

Jacob looked down at the dead men at his feet. All around them, people were looking their way and pointing.

"What's going on?" Jacob asked. "Who were those guys?"

Chelsea finally managed to break free from Kelly's grip. She ran to one of the dead men and rifled through his clothes until she found his pistol.

"What are you doing?" Jacob asked. "What's going on?"

"We have to get out of here. Right now."

Chelsea ran into the street, right in front of a car, forcing it to a stop. She raised the pistol at the driver and motioned for the driver to get out.

A man climbed out, hands raised high.

"Let's go!" Chelsea yelled at them. "We have to go."

Jacob looked down at the men he'd just killed, then to Kelly.

A crowd was starting to gather.

"Jacob . . . ?"

He reached down for her hand. "I think she's right. Let's get out of here."

CHAPTER 5

Chelsea sped away as fast as the car could go. In the front passenger seat, Jacob held on to the dashboard with both hands as they slid around a corner, the tires shrieking against the pavement, terrified pedestrians jumping away from the curb. The car's back end fishtailed from side to side as Chelsea struggled to get it back under control. In the backseat, Kelly was screaming. She was getting thrown around back there, trying desperately to find something to hold on to. They went through four more turns before Jacob finally started to yell, "Chelsea, slow down! You're gonna get us killed."

But Chelsea was too terrified to back off. Her eyes were wide and she was panting. She kept saying, "No, no, no!" over and over again, completely out of control.

Jacob grabbed for the wheel. "Chelsea, stop!" He yelled in her ear. "Chelsea!"

She looked at him then, and he could see the light of clarity coming back into her eyes. "Jacob?"

"Yeah, now slow it down. That's it, that's good."

Chelsea eased the car down and steered through the streets.

"Where are we going?" Jacob asked.

Chelsea shook her head. "I don't know." The look of panic flooded back into her face and Jacob felt the car tremble as she dug deeper into the throttle.

"Easy," Jacob said. "Chelsea, easy. Pull over, okay?"

"We have to get out of here."

"I know," Jacob said. "But for right now, just pull over."

Chelsea eased the car to the curb. She looked like she was about to say something, but then the stress and fear and panic all caught up with her and she collapsed, her chin sagging to her chest, making her look like a balloon going flat. She put her face in her hands and cried.

Jacob glanced at Kelly in the backseat and shrugged. Kelly leaned forward and put a hand on Chelsea's shoulder. "Chelsea, baby, what is going on? Who were those men?"

Chelsea just shook her head.

"Why were they after you?"

"I don't know."

Jacob picked up the pistol he'd taken from Chelsea's attackers and tried to find a brand name on it someplace. There was none. "This weapon . . . I've never seen anything like it. Where were they taking you?"

"I don't know," she said again. She was starting to whine. "Stop asking me."

Kelly squeezed the younger woman's shoulder again and said, "Chelsea, please, you have to tell us what's going on. We're caught up in this, too, now."

Chelsea took a few deep breaths. Her face was shiny with tears and her eyes bloodshot. She wiped her nose with the back of her hand, then took the pistol she'd taken off her attackers and handed it to Jacob. "You keep that," she said. "I . . . I can't."

"Chelsea," Kelly said, "those men. What do you mean, they are enemies of your father? You told us your parents both died when the *Darwin* crashed."

"They did."

"I don't understand. If your father's dead, why would those men be after you?"

"Do you remember the notebooks I showed you, back on the *Darwin*?"

"Yes, of course. Your father's work on morphic field theory."

"I took them. Those men want them back."

Kelly frowned. "Chelsea, I read those notebooks. Your father had pretty much figured out how morphic fields could be used to control zombie behavior. That's a huge discovery. Why would anyone want to kill you for that? Wouldn't they want the world to see it? A lot of lives could be saved."

"That's not it," Chelsea said, shaking her head. "Morphic field theory is the technological basis of our society. It runs our aerofluyts and powers our cities. It's even powering this car. But there's a downside, and it's a big one. My father's work showed that morphic fields were doing more harm than good. They're cooking us from the inside out and changing the structure of our brains. My father predicted we'd have the collective thinking power of a turnip within two generations. A lot of people make a lot of money off of morphic field power. My father's work was going to blow all that apart."

"Oh," said Kelly. She sat back in her seat and traded a worried look with Jacob.

"What did you do with your father's work?" Jacob asked. "Did you try to show it to anybody? One of your father's friends, maybe?"

"Friends of my father's are hard to come by these days," Chelsea said. "The same people who want my father's research have been smearing his name all over the place. They're blaming him and his research for the wreck of the *Darwin*."

"Oh God," Kelly said. "Baby, I'm so sorry."

"And so that's it?" Jacob asked. "There's nobody you can turn to?"

"When they caught me, I was at the Terminal. I was going to see my aunt Miriam. She works in the shipyards in El Paso, where they make the aerofluyts."

"What did you do with your father's research?" Kelly asked.

"I wedged the notebooks behind a toilet in the women's bathroom."

Kelly raised an eyebrow.

"It was the only choice I had."

"We'll make it work," Jacob said. "We get the notebooks back and get them to your aunt Miriam. Is that the plan?"

"I can't ask you guys to help me," Chelsea said. "These people are trying to kill me."

"And they just tried to kill us, too," said Jacob. "The way I look at it, we don't have any other choice but to help you. Kelly—what's wrong?"

In the backseat, Kelly suddenly looked ill.

"What is it?"

"We have to ditch this car," Kelly said.

"But why?"

"Jacob, look around you," Kelly said. "Don't you think they can track this car? I bet they're on the way here right now."

She was right, of course. Jacob had learned that about Kelly over the years. She usually was right, and she never failed to remind him of that.

He patted Chelsea's shoulder and pointed toward a narrow lane behind some nearby houses. "Pull the car into that alley over there. We'll leave it behind all those bushes."

"But she can't walk to the Terminal," Chelsea said. "It's on the opposite end of the island from here."

"We'll figure something out," he said. "Now hurry. Let's hide this thing."

Chelsea drove into the alley. It was dense with brush and swallowed the car almost immediately. Jacob moved a few branches around to cover the back end, and together they headed back for the main road.

No one seemed to notice them. The street was quiet. There were a few pedestrians walking the sidewalks, but they all seemed absorbed in their conversations. A few cars went by, but nobody stopped, or even slowed, to check them out.

"Where to?" Jacob asked.

Kelly pointed to a restaurant halfway down the block. A hand-painted sign hanging above the door said SEAWALL COFFEE HOUSE. "There, I guess? We can get out of sight, at least."

"If they're really looking for us, they'll go door to door," Jacob said. "A public place like that will be one of the first places they look."

Jacob pulled his shirt over the pistols as best he could, hoping the bulges wouldn't show. The last thing he wanted to do right now was attract attention.

"Probably. But they'll definitely see us if we wait out here."

"Yeah," he said. "That's true."

The restaurant, which must have been built to be someone's house many years earlier, was now a coffee shop and bakery, with tables and chairs crammed together in the front rooms and black-and-white pictures of Old Galveston hanging on the walls. A long, low counter stood off to their left, and Jacob could see loaves of artisanal bread and cookies and muffins in the glass cabinets. One of Jacob's favorite memories from growing up in Arbella was riding his bike through the streets just after dawn and smelling the odor of fresh-baked bread in the air. The same odor hung in the air here, as well, but it was faint, as though all the baking had ended hours earlier.

Very few of the tables were occupied, and no one seemed to pay them any mind as they walked inside. One table, though, with an older Asian couple, glanced at Chelsea with a worried frown.

Jacob followed their gaze and instantly understood why. Chelsea's face was still wet and red from the tears she'd shed in the car. That was going to be a problem.

But before he could say as much to the girl, a very skinny, but still quite pretty dark-haired woman in a green apron approached them. It looked like she was about to ask them if they'd like to sit down, but then she saw Chelsea. "Is there a problem?" the woman asked.

Kelly put a hand on Jacob's arm. "I got it," she said.

She leaned in close to the woman in the green apron and whispered something in her ear that Jacob couldn't quite make out.

"Oh," the woman said. She turned and pointed down

the hallway that led to the back of the restaurant. "Sure, yeah, of course. It's straight back through there, second door on the left."

"Thank you," Kelly said.

"If you look in the cabinet under the sink you should find some complimentary ones, if you don't have what you need."

"Perfect," Kelly said. "Jacob, will you find us a seat?"

"Uh, sure," Jacob said.

Kelly put her arm around Chelsea and led her away.

The hostess motioned toward a table in the corner. "Will that work for you guys?"

The table was right next to a window. At a glance, Jacob could see a wide section of the street to the west of them, and the mouth of the alley where they'd hid the car to the east. "Yeah," he said, forcing a smile. He was anxious, his nerves a wreck as he started to come down off the adrenaline dump he'd experienced during the gunfight and their escape. But he knew he had to hold it together. "Sure. This is lovely. Thank you."

"Can I get you a drink?"

He ordered a glass of sweet tea with some lemonade in it. After the hostess left him, he sighed heavily and sank into himself. He closed his eyes and let go of as much of the built-up fear and confusion as he could. It helped a little, but not much. He still felt like a live wire had been wrapped around his skin.

He ran a finger across the clean, white tablecloth, over the shiny silverware, watched the sun sparkle in the empty glasses. Everything was so clean and fancy here in Temple. This was a rich and powerful society, and the truth was, they had him by the balls. Jacob and Kelly were completely lost here. Kelly hardly knew her way around at all, and Jacob certainly didn't. Chelsea had no doubt spent some of her time since returning to Temple getting reacquainted with her old home, but even her knowledge of the place couldn't get them far, and he began to wonder what a culture that despised police officers did with murderers like him.

Outside, a large shadow crossed the street.

Jacob craned his neck forward, so he could see the sky. A large black, wasp-looking aircraft was circling overhead. Gooseflesh suddenly broke out all over Jacob's skin. His hands went numb. They'd caught up with them already.

As he watched the sky, two more of the wasp-like aircraft appeared. The three of them circled above the alley near where they'd ditched the car, and Jacob realized to his horror that Kelly had been exactly right. She'd no doubt saved their lives.

Now it was up to him to get them the rest of the way.

He rose from his chair, and as he did, two of the aircraft veered off and started making slow circles of the surrounding area.

A fourth aircraft, larger and boxier than the first three, its engines roaring, touched down near the entrance to the alley. A door opened on one side of the aircraft and a dozen men climbed out. Jacob had seen their like before, all of them tall and lean, highly focused, like soldiers. They disembarked, scanned the surrounding street, then began to fan out in groups of twos. Jacob didn't see any weapons on the men, but he knew they were there.

He reached around and adjusted the pair of pistols he'd secreted away into the waistband of his pants. If he had to take the fight to them, he probably wouldn't last long. After seeing what these strange pistols could do, he had no doubt that a group of well-trained men could make short work of him. And those wasp-like aircraft, whatever they were, looked like military hardware. If the soldiers didn't get him, the aircraft certainly would.

He had to find another way.

He went to the back of the restaurant and found the door the hostess had pointed out to Kelly a few minutes earlier. He knocked on the door.

"Kelly," he whispered.

Kelly opened the door. Behind her, Jacob saw Chelsea drying her face over the sink. "What is it?" she asked.

"We've got trouble," he said. "A lot of it."

"They're here already."

"Yeah. We can't go out the front. They're all over the street. We need another way out."

"I saw the back door was open," Kelly said, and nodded toward another hallway.

"What's going on?" Chelsea said from behind Kelly.

"We need to get moving," Jacob said. "We're going out the back."

He held the door open and waved them out. As he let it close, he happened to glance toward the front of the restaurant. Two of the soldiers were coming in through the doors.

He watched one of the men signal for the hostess. The woman in the green apron nodded at whatever the man said and pointed toward the corner, where she'd seated Jacob.

"Crap," Jacob muttered. He ran after Kelly and Chelsea, catching up with them right as they reached the back door. "We have to clear out," he said. "They're gonna be coming back here any second."

"Where do we go?"

The alley behind the restaurant was wide. Every building, every fence, every balcony, was festooned in vines thick with red and yellow flowers. The only thing out of place was a big, square-shaped truck. An employee of the restaurant was hauling a basket of towels and linens to the open back end of the truck. He hadn't noticed them.

"Jacob?" Kelly said.

There was enough cover, Jacob thought, that he might be able to get the jump on the two soldiers about to rush through the restaurant. But that was no good. As soon as he took them out, provided he could even do that, he'd have to deal with the aircraft circling overhead. The pilots would see them for sure, and they'd be done with moments later.

He wouldn't even be able to set up a diversion that would allow the girls to escape.

"That's an Oppe Linens truck," Chelsea said. "They converted the old Oppe Elementary School into a laundry. They're right next to Scholes."

"Would the driver give us a ride?" Kelly asked.

"There is no driver. All work trucks are automated. They do their rounds and eventually end up back at the laundry." She pointed to the employee who was dumping linens into the back end of the truck. "All we have to do is wait for him to finish and then go up front and pay the drop fee."

Jacob glanced back toward the front of the restaurant. "Let's hope he hurries."

"He's done now," Chelsea said. "See, he's going up front."

Jacob turned back to the alley just as the man was disappearing around the far side of the truck. "Okay," he said. "Go!"

The three of them ran for the back of the linen truck as quietly as they could. He could see the feet of the restaurant's employee up near the front of the truck. It didn't take him long to pay, and within moments he was walking back toward them.

Chelsea was already inside, worming her way under the mounds of soiled linens.

Jacob motioned to Kelly to hurry, and when she wasn't fast enough, he grabbed her legs and hurled her inside, wincing at her grunt of surprise.

He glanced again under the truck and saw the employee was almost to the back of the truck. Jacob threw himself into the back of the truck and landed hard right next to Kelly.

"Get the towels on top of us," he whispered. "Hurry!"

They pulled dirty tablecloths and soaking wet hand towels over their bodies, covering up just as the employee rounded the corner and slapped the button to close the back. Jacob peeked at the man, who looked bored and far away, and prayed for a break.

As the man pushed the button that raised the mesh screen over the back end, two of the soldiers came up on either side of him.

Jacob had Chelsea on his left and Kelly on his right. Both women turned stiff with fear. Chelsea was breathing so fast and so hard, Jacob thought for sure the men would hear her.

For a moment he thought of drawing his pistols. What harm could it do at this point anyway? They'd see the movement under the towels, but at least he had a chance of getting the jump on them.

"I haven't seen anybody," the restaurant employee said.

"How long have you been out here?"

"I don't know. Ten minutes, maybe."

"And you didn't see anybody at all out here?"

The man shrugged. "Nobody."

One of the soldiers stepped away from the truck and started to scan the alleyway. His partner hit the button to open the metal screen and, as it came up, pulled his pistol.

Jacob braced himself for the fight he knew was coming. He started to mentally rehearse drawing his gun, getting it on target.

The soldier poked at the mound of towels with the barrel of his gun, and even lifted a few of the towels out of the way. Beside Jacob, Chelsea felt like she was about to rattle herself to pieces. Jacob breathed in shallowly through his mouth, so as not to make a noise, the way Sheriff Taylor had taught him when he was first learning how to be a deputy and they were trying to sneak up on somebody who didn't want to be caught. He figured, if he had to, he could kick the gun away, which might buy him enough time to pull his own weapon.

He could probably squeeze off a shot on this guy, but after that, he'd be fucked.

The other soldier would blast him into a muddy red crater before he could even climb out of the truck.

"You got something in there?"

The soldier standing at the back of the truck poked the barrel of his weapon into the mound of towels again, then turned away. "No, nothing."

"Alright, secure the back door of the restaurant. I'll get us some more eyes out here."

The two soldiers split up, leaving the restaurant employee standing there by the back door of the truck. The man glanced from one soldier to the next, gave a barely noticeable shrug, and walked around to the front of the truck.

The next instant, the truck lurched forward, picking up speed. As the truck rumbled away from the restaurant, Jacob leaned forward just enough to watch the soldiers continuing their search.

For the first time, he thought they might actually be able to pull this off.

Beside him, Kelly sat up. "Are we clear?"

"For now," Jacob said. "But we need a plan."

CHAPTER 6

Two hours later the laundry truck lurched to a stop. It shook a little as something latched on to the front end, and then it settled with a pneumatic sigh. The vehicle had made four other stops after leaving the restaurant, with more linen heaped on them at every drop, so that now Jacob and the others were buried under a mountain of damp towels and tablecloths.

They waited for someone to come along, but after ten minutes, they were still waiting.

"I think we've made it to the laundry," Chelsea said. "That must have been what that jolt was. The truck settling into its charging station."

"Do you think it's safe?" Kelly asked.

So much laundry had been piled on top of them that Jacob could no longer see the back door. "Hold on, I'll check," he said, and pulled himself free. He crawled over to the back door. He scanned as much of the loading dock as he could through the metal screen, then pushed it open and stuck his head out.

He didn't see any workers.

Any human workers, anyway.

He did see several unmanned wagons trundling around the larger trucks, though. As he watched, one of the wagons slid underneath a truck, clicked into place, and waited for the larger vehicle to empty its cargo through a chute at the bottom. That done, the wagon pulled out, made its way up a concrete ramp, and continued on and out of sight through a hallway. There were four other trucks nestled into docking stations next to theirs, and robot wagons came and went with the regularity of the figurines in a cuckoo clock.

"Wow," Jacob muttered.

"What is it? Are we okay?" Kelly asked.

"I think so. I don't see anybody."

"Good," Chelsea said. "Let's get out of here. This smells gross."

"Beats being dead," he said.

He climbed out of the truck, then helped Kelly and Chelsea out. Kelly started to ask Chelsea which way they were supposed to go, but stopped when she caught sight of another unmanned wagon collecting its payload. Her mouth fell open, and she watched the automated operation in stunned silence. Once again Jacob had to suppress a smile. Even as a horny kid, who at sixteen hadn't thought much beyond talking Kelly out of her bikini, Jacob had known she was something special. Smart as a whip. That was what his momma always used to say about her. But she was born in the wrong place. A woman like her, smart as she was, should have been born here, in Temple, where her mind could swim in wonders like this.

"I can't believe this," she said. "How is this even . . .

Chelsea, how did your people do all this? How did this kind of technology survive? It's incredible."

"It's a laundry," Chelsea said.

"Yeah, but . . ."

"Seriously, it's a laundry."

The trucks came and went on a driveway that curved around the edge of the loading dock. Chelsea made her way around the driveway without waiting on the others. Jacob watched her go and marveled at how easily the girl seemed to have adjusted to coming back home. When he'd met her in the Slaver caravan, she was so sick she couldn't even stand. Nick had been forced to carry her as the Slavers drove them from one campsite to the next. She'd been a mangy-looking wreck then, so downtrodden and beaten that he'd mistakenly thought she'd been born into slavery. But now, barely a month back in civilization, she'd put on enough weight to look healthy and she seemed in control, in her element. She was taking on the world, fighting the power.

Of course, she was only seventeen.

Jacob still remembered being seventeen. He'd been bulletproof at that age. He could go weeks at a time out in the Zone, working with the salvage teams, dodging zombies and wild animals, sleeping on the ground and carrying a hundred pounds of scrap on his back, and then come back to one of his mother's home-cooked meals in Arbella. Nothing got to him back then. He could work all day and play all night and never miss a beat. He'd been so rock-solid back then he'd even thrown away the love of his life, and laughed about it with his friends.

With Nick.

Yeah, back then he'd been bulletproof.

He touched Kelly's shoulder. "We need to go," he said.

She nodded.

Together, they walked up the driveway and into the bright glare of the afternoon sun. Stretched out before them was Scholes Field, the air travel hub of Chelsea's world. The rest of Temple, at least the parts he'd seen, had embraced the look and feel of Old World Galveston. He'd seen street after street of wooden houses painted in pastels, vibrant as Easter eggs, and big, blocky government buildings made of dust-colored Texas granite, all relics of a distant, more glamorous time. But he'd seen nothing on the island like the Scholes Field Terminal. It looked like a giant stone octopus rising from a field of coastal grass. Huge, curvy arms, tentacle-like, radiated out from a central building five stories high. Docked up and down the length of the various arms were small aircraft the size of railroad boxcars. Scanning the field, Jacob saw dozens of different designs and configurations. Some looked sleek and fast, their hulls shaped like teardrops and glistening in the afternoon sun, while others looked boxy and powerful, obvious workhorses. And above them, thick as noodles in places, gleaming white trains hissed quietly along monorail tracks.

But the thing that dominated his attention was an aerofluyt half a mile away, just beginning to lift off. It was magnificent in the sunshine, as huge as the ruined skyscrapers he'd seen in Little Rock. It rose from the field on a shimmering cushion of air. Bright lights shone down its thousand-foot-long flanks, glowing, even in the glare of midday. Just days out of Arbella, back before the Slaver caravan had taken his friends, back when he still held on to the hope that he could do great things, Jacob had seen an aerofluyt like this one glide overhead. It hadn't made a sound, and yet, every piece of metal, from the window frames of the gas station where he and his party had taken shelter for the night, to the forks and spoons on their plates, to the old-fashioned metal signs on the wall, had started to dance and shake and rise into the air. His teeth shook in their sockets. His stomach had turned queasy, like he was looking down from a great height. He felt small and helpless and terrified.

He didn't feel that way now, though.

Now, watching the behemoth rise from the grassy field, he felt only awe, and wondered how such things could possibly be.

"It's your turn," Kelly said.

"What?" Jacob said. He was surprised to find that he'd been holding his breath.

"To be amazed," she said. "It's incredible, isn't it? How is it that we still have to wash our clothes in buckets, while they can make something like that fly?"

"It is incredible," he agreed. He turned back to the aerofluyt and shook his head. "Chelsea, where do you think that thing's headed?"

The younger woman was twenty yards ahead of them. At the sound of her name she stopped and turned impatiently. "Who knows?" she said. "They go all over the world. They can stay aloft for twenty years at a time, if they need to. The only reason they ever land is to load and off-load passengers."

"All over the world . . . you mean . . ."

"Mexico City. Wuchuan, China. Wellington, New Zealand. Salt Lake City. All over the world. Wherever my people have outposts."

Jacob shook his head. "Incredible."

"Yeah, I guess," Chelsea said with a shrug. "You mind if we go now? We've still got to find a ride out of here."

Jacob nodded.

"Okay. And listen, the two of you need to get your collective shit together, okay? All this, everything you see, it's all normal. There's nothing here that my people haven't grown up with. If you gawk like idiots, you're going to get us caught."

Jacob traded a glance with Kelly.

She smiled back at him.

"Yeah," he said to Chelsea. "That sounds fair enough. Lead on. We promise not to behave like a bunch of slack-jawed yokels."

Chelsea frowned at that, not getting it, but evidently decided it wasn't worth the effort. She started walking the long road that led to the airfield's main terminal.

"Jacob, is this safe?" Kelly asked. She looked around nervously. "Being out in the open like this?"

Jacob looked around. A long line of cars slid silently by, but nobody seemed to be paying them any attention. He realized he'd been bracing himself for one of those cars to suddenly veer to the curb and for armed men to jump out. He had no idea what they'd do if that happened. Out in the open like this, there was no way for them to run.

"I don't like it, either," he said. They weren't far from the terminal now, and he nodded toward it, where large crowds of people were hurrying about their business. "Something goes wrong, I say we run that way, try to get lost in the crowds."

"You think that'll work?"

"I think we'll be okay," he said.

She frowned at that. "Do you really, or are you just saying that?"

He didn't answer. He'd managed to break her heart, all those years ago, but he'd never been able to lie to her. She had a way of seeing right through him.

He followed after Chelsea, and after a few steps, Kelly rushed forward to walk with him. Within a few moments they'd started to merge with the crowd. Jacob had lived in Arbella nearly his entire life. He was no stranger to crowds and markets, but back home the markets were noisy, happy places, with children running everywhere and vendors calling out to their friends and neighbors, trying to arrange trades of produce or chickens or whatever they had to barter with.

The mood here was very different. All around him, the main hall bustled with travelers as they pressed impatiently through the crowd. Everybody seemed to be in such a hurry. Chelsea had said this was the hub for travelers from all over the world, and he no longer doubted that. Such wild clothes. So many unusual faces. They walked around him, speaking languages he couldn't recognize. He turned and tried to take it all in, his smile growing wider.

There were food booths all along the walls, and the smell of roasting meats and spices and fresh baked bread was overpowering. He saw chicken cooking on grills and meat being sliced from long sword-like skewers and huge shallow pans with a reddish-yellow rice dish piled high with chunks of seafood. He'd seen pictures of squid, back in school, but he'd never seen one in real life until now. He was simultaneously disgusted and intrigued. It smelled so good.

The woman sitting on the far side of the shallow pot smiled at him. "You like paella?" she said.

"I don't know," Jacob admitted. "It smells amazing."

"You try," the woman said. "Five BCs. I make you a big bowl."

"BCs?" Jacob said.

Kelly touched his shoulder. "They use money here, Jacob."

"Oh," he said. He turned to the paella woman. "I'm sorry, I don't have any money."

The woman's expression hardened for a moment. But when she turned to other passersby, her smile returned. Jacob stood there in surprise for a moment, a little taken aback by the transparency of the woman's feigned friendliness.

"Hey," Kelly said in a whisper. She gave his arm a nudge. "We're supposed to look like we do this every day, remember?"

"Yeah," he said. "Sorry, but that just made me realize something. How are we going to get a ride to El Paso without any money?"

Chelsea had been over at a bank of video monitors, but she returned in time to hear Jacob's question. "We have plenty of money," she said. "From my dad."

"But I thought your dad didn't have any friends left here," Kelly said.

"He doesn't. But he was a wealthy man. We have all the money we need. What we don't have is a lot of time." She nodded toward the black glass globes on the ceiling. "See those? Those are video cameras. This whole place is being watched. And if those men work for Lester Brooks, they'll have access to facial recognition software. It'll only be a matter of time before they show up here."

"How long?" Jacob asked.

"How should I know?" Chelsea said. "Could be ten minutes from now, could be right now. But that's not our only problem. Come over here and watch this."

She led them to the video monitors.

Every screen played a news feed in some foreign language. He couldn't understand any of them. But the images needed no translation. He saw teeming masses of ragged zombies, thousands of them, advancing through ruined suburban streets like rivers, devouring everything in their path. Aircraft, similar to the ones that had hunted them just a few hours earlier, circled overhead. The camera panned back, revealing a tide of living dead that stretched far off into the distance, and Jacob realized that what he was seeing was just the tip of some gigantic iceberg. He'd never seen so many zombies, even in the pictures they'd shown him back in school of the First Days.

"Kelly," he said, pointing at the monitor.

She was looking at a different monitor, but it displayed an image much the same as what he was seeing. She nodded, too stricken to speak.

To his left, two bearded men were pointing at the screens and talking loudly in yet another language he didn't recognize. He could tell they were angry, though.

A lot of people watching the monitors looked angry, in fact.

"What's going on?" he said to Chelsea. "What is this?"

"That's El Paso," Chelsea said. "The outskirts of it, anyway. The Technology Yards are closer in to the center of town, behind the defenses. The city's been put on lockdown. All travel in and out has been cancelled."

"So we're stuck here?" Kelly said. She gestured at

the crowd gathered around the monitors. "Is that what all these people are so angry about?"

"With good reason," Chelsea said. "Those zombies you see there, that's just a satellite of the Great Texas Herd. My father used to say that was the biggest herd in the world. He said they were more than a hundred million strong."

"But I don't understand," Jacob said. "When we were being held by Mother Jane and her family, we saw one of those aerofluyts steer a giant herd away from the camp. Can't they do that here?"

"They tried that already." Chelsea pointed at a pretty young Asian woman in a red suit, her image superimposed over an aerial image of a slowly advancing zombie horde. "That's what this newswoman is saying. The *Newton* has already made multiple sweeps overhead. Ordinarily, an aerofluyt's morphic field generator can be used to shepherd herds wherever you want them to go, but it's not working."

Chelsea turned back to the monitor and listened for a moment.

"Now she's saying that El Paso has been attacked before, but always by satellite herds, never like this. Their automated defenses have held in the past, but they don't think they can handle a herd this size. They're directing all personnel into the tunnels beneath the city."

"They've got aircraft," Jacob said. "Why don't they just fire-bomb them from the air? With the technology you people have, you could wipe them out in minutes."

"Be quiet," Chelsea said in a stage whisper. "People will hear you."

"So?"

"So, we don't have a military here in Temple. We don't believe in guns."

"Are you fucking kidding me?" Jacob said.

"Keep your voice down," Chelsea said.

Kelly put a hand on his shoulder. "Jacob," she said. "We need to work this out."

"No shit," he said. He turned to Chelsea and shook his head. "Look, I'm sorry. But what the hell are we doing here? No guns. Really? Chelsea, we were chased by the same guys, right?"

She crossed her arms over her chest. "I don't know who those men were. I don't. I think they work for Lester Brooks, but I don't know that for sure. Those weapons are only supposed to be available to exploration parties on the aerofluyts. They shouldn't be here in Temple."

"Yeah, well, guess what. I don't think they care about your fucking rules."

"But they shouldn't be here."

"Okay, but they are here. Why are we arguing about this?"

Chelsea looked away. "This shouldn't be happening," she said.

Jacob was beyond frustration. "Okay, well, one thing is clear. We're not going to El Paso. We need to figure something else out."

Chelsea spun around, suddenly full of fury. "But we have to go there. Don't you see?"

"No, I don't," Jacob said.

"My family is there."

He pointed at the monitors. "Am I talking to a wall here? Chelsea, look at that. I see rivers of dead people. You tell me there could be a hundred million more on the way. I can't even imagine what that looks like, and you expect me to just dive on in because your family is there? No thanks. I've done my share of stupid things, but that is not going to be one of them."

Chelsea looked at Kelly, hoping for some kind of support.

"Chelsea," Kelly said, shrugging her shoulders helplessly, "I really don't—"

"But we have to get there. My aunt Miriam, she's the only one who can help us."

"She can't be the only one," Jacob said. "I mean, look at all these news feeds. Can't we just send a bunch of copies of your father's notes to these people and let them spread the word?"

"That wouldn't work."

"How do you know that? These people could clear your father's name with a single broadcast."

"Yeah, maybe, if it ever got to them. But it wouldn't."

"Why not?"

"You really don't understand how this works, do you?"

"How what works?"

Chelsea pointed at the screens. "This. The political part of this. Every station you see here, every broadcast, Lester Brooks controls them all. He sets the tone. He's the one who decides what the public hears."

"One man?" Jacob said. "Chelsea, I'm sorry, but that's kind of paranoid."

"But he does," Chelsea said. She was yelling loud enough to attract the attention of some of the others standing around them, and seeing that quieted her down. She waited until the people in the crowd went back to their own business before speaking again. "You have to understand," she said, "in the span of a few months, he managed to turn my father into the biggest villain

Temple has known since the initial outbreak. My father used to be a great man, but Lester Brooks has turned him into a monster. Ask anyone in this place, they'll tell you exactly what Lester Brooks has guided them to say."

Jacob could only shake his head. But he couldn't drop the point, either. "I think that's ridiculous, Chelsea. One man can control an entire world's worth of information. Do you really believe that?"

She smiled, like he'd fallen into some kind of trap. "What I think is that it's proof my father was right about the morphic field generators. They really are turning us into sheep. Don't you see? He was right."

"Chelsea, are you listening to yourself? Do you realize how para—"

She cut him off with a wave of her hand, then nodded at something over Jacob's shoulder. "We're out of time," she said. "Look."

Jacob turned. He scanned the crowd, and saw two men standing on the edge of the crowd, slowly and deliberately looking at everyone there. He saw two more pairs waiting at the side doors, and another standing near the bottom of the escalators that led up to the monorail trains.

"I have to get my father's notebooks," Chelsea said.

"And then what?" Jacob asked.

She pointed down a hallway behind the escalators. "Down there," she said. "We can find transport down there."

"But you just said all flights were cancelled."

"All manned flights, yeah, but not routine cargo deliveries. Those are unmanned freighters."

"I still don't think this is—"

"Would you just go, please? They're coming this way."

She was right. One of the men over by the main entrance was looking right at them. He touched his neck and started to talk, but Jacob couldn't read his lips.

He didn't have to, though.

It was obvious enough the man was calling them in. They had to move.

"How will we know what we're looking for?" Jacob asked.

"You'll know."

"And you? How will we find you?"

"I'll find you," she said.

With that she ducked into the crowd and silently slipped away. She was a small girl, just barely over five feet tall and hardly ninety pounds. She was gone in the blink of an eye.

"Jacob, what do we do?"

"We can't stay here. Those guys want her for the notebooks, but we're not worth anything to them. They'll kill us."

"Oh God," she said. "I don't want to be here."

"Me, either." He grabbed her shoulder and pulled her away from there. He glanced back and saw the men moving toward them at a trot, pushing people out of the way as they forced their way through the crowd.

They slipped around the escalators and fell in with the crowd moving toward the main passenger terminals.

He pulled her close and dropped his voice to a whisper. "Duck out here."

They turned into the empty hallway Chelsea had pointed out to them, but a fat man in blue robes was trying to get around them, and they nearly knocked him over.

"Hey," he said.

Jacob tried to guide Kelly farther down the hall, but the man was angry. He raised his voice. "Hey, you there."

Jacob looked back at the man. He was short and round, his skin a deep coffee color. His robes sparkled in the daylight. He wasn't going to move on, and meanwhile the men hunting them were getting closer.

He grabbed Kelly, spun her around, and pushed her up against the wall. Before she could say a word in protest, he pressed his lips to hers in a rough, clumsy kiss he tried to make look real.

She pushed against him, not returning the kiss at all, but it must have looked real enough, for the fat man stuck two fingers in the air at them and walked off.

Jacob released Kelly from the kiss.

He watched the man in the blue robes walk away, and then turned back to Kelly. He was about to tell her they had to start searching the corridor when she kicked his shin.

"Hey," he said.

"Don't you ever do that again."

"I was . . . I was just trying . . ."

"I don't care," she said, anger flashing in her eyes. "Don't you ever . . . Don't ever touch me like that again."

"Alright," he said. "Yeah, okay."

She pushed him away and smoothed out her blouse. She pushed the hair back from her forehead and gathered herself together. "Fine," she said.

He took a step back, and in that moment he realized

that she hadn't had the luxury of a disconnect the way he had. He'd had two long stretches of unconsciousness. But Kelly, she'd been awake the whole time. She'd lived first with Barry's death, and then with Nick's. She'd had lots of time to sit and stew in the misery and heartache of losing loved ones. His pain was still to come. But hers was an open wound, inflamed and burning, and raw.

"I'm sorry," he said again.

"Just shut up," she said. She grunted. "Oh shit."

Jacob looked up. Two of the men he'd seen following them were coming down the hallway. Both had weapons drawn.

One of the men, dressed in a white tunic and brown pants, raised a pistol at Jacob's face and gave it a flick, motioning Jacob down a side passageway. "Down there," he said.

"Yeah, right," Jacob said.

"Move," the man said.

"Kiss my ass," Jacob said.

The man rushed forward, his partner coming around him with his pistol raised. The first man shoved Jacob in the chest hard enough to send him crashing into the wall. Before Jacob could recover, the man got in close, dug his fingers into Jacob's underarm, and pushed him deeper into the corridor. He was trying to push Jacob around the corner, out of sight of the crowd. As soon as Jacob realized what the man was doing, he fell backward, sending his attacker off balance.

The man stumbled forward, and when his pistol dipped, Jacob chopped down on the man's wrist.

The pistol clattered to the metal floor.

The man tried to reach for it, but got Jacob's knee to his nose instead. The blow landed perfectly. The man stumbled backward on uncertain feet, his eyes staring at nothing as he fell over. He lay there, unable to stand, twisting from side to side like a man too fat to pull himself to his feet.

Jacob rushed forward, grabbed the fallen man's pistol, and fired it at the man's chest.

Again, there was no sound. The weapon kicked in his hand, but it didn't let loose the familiar bark of a pistol. He did see the round leave the barrel, though. It was just a flash, but Jacob saw it smack into the man's chest and explode.

The man was dead the next instant, his chest suddenly nothing but an empty hole, like the belly of a canoe. Bits of blood and bone went everywhere. It splashed onto Jacob's face and clothes, spattering him in gore.

Jacob turned toward the main hallway, but he was too late. The second man was already there, his pistol raised at Jacob's forehead. "Stop right there," the man said. "Drop the pistol."

Jacob hesitated. With one flick of the wrist he could bring his weapon to bear on the man. If he combined that with a jump to the left, he stood a chance of getting off a shot first.

"Don't do it," the man said, as though reading Jacob's mind. "These things don't cauterize. Even a glancing blow would cause you to bleed out. Get down on the ground. Let's go, facedown."

Jacob tossed his weapon to the floor. "Yeah, okay," he said.

He went to one knee. The man held the pistol in his right hand. With his left he reached into a back pocket and produced a pair of handcuffs.

"Hands behind your back," he said.

"Okay," Jacob said. "Okay, just don't shoot."

Jacob bent his other leg as though to go to the ground, but instead planted it in a sprinter's ready position and then bum-rushed the man. He managed to get under the man's gun hand just as he discharged the weapon. Distantly, Jacob heard it smack against the wall and explode harmlessly with a muffled *pop*.

He tried to lift the man off the ground and throw him onto his back, but the man recovered in time and threw his weight backward, landing with his feet spread wide apart. He raised the weapon toward Jacob, but he wasn't fast enough. Jacob was already throwing a chop down on the man's wrist, a blow that knocked the weapon to the ground at Kelly's feet.

Jacob rushed forward again, trying the same flying tackle, but the other man was ready for it. He elbowed Jacob in the back and caused him to collapse.

Jacob fell to his knees, the wind knocked out of him.

The other man lost no time at all. He grabbed Jacob by the shoulders and threw him onto his back. Then he climbed on top of Jacob, his knees holding Jacob's arms down as he began to throw punches at Jacob's face.

The man clearly knew how to work a speed bag. The punches came that fast, and every single blow felt like a cinder block crashing into Jacob's face. He raised a hand to block the punches, but the other man knocked it away and kept on pounding on his face. And somewhere during the pounding Jacob stopped feeling the blows. His mind went off its rails and he started to sink into unconsciousness.

Jacob didn't see the round hit the side of the man's head. He was too punch-drunk for that. One minute, he was looking up through a bloody screen at a steady roll of punches, and the next he was looking at a headless corpse, the man's fists going slack.

The man rolled off of him, landing in a clumsy heap on the floor. Through a haze of blood, Jacob looked up to see Kelly holding one of the pistols with both hands.

She was shaking.

"Jacob?" she said.

He groaned. He lifted a hand to her, but it fell to the floor. He couldn't stand up. His head was reeling, his vision blurry.

She tossed the pistol aside and knelt down next to him.

"No," he said. "Keep the pistol."

"Jacob, I hate guns. I can't."

"Might need it," he said.

"Jacob? Jacob, stay with me."

"I'm okay," he said. He tried to stand, but his arms felt like dead weight and he couldn't even feel his legs.

"Let me help you," Kelly said. She ducked under his arm, and somehow managed to lift him. "Jacob, can you put any weight on your feet? I can't carry you like this."

"Trying," he said.

She stiffened. "Oh crap. Somebody's coming."

Right on cue, he heard the sound of running foot-falls coming from around the corner.

"Gun," he said. "Get your . . . gun up."

"Jacob, I can't do that again."

In his mind he formed the words: *Just do it. Don't think. Just pull the trigger.* But he couldn't speak the words. His mouth was a mealy mess, and he was still zoning in and out of consciousness. It took all the strength he had just to stand.

"They're coming," Kelly said.

"Shoot."

But it was Chelsea who came around the corner, the notebooks tucked under her arms like a student bringing home a satchel of books. She let out a whimper of surprise when she saw the gun pointed at her face.

Kelly lowered her weapon. "Oh God."

Only then did Chelsea seem to notice the bodies on the floor, the blood spattered all over the ceiling, all over the walls, all over Jacob's face.

"What happened?" she said.

Jacob and Kelly said nothing. They just looked at each other, both of them still in shock.

"Are you guys okay?"

Kelly nodded. "You said you knew how to get us out of here."

Chelsea pointed toward the nose of a blocky-looking freighter visible through the main corridor's windows.

"That way," she said. "That's our ticket right there."

CHAPTER 7

Flying wasn't that bad, Jacob decided. Takeoff had been a little rough. The freighter had climbed to altitude in a rush that had pressed him against the wall and set his heart racing. He hadn't been able to clear his ears. Chelsea showed them how to hold their nose and blow, forcing their ears to pop, but Jacob couldn't do it. He'd taken a pretty hard beating back at Scholes Field that had left his eyes almost completely swollen shut, his mouth a pulpy, bloody mess, and his nose filled with drying blood. It was probably broken. It hurt like it was broken. Still, despite his discomfort, the flight hadn't been that bad. At least his nerves had settled to the point he didn't need to vomit.

But going down was bad.

Really bad.

First, the quiet was broken with an alarm, three short bursts from a siren, and before Jacob had a chance to ask what it was, the bottom dropped out from under him. His stomach rose into his throat. He groped at the walls, at the floor, desperate for something to hold on to, but there was nothing.

"What's happening?" he said. He heard the fear rising in his voice, but he couldn't hold it in check.

Kelly grabbed his hand.

He squeezed back.

The two of them huddled together, their backs pressed flat against the wall, both too scared to breathe.

"Chelsea, what's happening?" Jacob said again. His voice was cracking, but he was past caring.

"Settle down," Chelsea said, sounding thoroughly bored. "We're on final approach. We'll be landing inside of a minute."

Kelly squeezed Jacob's hand hard, but when he looked at her, she wasn't looking at him. She wasn't looking at anything. She had her head back, eyes shut tight. He couldn't tell if she was trembling, or if she was just being jostled by the buffeting of the aircraft. But he was trembling. No doubt about that.

Kelly and Chelsea had been forced to carry him in order to get him onboard. He'd barely been conscious. They'd led him down into the freighter's hold and propped him up against the wall, in the corner. Kelly sat down next to him, but Chelsea had positioned herself several feet away from them, near the stairs. At first Jacob thought it was because she didn't want to answer any more of their questions, but he could see plain enough why she'd done it now. She was holding on to the railings, nice and secure, not getting jostled around at all, like she knew this would happen.

"Is it always like this?" Jacob asked.

"Is what always like this?"

"Landing."

"No," Chelsea said. "This is supposed to be an unmanned freighter. If there were people onboard, the aircraft would be coming down in a soft landing. But, right now, with El Paso on lockdown, they don't have the time for soft landings. Don't worry, we'll be fine."

"Great," he said. He glanced again at Kelly, her breaths coming fast and shallow, eyes still shut tight, and squeezed her hand.

The aircraft shuddered. There hadn't been any sound through most of the flight. He'd heard a low muffled roar as they took off, but that had faded into the background once they made altitude. Now he was hearing it again, only this time, there was a high-pitched whining sound behind the roar.

"What is that?"

"The morphic field reactor," Chelsea said. "Would you please relax? We're fine. We're almost on the ground."

The aircraft shook again, and then went still. No falling, no sense of movement. The freighter hung in the air, then gently touched down with a soft bump.

Chelsea jumped to her feet. "See? What'd I tell you? Nothing to it."

She started to climb the stairs toward the exit.

"Hey," Kelly said. She stood up, balanced on unsteady legs. "Where are you going?"

"To find my aunt Miriam."

"Just like that?" Kelly asked. "We're just going to walk right out of here and head to your Aunt Miriam's place?"

"Yeah. Why not?"

"Why . . . ?" Kelly glanced at Jacob incredulously. "Chelsea, are you serious? This city is on lockdown. How are we supposed to walk across a city on lockdown? Especially when we're about to be overrun by the biggest herd of zombies on the planet?"

"We're not going to be walking through the city. I told you, we'll take the tunnels."

"The tunnels?"

Chelsea stepped off the stairs. "Really? I told you, there's a whole network of tunnels underneath El Paso. The city was chosen as our construction yards because of that. Anytime there's a lockdown, everybody goes underground. It happens all the time."

"And you know this how?" Jacob asked.

"My aunt Miriam," Chelsea said. "She's like an expert on it or something."

Jacob grunted. "What do you mean, *or something*?"

"I mean, it's like her hobby. She told me all about it last time I was here."

"That was seven years ago," Jacob said. "You were ten."

"I remember it just fine."

"You remember this place well enough to get us to her lab? Is that really what you're telling us?"

"There'll be signs. There's a whole rail system. It'll take us anywhere we need to go. Honestly, what is the big deal?"

"The big deal is, I don't want to get killed," Jacob said. He hooked his thumb at Kelly. "I don't want her to get killed. We've been with you for less than a day, Chelsea, and so far we've almost been killed twice. Now, I'm sorry if this upsets you, but we need a fucking plan."

"I have a plan," Chelsea said.

"Which is exactly what?"

Chelsea looked from Jacob to Kelly. Her anger seemed to ebb, replaced by uncertainty. "There are maps at all the rail stations," she said. "We just follow the maps."

Jacob waved her off and turned away in frustration.

Kelly let him go. She climbed the stairs and took Chelsea's hands in hers. "Look, Chelsea, you haven't thought this through, and that scares the hell out of us. We need to have a plan."

"You want a plan?" Jacob said. "We have to figure out a way to get back home. We can't stay here. Staying here is stupid. She's going to get us all killed."

"I will not!" Chelsea said. "I know the way."

"Bullshit," Jacob said, wheeling around to face her. "You don't know shit. I've followed you halfway across the fucking continent because I didn't have any choice, but now I've got a choice. You hear me? I have a fucking choice. And I say you're full of shit. You're a goddamn ignorant teenager without the common sense God put in the ass end of a goat, and I for one have no intention of getting myself killed because your people are fucking lunatics."

"My people?"

"You heard me. Your fucking people."

"My fucking people don't kill their best friends," Chelsea said.

That stopped Jacob cold. "Who the fuck do you think you are? Nick was my best friend. He was my friend!"

"And you fucking shot him in the face, you bastard!"

Chelsea turned away. He could hear her sobbing.

"He was my friend," Jacob said to Kelly. "She has no right."

"Jacob," she said, whispering. "Please. This isn't helping."

"But what fucking right does she have? Look, you can coddle her all you want, but this dumb kid is going to get us killed, and Kelly, I can't do that again. I can't bear that kind of responsibility again. I already hurt enough."

"You're not the only one hurting."

"I know that," he said. "Don't you think I know that? I just can't be the one who leads us into death. Not again."

"No one is asking you to lead, Jacob."

Kelly turned away before he could answer her, which was probably just as well. He was totally lost, and he always managed to say the stupidest things when he was lost. It was what had ended what they had seventeen years earlier, and he couldn't go through that again, either.

"Chelsea," Kelly said, "can you come down here, sweetie? We need to figure this out."

"There's nothing to figure out," Chelsea said. She charged down the stairs. "Why can't you two hear what I'm saying? There's nothing to figure out. I'm going to take these notebooks to my aunt Miriam, and she's going to figure out how to save my father's name."

"But you don't even know whether your aunt will help you," Kelly said.

"She has to. She has to, don't you see? She has to."

"Chelsea, please, don't shriek at me."

"I'm not shrieking!"

Chelsea stopped there. Kelly tried to put a hand on her arm, but Chelsea pushed her away.

"Don't you see? She has to help. If she doesn't, I've got nowhere else to go. I'll be ruined. She has to help."

Kelly frowned. "What do you mean, you'll be ruined? I thought you said you had your father's fortune to fall back on."

Chelsea was crying, not even trying to hold back

the tears. "I lied, okay? Are you happy with that? I lied. They've locked up my father's accounts and seized the money. I got a few thousand BCs out of the bank before it happened, but not enough to live on. They destroyed my father's name, and now they've left me with nothing."

Kelly looked confused. "But, Chelsea, why would you lie about something like that?"

"Because I didn't think you'd help me otherwise."

Kelly glanced back at Jacob for just a second, and in that moment he saw so much of the girl he'd known way back in their younger years. He saw her kindness, and her ability to adapt, to forgive, to make bridges out of blasted roads. It was strange, he thought, how he'd been forced to travel halfway across the continent, and across two decades, to see that girl again. But that was the way of things, wasn't it? You had to go far afield to remember where you lived.

Kelly went after Chelsea. "Oh sweetie," she said. "Come here."

But Jacob had had enough of the touchy-feely crap, and he didn't trust himself to speak again. Not without starting up the screaming match all over again. He went to the rear of the compartment and sulked. Let the two of them work their shit out, if they could.

He doubted it, though.

In the meantime, he'd sit in the dark and figure out how in the hell they were going to get back home. Texas was eight hundred miles across from border to border. That meant eight hundred miles, on foot, while fighting their way through the Great Texas Herd.

Wasn't going to happen.

And they couldn't just go to the authorities. The authorities were the ones looking to kill them.

Which left—

The door at the top of the stairs hissed open, breaking his thoughts off clean. A man appeared there, wearing yellow overalls with blue sleeves and a blue hard hat. He was holding a wrench in his hand, and looking like he had every intention of using it to bash somebody's head in.

"What's going on in here?" he demanded.

Kelly and Chelsea put their hands up and started backing down the stairs.

"What are you doing in here?" the man said. "Who are you people?"

Goddammit, Jacob thought. Was this really how it was going to be? Was this really how his luck was going to run?

He pulled one of the pistols from behind his back and hustled toward the stairs. The man was still coming down the stairs, the wrench held low.

"Who the hell are—"

He didn't finish the rest of his sentence. Jacob stepped between the two women and pointed the pistol right between the man's eyes.

The man made a startled, strangled sound.

"You don't have to die today," Jacob said. "But I will kill you if you don't cooperate."

The man nodded.

"Good. Drop the wrench."

The man tossed it away.

"Where are your keys?"

"Keys?" the man said. He looked genuinely confused.

"To get underground. This place is on lockdown. Where are your keys to get underground?"

Real terror had crept into the man's voice now. "I don't have any keys!"

Jacob pressed the barrel of the weapon right between the man's eyes. "I am not playing with you. Give me your keys now!"

"I don't have any keys," the man said again.

"Jacob, wait!"

It was Chelsea. "How do the doors open?" she asked. "Do they key off your Life Alert?"

The man nodded.

"Then take us to the doors."

"Please," the man said. "I have a family."

Jacob pushed Chelsea out of the way and stuck his weapon back in the man's face. "Then unless you want to be sent back to them in a bucket, I suggest you get your ass back out that door and take us underground."

"Okay," the man said. "It's this way."

They followed the man outside. Hot desert air hit them in the face, carrying with it the smell of dust and a faint, lingering reek of decay. The evening sun was low over the buildings of downtown, coloring them with shadows. In the far distance, a line of black mountains shouldered up against the sky.

"Lead on," Jacob said.

"Okay," the man said.

They were on the ground level of a large port. Their freighter had docked at what looked to Jacob to be a huge open-air hangar. There were a dozen more freighters like the one they'd just climbed out of sitting at stalls up and down the rows. He saw trucks and robots parked in stalls in the center of the hangar, but none of them were moving. Must be parked for lockdown, he thought. The zombies were attracted by movement, even that of machines.

"It's this way," the man said.

He led them up a flight of stairs, across a loading platform, and stopped in front of a doorway.

"This is it."

"Open it," Jacob said with a wave of the pistol. "Hurry it up."

The man waved his left arm over a black plastic pad next to the door, causing it to crack open with a sigh. The man pushed the door open, stepped inside, and then wheeled around fast, shoving the door back in Chelsea's face.

Jacob was ready for it, though. He jammed the barrel of his gun into the doorway and prevented it from closing. The man shoved even harder on the door, trying to keep them out. But when he realized he couldn't close the door, he glanced to one side and slapped a big red button on the wall.

Right away, sirens started to sound.

"Crap," Jacob said. He shoved Chelsea to one side. "Get out of the way."

The girl stepped to one side, allowing Jacob an open shot on the door. He took a step back and slammed his heel into the edge of the door, knocking it into the man's face. The dockworker fell onto his back as the door flew open. The man tried to scramble to his feet, but Jacob was faster. He pushed his way through the doorway and pointed the muzzle of his pistol right between the man's eyes. The man stayed on his back, his breath wet and congested as he struggled to breathe through the blooming flower of blood that had been his nose only moments before.

Kelly put a hand on his wrist. "Jacob, no. Don't kill him."

Jacob looked at her, but didn't take the pistol away. He was mad, and he was sick and tired of assholes.

"Please," Kelly said. "Not unless we have to."

Jacob turned back to the man on the floor. He met the man's terrified gaze, and in that moment, he got a glimpse of himself. He realized he wanted nothing more than to pull the trigger. He was honestly hoping that the man would make some stupid move, do something that would give him the excuse to pull the trigger.

Jacob tried to take a step back from the horror of his self-realization, but he couldn't.

He *wanted* to kill this man. He was so angry, he was willing to turn the man's head into a muddy puddle of brains and blood on the floor.

And for what?

The man had hit an alarm button. Nothing more. Did he really deserve to die?

And wouldn't Jacob have done the same thing?

Wouldn't Nick have done the same thing?

"It's this way," Chelsea said.

Startled out of his thoughts, Jacob looked up. Chelsea had moved down a side hallway. She was waving for them to follow.

"Jacob?" Kelly said.

Jacob looked back down at the bleeding man and cocked his head to one side. "Looks like it's your lucky day," he said, and lowered the pistol.

CHAPTER 8

The alarms echoed off the walls.

Jacob had never heard anything like it.

It hurt. His head felt like it was going to cave in. Not even covering his ears helped.

But he couldn't stop running. Despite the pain, he couldn't even slow down. He was bringing up the rear, and falling farther and farther behind with every step.

Chelsea was running full speed ahead, tearing around corners and running down hallways, not even bothering to see whether Kelly and Jacob were still behind her. Kelly was keeping up, but only barely. Between the noise of the sirens and the ringing in his ears from the beating he'd taken earlier that day, Jacob's head was swimming.

He yelled at them to slow down, but if Chelsea heard him over the shriek of the alarms, she made no sign of it.

"Chelsea, stop!"

Again, no response. The girl kept running. They

were moving through some kind of warehouse. The walls, the floor, the metal office doors: Everything had a grungy, worn-down look to it, like it was decades old and used hard every day. They'd passed an opening that looked out onto a wide room, two stories high, with metal girders in the ceiling and row upon row of boxes and wooden crates. Heavy-loader machines sat motionless in the shadows, the only light coming from the red emergency lights flashing overhead. Every door, every opening off the warehouse floor was covered with a heavy metal mesh gate.

"Where are we going?" he yelled at her.

"This way," she said, and turned another corner.

He reached the corner a moment later, rounded it, and froze.

A heavily armored figure was walking toward them. His armor was as bulky as a space suit, with a heavy nylon web bib in front that looked to be part body armor, part utility belt. Near the figure's shoulders, the bib formed a high, stiff collar that protected the back and sides of his neck. He wore a thick helmet with a copper-colored glass plate that hid his face from view.

Every inch of him was bulletproof.

Jacob knew that from personal experience.

Back on the wreck of the *Darwin*, he'd emptied two full magazines of .22 long-range rifle ammunition into the face and chest of a zombie wearing a similar suit. The bullets bounced harmlessly away, and the zombie trudged forward, clumsily, but steadily, every step and every swing of its arms sounding the odd, hydraulic groan of mechanical assistance.

Those same servos in the arms and legs augmented the strength of the wearer.

He'd seen the same zombie rip an arm off of a full-grown man.

But even though he'd seen the gear before, the sight of the hulking figure bearing down on them terrified him. There was no way he could win this fight. He'd already seen the rounds his stolen gun fired bounce harmlessly off a car's windshield. And he'd already seen what little good a .22 rifle did against a suit like that. He had little doubt the pistols he carried would be equally useless.

But then the armored figure surprised him.

"Who hit the alarm?" the man said, his voice, also augmented, sounded harsh, powerful, mechanical.

Jacob moved forward, his hand reaching back for one of his pistols even though he knew it would do no good.

But Chelsea was faster.

She stepped in front of the advancing figure, like she was the boss. "It was back there," she said. "I heard a man screaming."

"Okay," the figure said. "Keep moving. Go underground."

"Yes, sir."

The armored man trundled forward on his servo-powered legs. He passed by Jacob, gave him a second, curious, and maybe worried glance, but pushed on, making his way down the tunnel to the main exit leading into the freighter yards.

Chelsea watched him until he was out of sight, then motioned for the others to follow. "If we're gonna go," she said, "looks like now is the time."

"Agreed," Kelly said. "Chelsea, that was incredible. You really kept it together there."

The younger girl shrugged. "All you gotta do is make 'em think they're looking for somebody else. It's not that hard."

"Well, yeah . . ."

But Chelsea had already started running again.

Jacob watched her go and could only shake his head in frustration. He wanted to strangle the girl for her recklessness.

"What do we do, Jacob?" Kelly asked.

"Follow her," Jacob said. "We don't have any other choice."

"I hate this," Kelly said. "I feel like we're being sucked down into something we can't control."

"I know," he said. He put a hand on her wrist, and when she didn't pull away, he squeezed, gently, familiarly. "I feel the same way. But we don't have any other choice. We either follow her, or take our chances on our own. And we don't know the first thing about how these people run their business. We'd be lost here. What's the saying, strangers in a strange land?"

She nodded. She didn't say anything, but she did pull her wrist out of his hand.

It was enough.

Too soon.

Or maybe it would always be too late for them. He didn't know anymore.

She followed after Chelsea. Jacob was right on their heels. They rounded a corner and found themselves facing a large, open terminal. Men and women in different-colored work uniforms hustled for the exits. A few paused long enough to give Jacob's battered face a curious stare, but otherwise, nobody paid them any mind.

"Which way?" Jacob said.

There was an information desk on the opposite side of the room. Wide doorways opened up on both sides of the desk, and through those they could see workers hustling toward wide stairwells.

"There has to be a safe area or something through there," she said. "Some place where all these people are supposed to go when the breach alarm sounds."

"Is that where the train is?"

Chelsea shrugged. "I don't know. Probably."

"Probably?"

"Yeah, that's right. I don't know," she said again. "Let's go see. We can't stay here."

That, he couldn't argue with. He and Kelly followed her through the doorways and found themselves on the top level of a train station. Signs in English, Spanish, and Chinese directed them down the stairs. They pushed their way through the crowds of uniformed workers, down a wide, curling staircase, and stepped off on what the signs called the Tube Level.

"This is it," Chelsea said. She turned and gave Jacob and Kelly an *I told you so* look. "There's a map over there. It'll tell us where to go."

Jacob looked around. The place was packed. He'd caught a few glimpses of El Paso as they'd left the freighter, and he'd seen a few big buildings in the distance, but it was hard to imagine that so many people could come from so few big buildings. But they were here. They were everywhere.

As far as he could see, the floors, the walls, and the ceilings were done up in the same white, small square tile. There were support pillars at regular intervals up and down the station. They curved to meet the ceiling, like a tree trunk spreading out its branches. Metal benches circled the bases of the pillars. Everywhere he looked, up and down the platform, he saw people sleeping on those benches.

It struck him then, the shock that those people had no homes.

Looking at them, he realized he was seeing people who lived on the fringes, people who were desperately in need of help, of purpose, and yet got none.

How could a civilization so advanced, so capable of digging wonders like this out of the earth, fail to care for the ones who couldn't care for themselves? There were people like these back in Arbella, people with mental problems, people with substance abuse problems, people with too many problems to count; and yet, in Arbella, they were given jobs. Nobody rode for free. Nobody ate for free. Everybody worked. Everybody mattered.

They weren't allowed to go wasted and forgotten like this.

Thinking about it made him homesick, which was funny.

Ever since his teenage years, back when he was working with Arbella's salvage teams, he'd believed with the conviction of the faithful that his community needed to expand beyond its walls if they were to survive. In the time since, he'd seen wonders few of his generation had been privileged to see, from giant aerofluyts that filled the sky to electric cars to buildings that could clean the air and make it feel like spring, even in the middle of summer. Twice he'd been brought back from the brink of death by medical knowledge unheard of in his home. He'd seen glimpses of the Old World, the time before the living dead consumed the planet, and yet, even with his boundaries opened and so many wonders spread out before him, he found himself wishing for the simpler life he'd known back in Arbella. He wanted to be back there, where the nights were lit only by candlelight, and where life wasn't held so cheaply.

He was still lost in his thoughts of home as he followed Chelsea and Kelly to a large electric map on a nearby wall. It showed all of underground El Paso, all of the main tunnels, all of the train routes, everything. He'd heard Chelsea's remark that there were nine hundred miles of tunnels beneath El Paso, but looking at this map, he found it hard to believe it was only that. According to the map, not only did the tunnels extend under all of El Paso, but under the Rio Grande, as well. There were options to expand the map views into Juarez, and even beyond.

"Nick would have loved this," Jacob said.

Kelly glanced at him over her shoulder. "What did you say?"

"I was thinking of Nick."

She gave Chelsea a quick glance to make sure the girl hadn't heard, then stepped closer. "Don't beat yourself up about this morning. Dr. Brooks and the rest of the council had it in for you before you ever opened your mouth."

"Yeah, I know that's true."

"But that's not what's bothering you, is it?"

He smiled. "You know me pretty well, don't you?"

She shrugged and smiled back.

"I was thinking of Jerry Greider. I executed an innocent man."

"Jacob, that wasn't your—"

"I know that. Hold on, let me finish. I guess what's really bothering me is how I feel about it. Or how I don't feel about it. I killed Jerry, and even though I know now that he was innocent, that doesn't weigh on my conscience. I was doing what I was supposed to be doing. But what happened with Nick bothers me. I know he was guilty, and what I did was right, but it still hurts. It feels wrong, what I did to him."

"It doesn't bother you that Jerry was innocent?"

"Oh no, I didn't mean it exactly like that. I mean, well, actually, kind of. With Jerry, I had made my peace beforehand. I was ready for it, you know? Even with Amanda screaming at me that I was putting the wrong man to death, I believed in what I was doing. With Nick, I just felt like . . . I don't know, like it was personal somehow. That was what made it wrong, I guess. The feeling that it was personal."

He glanced over her shoulder at Chelsea. The girl was still studying the map, trying to figure out where they needed to go, oblivious to their conversation. That was good. If what Kelly said was true, Nick had meant a lot to her. She still couldn't wrap her mind around why Nick had to die, and there were moments, when she caught Jacob's eye, when he could see her confusion, and her hatred for him, and the bitterness burning inside her.

"Jacob," Kelly said, "I don't know how to guide you in this. But we executed an innocent man. When we get back to Arbella, that has to come up. We have to acknowledge that in some way. To me, it's a scary indictment on the Code itself. It makes me sick knowing what happened to him. It really doesn't bother you?"

"Of course it bothers me. I just meant . . . hell, I don't know what I meant. I don't know much about anything anymore. Not since we left home. That's why I brought you along. You're the smart one."

"God help us all if I'm the smart one." She smiled again, but it looked forced. "But I'm serious, Jacob.

We need to have this discussion. All of Arbella needs to have this discussion. Innocent men shouldn't die in the name of justice."

Jacob didn't really know how to respond to that. That was the thing about Kelly. She made his brain hurt. But Chelsea stepped between them the next instant, sparing him the embarrassment of saying something stupid.

"Everything okay?" the younger girl asked, looking from Jacob to Kelly.

"We're fine," Kelly said. "Just feeling like strangers in a strange land is all."

Chelsea nodded. "It is a lot to take in."

"I'll say." Jacob nodded toward the map. "I have to be honest, Chelsea. When you said there were nine hundred miles of tunnels under El Paso, I didn't believe you. Even after being onboard that aerofluyt, and seeing Temple, I wouldn't have believed all this. It's incredible."

"Isn't it?" she asked. "It's just like I remember it, too."

"Did your people build all of this?"

"Not all of it. A lot of it was here before the Outbreak. The way it was explained to me, these tunnels are a network of naturally occurring caves, primitive tunnels dug hundreds of years ago by the Native Americans, larger tunnels dug by Mexican revolutionaries, drug smugglers and human traffickers, and even larger tunnels made by the U.S. Army back in the late twentieth century. When my people came here, they just enlarged and stabilized those existing tunnels and turned them into a mass transit system. You should ask my aunt Miriam about it. She's the real expert. It's like her hobby."

Chelsea went back to the map and motioned for them to join her.

"See this?" she said, pointing to the large dot that marked the southern end of a long red line. "This is where we are. We're immediately below what used to be the El Paso International Airport. We need to take the Red Line Tube to here, beneath the old Biggs Army Airfield. That's where my aunt Miriam's shop is located."

"How do you know she'll be there?" Kelly asked. "I mean, she doesn't live in her shop, does she?"

"No, of course not. But the city is on lockdown. Knowing her, she'd rather be stuck at her shop than in her apartment. And if what we saw on the news is true about the *Hawking*'s failure to shepherd the herd with their morphic field generators, I can pretty much guarantee you that's where she'll be."

Kelly nodded.

She glanced at Jacob and he nodded back. It was the closest they'd come to a commonsense plan all day, and for the first time, Jacob was feeling pretty good about their chances. "So how do we get to the Red Line?" he asked.

Chelsea pointed at a sign over his shoulder that read RED LINE, LEVEL FOUR. "We go down those stairs there, I guess."

"Okay," Jacob said. "Excellent."

At the bottom of the stairs they joined a small crowd. Most were trying to work their way onto a sleek white train with black windows. Nearly everyone on the platform was dressed in some type of work uniform, lots of blue and yellow dungarees and lots of hard hats. Kelly wore a white blouse and tan-colored slacks. Chelsea also had on a white blouse, but she wore it untucked over a knee-length green skirt. They both fit in well enough. Jacob, on the other hand, wore a red jacket over the white shirt and pants they'd given him at the hospital. He was the only splash of red on the whole platform, and between that and the bruises to his face, he drew more than a few stares.

He just ducked his head and followed Chelsea through the crowd. The nearest open car door was directly ahead, and Jacob stood to one side to let the ladies get on first. Kelly and Chelsea found seats on the far side of the car. Kelly put herself on Chelsea's right and patted the empty seat next to her for Jacob to take.

"Jacob, what is it?"

He motioned for her to be quiet. He was still standing on the platform. From where he stood, he could see down the length of the train. The platform extended almost two hundred meters in that direction. There was another stairwell at the far end of the platform, but the crowds there weren't as heavy as where he was standing. It allowed him to see the pair of men hovering near the car doors nearest them. Both had the hard stare and chiseled toughness that he'd seen back on Galveston Island.

And they were staring right at him.

"Shit," he muttered.

"Jacob?" Kelly said. "What's wrong?"

He ignored her question and stepped onto the train. Then he craned his head forward so that he could see down the inside of the train.

Four cars down, the two men stepped onto the train.

Jacob stepped back off the train, his gaze still fixed down the length of the platform.

The two men stepped back off the train.

"Jacob, what are you doing?" Kelly asked.

"Chelsea," he said. "Let me have the notebooks."

"What? No."

"Chelsea, we don't have time for games. Give me the notebooks."

"What are you going to do with them?"

"Hopefully keep us from getting killed. Now come on, hand them over. We don't have a lot of time."

Kelly nudged Chelsea in the ribs. "Better do it."

Chelsea clutched the notebooks to her chest like they were asking her to give up her newborn child.

"Come on," Jacob said. "We do this right now or we're going to get killed. There are two more of those men down there."

"Where?" Chelsea said.

She leaned forward, and when she did, Jacob grabbed the top of the notebooks.

Chelsea wouldn't let them go.

"Chelsea, come on. You have to give them to me. They're coming for us right now. Please. You have to trust me."

There was no trust in her eyes. Certainly no forgiveness. The look she gave him could have cut glass. But she let the journals go.

Jacob took them. "Thanks," he said. "I promise you'll get them back."

"Where are you going?" Kelly asked.

"I should be right back," he said.

He looked back down through the cars. The two men had reboarded the train, and they were watching him. Jacob held up the notebooks and used them to give them a mock salute.

Then he ran from the train.

When he glanced back over his shoulder, the two men were spilling out of the car, pushing their way through the crowd as they charged after him. Jacob quickly ran down his options. He still had both pistols. He could fight his way out of this. But even if he won the gunfight, doing it here, on this platform, in front of hundreds of people, was just as good as getting caught.

So if he couldn't fight, that left running.

And there were two ways he could go.

He could go back up the way they'd come and hope to get lost in the crowds. His chances of escaping were better that way, but he'd be lost trying to find Kelly and Chelsea again. Maps had never really been his thing, even back in his days with the salvage teams.

His only option was finding a way back on the train and rejoining Kelly and Chelsea, so he needed another way out.

He found it near the front of the platform. People in white and gray uniforms were filing down from the main level, packing themselves onto the train.

A warning chime sounded over a PA system, followed by a woman's voice. "One minute to departure," she said. "All doors to the Red Line will be closing in one minute."

He glanced back to the rear of the platform and saw the men getting closer.

Whatever he was going to do, he had to do it fast.

He ran toward the front of the platform and turned up the tunnel he found there. It was packed with people, all of them in the white and gray uniforms of their company.

Jacob moved quickly. He ran halfway up the length of the tunnel and stopped at a trash can. He pulled off his jacket and stuffed it into the can. Then he pressed the notebooks against his right thigh, merged in with the crowd moving toward the platform, and lowered his gaze.

The two hired men rounded the corner a second later. They pushed workers out of the way and jumped up and down to try to catch a glimpse of Jacob. When that didn't work, they ran up the tunnel.

Jacob, his head down, using passersby to block him from view, glanced left just long enough to see the men run past. Once they were out of sight, he hustled forward and got back on the train.

The doors closed right behind him.

Kelly was at his side a moment later.

"What in the world was that about?"

"Look there," he said, and nodded up the tunnel.

The two men had stopped next to the trash can. One of them had fished Jacob's jacket out of the trash and held it up for the other one to see. They gestured at each other, then ran toward the train.

The train was already moving by the time the two men reached the platform. They tried to look through the windows, but couldn't.

Jacob held up one hand and gave them a wave as they slid by.

"Jacob, don't!" Kelly said, grabbing his hand.

"They can't see us. We got away."

"We got lucky."

It was Jacob's turn to shrug. "Yeah, but we got away."

Chapter 9

They were the only ones left on the train when it glided into Industrial Yards Station half an hour later.

Glancing out the window, Jacob got the feeling not too many people made it this far down the line, even when the city wasn't under lockdown. The Airport Station, where they'd boarded the train, was enormous. There'd been room on the platform for hundreds of people. And the place was clean and well-maintained, despite all the homeless people he'd seen there.

Industrial Yards Station, by comparison, seemed like an afterthought. The platform was barely five meters wide, and at most forty meters long. Benches lined the back wall. There were trash cans in between the gaps in the benches with paper and cups spilling out of the top. The walls, the floor, the grout in the tile: Everything had a worn-down, grungy appearance.

"This is where your aunt works?" Jacob asked, trying, unsuccessfully he thought, to keep the doubt out of his voice.

"Near here, yeah," Chelsea said. If she'd noticed his tone, she made no sign of it. "We have a little walking to do, I think."

"Okay," Jacob said, glancing at Kelly. "I'm ready if you are."

Kelly nodded.

But as soon as the doors opened, Jacob knew it wasn't going to be easy. They were greeted by a blaring alarm, five long blasts of a high-pitched siren. As soon as the last one sounded, a woman's voice came over the overhead speakers: "This area is under lockdown and has been restricted to authorized personnel only. All exits to the surface have been sealed. All surface travel has been suspended until further notice. If you notice any signs of incursion, report it immediately using the call boxes located throughout the station. Thank you."

The message repeated twice more, once in Spanish and again in Chinese.

"Come on," Chelsea said, stepping off the train.

Jacob and Kelly glanced at one another, and he saw her swallow a lump in her throat. She was scared, and so was he. Everything about this felt wrong.

But Kelly was the first to move. She stepped off the train and starting walking toward the nearest passageway off the platform.

Jacob followed.

Chelsea and Kelly rounded the corner and stopped. Kelly looked back at him and said, "Uh, Jacob. I think we have a problem."

He hurried around the corner and immediately saw the problem. A thick metal roll-down door covered the entrance.

"Jacob, what do we do?" Kelly asked.

"There's another entrance farther down," he said. "We'll try that one."

He made his way down the platform to the other entrance. Like the first, a metal roll-down door blocked it. But it looked to be in bad repair. As Jacob studied it, the women came up behind him.

"Jacob, are we stuck here?" Kelly asked. "I think the train is going to leave soon."

"I don't think this is a problem," he said.

His earlier impression that the Industrial Yards Station was not much on anybody's mind when it came to upkeep was true here, as well. The pull-down door was battered and bent, and it didn't even latch securely to the floor. Against a small group of zombies, it would probably offer adequate protection. But to a living person, somebody with a desire to break through, the door was nothing.

It didn't even fit flush with the floor.

Jacob motioned for the women to stand aside and went back to the platform. At the far end of the platform was a custodial station, and he rummaged through that until he found a broom. He brought it back to the roll-down door, then wedged the handle under the opening at the floor. He used his knee as a fulcrum and pushed down with everything he had.

The first push didn't work.

He tried again.

"Jacob, what are you doing?" Kelly asked.

He glanced up at her through his bruised and swollen eyelids. "What did Archimedes say about a lever?"

Kelly frowned. "I thought you slept through physics."

"I paid attention during the important parts. You're the smart one, so you tell me."

"He said that if he had a lever, he could lift the world," Chelsea said. "Jacob, can you get us out of here?"

He didn't answer. Instead, he bent his back into the broom handle and pushed.

The door gave way a moment later.

Jacob threw it open. "There we go," he said.

Kelly shook her head. "You're good," she said, and hurried through the door.

Chelsea followed right after her. Jacob came through right after Chelsea and pulled the door down.

"Can you seal that back up?" Kelly asked.

"On it already," Jacob said.

Jacob grabbed the bottom of the door and gave it a good hard tug, then slid the broom handle through the lock on the door and a groove on the wall. He pulled at the bottom of the door, but it didn't budge. "I think this is good," he said, and motioned them through the short corridor to the main concourse beyond.

He followed them through the hallway, and stopped.

The women stopped, too.

Ahead of them was a narrow, hangar-shaped concourse, with a pair of ramps leading up to a higher level. Midway down the concourse, Jacob could see a pair of metal staircases leading out of sight. But his attention was focused much closer than the stairs. On the far left staircase, he saw five dead bodies. On the right were two more.

There was no doubt they were dead.

Most were lying in dried puddles of their own blood, their faces and the backs of their heads ghastly open wounds.

"Oh God," Kelly said, covering her mouth.

Jacob walked to the nearest body and knelt by the woman's side. She was dressed in a blood-spattered white jumpsuit. She hadn't been dead long, though—maybe a few hours at most. Her face had started to go pale, and even yellow in a few places, a sure sign that most of her blood had pooled down at her feet. She was wearing black boots under her white jumpsuit, and he knew what he'd see if he pulled those boots off. Her feet would be swollen and purple from the pooled blood, filled to the point they might even pop. A bunch of times over the years he'd seen a fresh zombie like this leaving a thick trail of blood slime from ruptured feet.

But it wasn't that she had been a zombie that really bothered him.

The bullet holes in the woman's forehead were a much bigger deal.

And they *were* bullet holes.

The weapons he'd taken off the hired hit squads back in Temple didn't fire rounds like this. On the train ride up here, after the last of the passengers disembarked and they had the ride to themselves, he pulled the pistols and studied them. They worked much like the weapons he'd been firing all his life. The sights were the same, the trigger, the magazine that slid in and out of the receiver. It was all very familiar.

The real difference was the ammunition. Rather than a traditional bullet pressed into a cartridge, the Temple gun held about fifty very small rounds made of some sort of plastic. They looked a lot like the .22-caliber rifle rounds his mother had taught him to shoot back when he was seven.

But they weren't the same.

Chelsea had caught him studying the round and told him they were fired by compressed air. "That's why they're so quiet," she said.

"Why do they explode?" he asked. "That man's head back in Temple. It just blew up."

"Compressed air again. It explodes on impact."

He studied the round anew after hearing that, and his awe for the technology that went into developing such a weapon ratcheted up another notch.

It was the perfect zombie-killing weapon, he thought. The fired rounds were completely silent, and the weapon could carry an enormous quantity of ammunition in a normal-sized magazine. It was limited in its range, that was true, kill-capable to only a maximum of maybe ten meters, maybe twenty at best, but it was able to thoroughly devastate anything it hit within that range. Even a glancing blow, especially one to the legs, would cause so much damage that a zombie would be unable to pursue the human firing the weapon.

The trouble was, those amazing compressed air rounds hadn't killed these people.

These folks were slaughtered by good old-fashioned gunfire.

Jacob rocked back on his heels and glanced up and down the concourse. There were signs at the far end, but over the last few years his vision had kind of gone to the dogs. The signs were just blurred garble to him.

"They were zombies, weren't they?" Kelly said.

"Yeah," Jacob said absently. "They probably were."

"Somebody killed them," Chelsea said. "Whoever did this obviously walked away from the fight, right? I wonder why they didn't use the call boxes to report an intrusion."

Jacob said nothing. He went back to studying the concourse.

"Well, those zombies obviously came from someplace," Kelly said. "We already saw how flimsy that one door panel was. Maybe there's a surface entrance somewhere around here that they were able to penetrate."

"Those aren't members of the Great Texas Herd," Chelsea said. "Look at the way they're dressed. They didn't come from the surface."

"She's right," Jacob said. "Their clothes. These wounds. Everything's too fresh."

"So where did they come from?" Kelly asked.

"From here, I guess."

It took Kelly a long moment to process that. Longer still to finally speak. "But that's not what's got you spooked, is it? What's wrong, Jacob?"

Jacob used the barrel of his pistol to turn the woman's face so Kelly could see. He held up the gun and said, "A weapon like this didn't do this. This is rifle fire. A .223 or 5.56, probably. Old-fashioned, pre–First Days military hardware. It would have to be something that big to cause this kind of damage."

"I don't understand. They were shot. What difference does the bullet make?"

"A whole lot," Jacob said. "Chelsea, didn't you tell me there were no guns in Temple?"

The girl nodded. "Just the ones like you've got, which are used by the surface teams assigned to the aerofluyts. Guns of every kind were outlawed when my people left Mill Valley."

"Well," Jacob said, letting the dead woman's head slump back to the tiled floor, "looks like somebody's not playing by your rules."

Jacob wiped the barrel of his gun off on a clean section of the dead woman's clothes and stood up. He pulled the other weapon from the small of his back and handed it to Kelly.

"I don't want that, Jacob. I can't . . . I can't kill again."

"Take it," he said.

"I can't."

"You're gonna have to," he said. "Look at these zombies. They all had to have turned in order to get these head shots, right?"

"Yeah."

"So how did they die?" Jacob extended the gun to her. "Somebody had to kill them first in order for them to turn, right?"

With a darkly worried expression, Kelly took the gun. "Yeah," she said. "I guess so."

CHAPTER 10

Halfway down the concourse they came to a wide stairwell. Signs hanging from the ceiling indicated that they led to the main tunnel network, two levels above them. At the far end of the concourse, tunnels branched off in three different directions. Another set of signs above those tunnels directed them to surface access, the airfields, and a series of research labs with long, confusing titles that Jacob didn't even try to figure out.

Jacob walked a little farther down the concourse and squinted at the signs. "Chelsea, what's your aunt's lab called?"

"Morphic Field Studies and Application."

Jacob shrugged. "I need somebody with better eyes than me. I can't read those signs."

But behind Chelsea, Kelly looked terrified. She was staring up the escalators, wide-eyed, shaking her head.

She turned to Jacob, held up her fist, and clenched it four times.

The nonverbal sign everybody in Arbella was taught to give to the rest of their party when there were zombies close by.

Jacob advanced on her position.

Sure enough, coming down the stairs were three zombies in tech uniforms.

A fourth appeared at the top of the stairs and started down after the first three. They had only recently turned, and like the dead bodies Jacob and the others had come across, they showed no signs of injury. That meant they moved fast, and they were still strong. Running from them wasn't an option. He had to engage them right now. If he didn't, they'd start to moan and their hue and cry would bring every other zombie within the sound of their voices over to them immediately.

Jacob ran up the stairs, got just out of arm's reach of the nearest zombie, and fired right in its face.

The woman's head burst open in thick clumps of hair and bone and blood that oozed down her shoulders before her body even got the message to fall to the ground.

Jacob sidestepped the corpse and bumped into the metal handrail that ran down the middle of the stairs. He'd wanted to get above the man in the yellow flight suit in order to put him off balance, but the zombie was faster than Jacob expected, and it closed the distance between them with a few quick steps.

It lunged for Jacob, like it was trying to tackle him to the ground.

Jacob ducked under the man's hand, grabbed the front of his flight suit, and pulled the zombie down so that it ended up bent over the railing.

Off balance, Jacob went for the shot anyway. He couldn't afford to let this one stand back up. It was too fast. He fired and landed a glancing blow across the back of the zombie's shoulders. Bits of the back of the man's head splashed onto the stairs below him, along with part of his left shoulder.

He turned to face Jacob, his dead eyes showing no pain, no surprise. The zombie collapsed the next instant and rolled down the stairs, landing in a heap on the tiled floor below.

The other two zombies were caught on the opposite side of the railing. They charged Jacob, only to run right into the handrail. They reached for him, tore at the air. They snarled and snapped at him like rabid dogs.

But they couldn't reach him.

Before they had a chance to figure out how to get to him, Jacob took a step back, leveled his weapon, and fired two quick head shots. Both zombies collapsed onto the handrail and then slid harmlessly to the floor.

Jacob glanced toward the foot of the stairs and saw Kelly staring at the second zombie he'd killed. She and Chelsea were okay. Moving quietly and staying low, he climbed the stairs to see where the zombies had come from. Near the top of the stairs he got down on his belly and poked just enough of his head above the top step to see the large junction beyond. It was a huge circular room, probably a hundred meters across, with eight passageways leading off in different directions. A few zombies were milling around the right side of the room, exploring, hunting for noise. Beyond them, filing out of most of the passageways, were more zombies. Too many to count. More than a hundred, though, certainly.

"Shit," he muttered.

He slid away from the top stair, then rose to a crouch and hustled down the stairs. Kelly was kneeling next to the zombie he'd killed, studying the dead man's face.

"We need to get out of here pretty damn fast," he whispered. He hooked his thumb toward the stairs. "We're about to have a whole lot of company from up there."

"How many?" Chelsea asked.

"No idea," he said. "I saw maybe a hundred, but there's probably more. And if we make any noise we're probably going to get a whole lot more."

"Jacob," Kelly said.

He knew that tone. She was worried.

"What is it?" he asked.

She turned the dead man's face toward him. "Look at that. There, around the mouth."

There was a faded, uneven blue ring around the man's mouth, like he dove face-first into a blueberry pie and hadn't done a very good job cleaning up after himself. "What is that?" Jacob asked. "Some kind of bruise?"

"Cyanosis," Kelly said. "That's one of the leading indicators of death by asphyxia."

"You mean somebody strangled him?"

"More like poisoned him with some kind of nerve agent, like a poisonous gas."

"Gas?" Jacob grabbed his shirt collar, ready to pull it over his mouth. "Are we in danger?"

Kelly shook her head. "These people look like they've been dead several hours. That would be enough time for it to dissipate. And we probably would have felt something by now if it was still a danger."

"I don't understand," Chelsea said. "You're saying somebody gassed all these people? Why?"

"I don't know. I don't even know if it was done intentionally. Maybe there was a massive carbon monoxide leak somewhere and these people just got trapped down here with it."

"But you don't sound convinced," Chelsea said.

Kelly shrugged. "It'd take an awful lot of carbon monoxide to kill this many people. But a concentrated nerve agent, like sarin or mustard gas . . . it wouldn't take much."

"Okay, well," Jacob said, "let's talk about it somewhere else."

"Which way?" Kelly asked.

To Jacob, the choice was obvious. They couldn't go back to the train. They'd be sitting ducks there. And they sure as hell couldn't go up the stairs. There was only one other way to go.

"That way," Jacob said, pointing toward the sign for the various labs and offices at the end of the concourse. "We go through there and figure out where your aunt's office is. Should just be a matter of following the signs, right?"

"No," Chelsea said. "I think we need to go topside."

"What?" Jacob said. "Are you crazy?"

"No," the girl said again. "Think about it. All these tunnels are connected. The same air circulates through all these vents. If these people really were gassed, the people through that corridor would have been gassed too. There are hundreds of people working in those labs. Maybe even thousands. We should go topside."

"But how will we get inside your aunt's building? With everything on lockdown, won't they be barricaded?"

"Only on the ground floor. Zombies can't climb the outside of buildings. My aunt's building has balconies all over it. We can just climb up."

"Chelsea," Kelly said. "I can't . . . that sounds like suicide to me."

Just then three figures emerged at the top of the stairs.

One of them let out a long, death rattle moan, and soon more joined them.

"Shit," Jacob said. He turned to Kelly. "You know what, I'm beginning to like her plan more and more. Chelsea, lead on."

They ran for the end of the concourse. Behind them, a large crowd of zombies spilled out of the stairwell, their death-rattle moans taking on the more urgent feeding call of a herd closing in for the kill. The three ran faster, charging toward an angry red sign that read: DO NOT ENTER—SURFACE TRAVEL PROHIBITED. Beyond the sign, the passageway that led topside was bathed in red light.

And a hurricane fence blocked the way.

"Jacob!" Kelly shouted.

Jacob had been checking their position. The zombies moved stiffly, awkwardly, yet a few of them were still fast enough to keep a running pace. They weren't catching up, but they weren't falling behind, either.

At the sound of Kelly's voice, Jacob turned. More zombies were emerging from the corridor that led to the research labs and offices. Chelsea was right.

"Keep going!" he said. "I'll cover you."

He veered off, putting himself between the women and the new herd of zombies coming at them from the labs. Two female zombies lumbered toward him. He stepped into the path of the nearest one and fired once at her face. The second one got on him before he could readjust. She put her hands on his shoulder and snapped her teeth at his face and his hands. He used her momentum to guide her to the ground, then stomped on her nose with his heel. Her head snapped back against the tile with a solid *smack*. If a living person had taken a blow like that, it would have put them out cold, but it didn't have any effect on the zombie. She just tried to get back up again.

Jacob broke away and put a little distance between himself and the fallen zombie. He raised his pistol, took aim, and turned her head into a puddle of dark red gore and bits of bone.

"Jacob, the gate is locked!" Kelly said.

He glanced her way. He'd seen lots of fences like that one in the little towns around Arbella, back when he was with the salvage teams. They were an effective visual deterrent for the zombies, who rarely tried to force their way through them unless they had their sights on a victim close at hand, yet they weren't very solid. They could be knocked down.

A large man in light blue medical scrubs staggered toward him. Jacob raised his weapon to the man's head, but didn't fire. Instead, he ran around the zombie and came up behind him before the dead man could turn around.

Moving fast, Jacob shoved the man toward the fence. He didn't let him fall, though. He caught the man's shirt in his fists and half-carried, half-shoved the big man headlong into the side of the fence, where it looked weakest.

The man's head crashed into the fence like a battering ram and plowed through. Jacob tried to pull the dead man back out and maybe ram him through again to widen the hole, but man's head was stuck.

"Jacob, they're close!"

"On it," he said. He pulled his pistol, put it up to the back of the zombie's head, and fired. The dead man's head turned to muck, and Jacob pulled the headless corpse out of the way.

He grabbed hold of the frame and used his leg to

push on the fence until one of the clasps holding it to the frame snapped.

It was an opening, but not big enough.

"Jacob!"

He spun around. Kelly and Chelsea were backing toward him. Three zombies were closing on them from the right, and two more on the left. Jacob slipped around Kelly's shoulder and shot the dead woman standing there. He looked left, then right, and shot at the woman coming up on his right. She was moving faster than the others, though, and his shot went low and to the right, hitting the dead woman in the shoulder. It separated her and spun her around, but she didn't fall. He fired again and this time landed a head shot.

But he had wasted seconds he didn't have, and by the time he turned on the two zombies coming out of the lab passageway, the first one was on top of him.

The dead man swiped at Jacob's face.

He ducked away from the zombie's hand, but it put him off balance and he nearly fell over backward. The zombie lunged for him again, carrying him further off balance. Jacob was bent over all the way now, forced to crab-walk away from the zombie with only one hand. He took the only shot he had. He hit the zombie in the left knee. The leg was blasted in half by the impact and the zombie pitched over. The dead man landed face-down on the tile and immediately tried to pull himself back up.

Jacob circled around the dead man, grabbed him by his hair, and pulled him to his feet. The zombies from the stairwell were closing on them, and Jacob hurled the one-legged man at their feet. It didn't knock them over, but it slowed them just enough. He turned and rushed back to where Kelly and Chelsea had backed up to the fence. Another man in soiled hospital scrubs was bearing down on them. Jacob ran at the man, got into kill range, and raised his weapon. But before he could fire, the dead man's head exploded.

As the body fell, he saw Kelly standing there, holding the gun in both hands. She was shaking, her eyes wide open and unblinking. The gun pointed directly at Jacob's face.

"Hey!" he said. "Whoa, hold up! It's me."

Only upon hearing his voice did Kelly catch herself. She gasped, and lowered the gun. "Oh God, Jacob. I almost shot you."

He smiled. "That sure would have sucked."

He rushed to the fence and kicked at it until another clasp snapped. From there it was easy to bend it over.

"Come on," he said.

He held the fence down as the women crawled through, then he climbed through himself. A dead woman tried to dive for him through the hole. Rather than risk catching her fingernails in his face while pushing her back through, he grabbed her hair and pulled her through. She landed facedown and he popped her in the back of the head. He grabbed the curved-over section of the fence and pushed it back in place. It wouldn't hold against even a single zombie, but if they couldn't see the hole, it might slow them down a second or two until they found it.

He raced after Kelly and Chelsea, and caught up with them at the end of the passageway. In the pale red glow of the emergency lights, he could see they'd reached another of the metal pull-down doors. Coming up beside them he saw that the door was rusted and dented all over, but it wasn't a weak link like the one they'd found back at the platform. This one would hold.

"Shit," he said. "Okay, okay, let me see what I can do here."

"This one's easy," Chelsea said. There was a large metal plate in the wall next to the door with a flat, square-shaped button in the center labeled EMERGENCY DOORS. Chelsea hit it with the palm of her hand and immediately a woman's voice came over the intercom. "Warning: Surface door breach. Warning: Surface door breach."

At their feet, an internal lock in the door let go with a loud click, and the door raised up an inch or two.

Jacob grabbed the handle and yanked the door open.

The bright light and the heat of the late afternoon desert sun hit them square in the face. After spending hours underground, Jacob walked into the street nearly blind. It took several long moments for his eyes to adjust. A dry breeze carried thick clouds of dust down the street. He could feel the grit adhering to the sweat on his neck and his face. And on the breeze he could smell something rotten.

All the buildings around them were made of red brick. They were small, not a one of them taller than six stories, and shaped like squares. Halfway down the block to his left he saw movement in the dust clouds. Shadowy figures stepped through the blowing dust. Looking around, he counted twenty-four zombies. Some looked like the techs and hospital staff he'd encountered down below, while others were badly decayed, hardly a stitch of clothes left on their withered bodies.

From behind him came the sound of Chelsea pulling the metal down into place.

"It locks automatically," she said.

Jacob pointed down the street. "See that? Those are zombies from the Great Texas Herd. Looks like they broke through the automated defenses."

"Oh no," Chelsea said. "That's bad. That's real bad."

"Yeah, that's one word for it. Just tell me which way we need to go. Which building is your aunt in?"

"I don't see it here," she said. "It's red brick like these, but it has white balconies in front of each of the windows."

Jacob glanced to his right, where the buildings started to give way to houses. The dust clouds were thicker that way, and he thought he had a pretty good idea why. He pointed toward the houses and said, "We can't go that way. The herd's coming from there."

"Okay, then," Chelsea said, turning to the left. "This way. It has to be around here somewhere with all the other buildings."

Together, they rounded the far corner and scanned a new set of buildings.

"Is that it?" Jacob said. He pointed at a building down the block from them.

"No, hers has white balconies."

"Not that one," he said. "Behind that one. See it there? You can just see the top level. Those are balconies, aren't they?"

"Yes!" Chelsea said. "Yes, that's it!"

Chelsea started to run for it, but Jacob grabbed her shoulder and held her back. "Wait," he said. He nodded to the right. "Look over there."

There were several large vehicles parked on the

street near a construction zone less than a block away. A few grotesquely broken and decayed bodies came limping through the gaps between the vehicles. More followed close behind.

A moment later, they began to moan.

"Oh God," Kelly said. "Why can't we catch a break? Jacob, why?"

"We'll make our own break," he said. He pointed to the left of the building directly in front of them. "We need to do a dead sprint around that side of the building. Everybody up for that?"

"Do we have any other choice?" Kelly said.

"Not really."

"Fine," she said. "Let's do it."

Jacob holstered his weapon and chased after the women. The three of them ate up the first hundred meters or so, but after that, all three had to slow way down. They were breathing hard and the bruised ribs Jacob got from the fight back in Temple earlier that day started to burn. By the time they came around the far side of the building, they were all slogging along at little more than a trot, all three of them breathing hard.

But the dead didn't know exhaustion. They were a relentless, unwavering, unending swarm that knew only the need to feed. Streams of zombies filled the streets like a flood, coming closer and closer to them.

Jacob was about to direct them around the back side of the building so they could find a way to climb up to a balcony, but then he noticed that a metal screen that was meant to protect one of the building's main entrances had only been pulled part of the way down.

"There!" he said. "Let's go through there."

Jacob tried to lift the metal screen, but it wouldn't budge.

He turned to face the crowd gathering around them. They were a mixture of recently turned techs and medical personnel from El Paso, and older, rotting corpses, the vanguard of the Great Texas Herd.

And they were getting too close.

"Chelsea," he said. "Can you roll under there and try the door?"

The girl dropped to the ground and rolled under the metal screen without effort. On the other side of the screen was a short passageway that led to a metal door. Chelsea pushed at the door and it swung open on groaning hinges.

"Jacob," Kelly said. "I don't like this. Why would those people get gassed? Why would these doors be left open?"

"I don't know," Jacob said. "Just get inside. Both of you. Find someplace to hide. I'll catch up with you."

"What are you going to do?"

"Buy you some time. Now go!"

"Oh God, Jacob."

A zombie in a gray, knee-length skirt and a red blouse darted out of the crowd and charged for Jacob. He saw her coming out of the corner of his eye and dropped her before she could get to him.

"Don't worry about it," he said. "Just go."

Three more zombies stepped over the fallen zombie and onto the sidewalk. Jacob raised his pistol and took deliberate aim before squeezing the trigger. *Rushed shooting is sloppy shooting*, he remembered his firing range instructor telling him back in grade school. *You get in a hurry, you get dead. Take your time. Find your shot. Squeeze the trigger.*

"Jacob, this is stupid. Come with us. While there's time."

"I know what I'm doing. Just get inside."

"God, you're a stupid man, you know that?"

"That's what you always told me. Go on. Get inside. Be right behind you."

Kelly crawled under the screen. With one last look back at Jacob, she went inside. Jacob watched her go, then wiped the sweat from his hands and got ready to fight. The faster zombies had broken out ahead of the main group and were bearing down on him. Behind them, swelling into the streets, were thousands more. Their moans bounced off the sides of the buildings, like echoes in a canyon, and for a moment, Jacob felt his courage waver.

He put his back to the metal screen, took a deep breath, and let the fast ones get in close. As soon as they stepped onto the sidewalk, they were his. He dropped five in rapid order, perfect head shots each. That left a gap between him and the leading edge of the coming herd.

Exactly what he was looking for.

He holstered his weapon, grabbed the nearest headless corpse, and pulled it toward the opening at the bottom of the metal screen. He did that again and again until finally he had nearly the entire gap blocked. Then he crawled through, turned, reached back through the hole until he found a dead woman's ankle, and pulled her body into the hole, plugging it.

He stood up just as the herd reached him.

A dark-haired woman in a red shirt lunged at him through the diamond holes in the screen, and he jumped back just in time to avoid getting a face full of fingernails. More zombies rushed his position, smashing the woman in the red shirt into the screen. For a hideous moment, he could see the metal wires cutting into her cheeks, but soon the weight of the herd behind her forced her down.

Jacob backed up to the door as more faces pressed against the metal screen. Their combined weight seemed to shake the entire building and he didn't know how much longer the screen would hold. He pushed the door open and was about to rush inside when he heard a snarling growl rise over the collective moans of the herd.

He turned toward to the screen, and to his horror saw the first who had been smashed against the screen digging at the barricade of bodies he'd used to block the entrance. She grabbed one of the bodies and pulled it free. Once the first one was out of the way, the others came loose easily.

The next thing he knew she was crawling under the screen.

When she stood up, her face was a bloody mess.

Jacob stepped forward, put his gun in her face, and fired, blowing her brains and blood all over the herd behind her.

He backed up again as her body fell to the floor.

Another zombie crawled through the gap, then two more behind it. Jacob shot all three, but he knew he had to get out of there. More and more of them were figuring out how to get through, and within seconds there would be far more than he could shoot.

And he'd long since lost count of how many rounds he'd fired.

He ran through the metal door and slammed it shut, but when he tried to lock it, he found the lock had been pried out of the door. The tool marks were fresh, too. No rust. It was at that moment that it hit him. He stood looking at the hole in the door where the lock had once been, and knew that Kelly was right. Something was going on here. The people in the tunnels deliberately gassed. The bodies with the bullet holes in their heads. So many defensive systems showing signs of tampering.

He tried to make sense of it, but at that moment bodies crashed against the other side of the door and he had to throw his shoulder into it just to keep it closed.

It was a losing battle, though.

There were too many of them. His feet started to slide across the hardwood floors as the zombies forced the door inward.

He glanced up the stairs to his left and saw Kelly poking her head around the corner. "Come on!" she said.

Jacob took a deep breath, then ran for the stairs.

A small crowd of zombies fell through the doorway while others scrambled over them. Jacob leveled the weapon at the first one to clear the tangle of bodies and shot her. The dead began to stand up all around him, even as more pressed through the narrow doorway. He climbed the first few steps and fired again and again.

He'd dropped eight more zombies by the time the weapon clicked empty.

"Jacob, come—"

Kelly's plea was cut off by a scream. It sounded like Chelsea.

Jacob raced to the first landing, expecting more zombies, but instead saw a figure in one of the big gray, armored space suits coming down the stairs. Its steps clanged against the floor, the servos that allowed its legs and arms to bend making pneumatic sighs. In its right hand the figure held a massive weapon, like a mini gun, of which he'd only seen pictures.

But it wasn't a mini gun. Rather than run separate, rotary barrels, like the mini guns he'd seen pictures of in Arbella's library, it had six small muzzle holes contained inside a single housing.

The figure raised the weapon, and Jacob threw his hands into the air. He twisted out of the thing's way and pressed his back against the wall.

The figure moved by him, and when the first zombies appeared at the foot of the stairs, the strange-looking mini gun jumped to life. In less than a second, six zombies were blown to bits against the wall. Another zombie rushed up behind the first six and tried to slash at the figure's copper faceplate.

Whoever was inside the space suit didn't even bother to shoot it.

With its left hand, the figure grabbed the zombie's face and pushed it to the floor, its augmented strength snapping the dead man's neck like a chicken bone. Jacob heard the dead man's neck break even over the moaning of the herd. The zombie landed on its back, unable to stand, unable to do anything but growl and snarl at the wall. It couldn't even turn over.

But the figure didn't pause to deliver the coup de grâce. Instead it raised its weapon and began mowing down the crowd pressing through the door.

Heads exploded.

Zombies dropped like wheat before a sickle.

And all the while, the figure advanced toward the door, crushing the dead beneath its lumbering stride.

Jacob stood in rapt fascination. He'd never seen anything like it. Once, when he was maybe eight or nine, and had begun to show some aptitude for building things out of scrap, his mother had told him about the robot armies the military had developed during the First Days, and how they had plowed through the zombie herds. After seeing Lester Brooks inside a similar suit just weeks before, he'd assumed the suits were merely suits.

A person inside.

But now, seeing this figure move with such precision, such complete and utter purpose, he wondered if he wasn't seeing some robot relic of the First Days.

The figure certainly moved that way.

Killed that way.

Chewed through the dead like a house on fire.

As the bodies fell, the figure continued to advance. And when they didn't fall fast enough, they were thrown against the wall like rag dolls. If he hadn't been so amazed, Jacob would have felt nothing but disgust for the violence of it. He'd seen bodies torn apart. Lots of them, in fact. But nothing like this.

The figure pushed through the doorway and into the passageway beyond.

Still firing, it cut through the crowd like a zipper, and when it reached the metal screen security door, it simply grabbed the bottom part of the frame and slammed it down to the ground, severing the fingers of one zombie that was trying to reach for the figure's feet.

Then it knelt to the floor, grabbed the latch that locked the screen in place, and wrenched it over into the closed position.

All the while, the herd was gathering at the gate.

The figure didn't seem to notice.

At least until it stood from locking the screen and fired another long burst from its mini gun. The firing went on for a long time. Jacob had no way of knowing exactly how long, but it felt like two minutes, easily.

And when the firing stopped, all that was left was a mound of the dead piled up in front of the metal screen.

That's how you do it, Jacob thought.

His plan had been to use a few zombies to plug the gap beneath the screen.

But whoever was inside that space suit had clearly intended something bigger, for the mound of dead men and women that now surrounded the main doorway was tall enough that it blocked his view of the main herd surrounding their building.

When the figure finally turned away from the metal screen door, it turned its copper-plated face shield toward Jacob. "You need to follow me."

The voice was oddly feminine, though still mechanical, amplified.

"You'll be safe," the figure said. "The doors are closed now."

And with that the figure pushed its way past Jacob and started up the stairs.

Feeling once again like a stranger in a strange land, not knowing what else to do, Jacob followed the space-suited figure up the stairs.

CHAPTER 11

They went up four flights of stairs, following the space-suited figure in silence.

Below them, the moans of the ravenous dead faded, leaving only the heavy clomping of the figure's foot-falls on the stairs. Kelly glanced back several times, sometimes checking on Jacob with a worried frown, other times looking past him, down the stairs. He knew what was on her mind. He, too, wondered how long the barricades would hold. But the thought didn't linger. Jacob was too exhausted for that. He'd been beaten and run ragged the entire day. He hadn't eaten since early that morning, and now, with evening coming on, and climbing all these steps, and the danger quieting below him, he was beginning to feel the adrenaline hangover. He had to stop.

"Jacob?" Kelly said. She was at his side a moment later, her hand on his shoulder.

Above them, the space-suited figure stopped and

turned. "Is your friend okay?" The voice, though amplified, was nonetheless unmistakably feminine.

"I'm fine," Jacob said.

"No, you're not," Kelly said. "God, Jacob, you're trembling."

"He looks like he's been run through a meat grinder," the figure said. "My office is on the next level. I have a cot we can put him on."

"Okay," Kelly said. "Jacob, can you make it?"

"I'm fine," he said again. But it was so hard to push off the railing. He felt strangely disconnected, like he didn't care. He just wanted to rest. For the first time in a long time, he felt like sinking to the floor and staying there.

"Get up," Kelly said. She pulled at his arms. "Jacob, get up."

He blinked in confusion. He was on his back, looking up at Kelly, with no idea how he got that way. He tried to ask her what happened, but he couldn't make the words come out. He could only stammer.

And then the space-suited figure was kneeling next to Kelly.

"I'll take him," the woman inside the suit said.

She scooped Jacob up like he was a puppy. He felt limp in her arms. He tried to struggle, but she held him fast.

When she turned to head back up the stairs, Chelsea was standing there.

"Aunt Miriam?"

Even through the suit, Jacob felt his handler stiffen.

After a long pause, the woman in the suit said, "Chelsea, is that you?"

"Yes," the girl said, breathless, overcome with emotion.

"Oh my," the suited figure said. Even with the mechanical amplification, her voice sounded tender and loving. "Child, I didn't recognize you. Oh my."

Chelsea rushed forward and threw her arms around her aunt. Or tried to. She couldn't get anywhere close to a real hug around the bulkiness of the suit.

"What in the world are you doing here, child?"

"Aunt Miriam, I need your help really bad. My daddy didn't wreck the *Darwin*. They're telling lies about him. I have these notebooks my daddy wrote, and they're all about his theory of what's going wrong with the morphic field generators and as soon as the council found out about them they sent men after me to get them and we've been running from them all day. Oh God, Aunt Miriam, I feel so scared. I didn't know where to go or who I could trust. I feel so alone."

Miriam put a huge gloved hand on the girl's shoulder and pulled her close. "You'll be okay here," she said.

"Will you look at the notebooks?" Chelsea said. "My daddy didn't wreck the *Darwin*. I know he didn't. He was just trying to show how dangerous the morphic field generators are. It's all there in the notebooks."

"I'll look at them, child. You did the right thing, coming here. Don't you worry."

The next thing Jacob knew he was being placed on a cot along the back wall of a large lab. The room was a mess. There were long tables along the far wall, piled high with papers and computers and electrical cables of all sizes. He saw half a dozen chalkboards spaced around the room. Only they weren't like the chalkboards he'd seen as a kid back in school. They were shaped like the chalkboards he remembered, and mounted on wooden frames with wheels, but the actual board part was a computer screen. They were covered with calculations so out of his league he barely recognized them as math.

Large windows dominated another wall. The sun was setting and the desert sky was on fire with molten tones of copper and red and yellow. There were plants clustered on the windowsills. An herb garden, well-maintained. A couch and a few armchairs were positioned around the windows, with leaning piles of books on the floor. It reminded him a little of the front parlor in his mother's house. The memory soothed him a little, and though he ached all over, he let himself sink into the cot as the tension started to ebb from his body. It was almost like a great weight was lifted from his chest.

Kelly was by his side the moment his head hit the cot, brushing his sweat-soaked hair from his face. Looking into her face, for just a moment, he caught a glimpse of the sixteen-year-old girl she had once been. He saw, again, the warmth, the affection, the mysteries of a girl turning into a woman, and he wondered if they could ever go back to that place on the banks of the Mississippi, where the two of them had been perfect.

But then she lifted his hand and searched out his pulse and began counting silently to herself, and the vision, the memory, the warmth of better times, faded.

He focused instead on the space-suited figure. Two of the ugliest, the strangest-looking people Jacob had ever seen guided her toward a rack where four other suits just like the one she wore stood empty and plugged into the wall. Jacob hadn't noticed them until that moment.

It was a man and a woman.

The man was tall and skinny. Not slender, but skinny. Almost freakishly so. His face looked like it had been squeezed in a vise. He wore a scraggly brown beard at the point of his chin, which made his face look even longer. The rest of his face was chalk-white with a splash of freckles across the nose. His brown hair was an unwashed mess. He had a sleepy, glassy-eyed look to him, and a slow, overly deliberate way of moving that made Jacob wonder if the man wasn't high.

The woman most certainly wasn't, though. At least not on weed. Where the man was slow and easy, she was frantic. Where the man was tall and slender, she was tiny. Her skin was as white as a plate, and her red hair had an oily, unhealthy look to it. She fussed like an old woman over every detail of the suit, checking every buckle and clasp until she found one that had snapped.

"Look here," she said. "It broke. I told you it had been stressed beyond tolerance. Didn't I tell you?"

"I'm sure it's fine," the man said.

"It's not fine. Look at this. The clasp broke, just like I said it would. Didn't I tell you this would happen? I stood right here and said this would happen, and now look. Just like I said it would."

"We got her dressed in a hurry," the man said. "Just calm down, will you? We probably just didn't fasten it correctly. Let's get her out of this thing and we'll see if it's really broken or not."

"I'm telling you it's broken. I'm looking at it and I'm telling you it's broken."

"Well then, let's take it apart and see why. Okay? It can't be that hard."

"Don't patronize me. If you'd just take the time to listen to me, you'd have been able to see this coming."

The woman in the suit raised one arm like she was cutting the air between them. "You two knock it off. I'm starting to get claustrophobic. Get me out of this damn thing."

"You got it, boss," the man said.

He guided Miriam to a vacant stall next to the other suits and attached a series of cables to her waist. Once she was hooked in, he and the woman started working on the buckles on the back of the suit, prying it open bit by bit until the woman inside was able to squeeze out. When they finally got her out, she was soaking wet with sweat. Her long gray hair was wrapped around her neck like a rope. She was a slender woman in her late fifties, and in her delicate face and well-muscled arms Jacob could see what Chelsea would look like in forty years. The similarities between them were striking. Like the younger woman, Miriam's natural expression seemed to be one of great sadness. In Chelsea, Jacob thought he knew the cause. Seven years in the shackles of a Slaver caravan had worn her down to the nub. Miriam carried the same road-weary expression, though in the older woman it seemed tempered by a kindness and a patience that Chelsea had yet to master.

Miriam gathered her hair in a ponytail. She wore a white tank top and black slacks, both of which were matted with sweat to her narrow frame. Even in her late fifties, she was an attractive woman. She certainly took care of herself.

But her only concern was for Chelsea. She paused only long enough to fan her face, then went immediately to the younger woman. The two crashed together in a hug that ended with Miriam planting a kiss on the younger girl's forehead.

"You're safe now," Miriam said. "Nobody can hurt you here."

Chelsea nodded into Miriam's shoulder.

"Now tell me," Miriam said. "What in the world are you doing here?"

"They're trying to frame my daddy for the wreck of the *Darwin*," Chelsea said. She was explosive, her words coming so fast she sounded hysterical. "But he didn't have anything to do with that. Aunt Miriam, you have to believe me. I have his notebooks right here. Read them. You'll see. They tried to kill me for them this morning. And then I saw Jacob and Kelly and I got loose and they've been chasing us—"

"Chelsea, easy, child. Easy now. Why would anybody want to kill you?"

"For the notebooks! Everything my daddy found out about the morphic field generators is right there. Go on and read them if you don't believe me."

"Easy," Miriam said. "Child, go easy. He was your daddy, but he was my brother. I know he was a good man. I know he didn't cause the wreck. I don't believe all the rumors I've been hearing—no more than you do. Now, can I see the notebooks?"

"Yes," Chelsea said. She pointed to Kelly. "She has them."

Kelly slid the satchel off her shoulder, opened it, and handed the notebooks to Miriam. From his cot, Jacob watched the exchange, and studied Kelly's face. He knew her, he knew every expression she made, and he immediately recognized the look on her face as one of distrust.

"It's okay," Miriam said. Perhaps she sensed much of what Jacob did, for Miriam was very deliberate in leaving the notebooks out in front of Kelly, as though giving her the chance to take them back if she wanted to. "Alfred Walker was my brother. I don't know if you ever had a brother, but that bastard and I fought over everything from where to sit at the table to the fundamental workings of morphic field theory." Miriam took a deep breath, then glanced around the room, her gaze finally settling on Chelsea. The two shared a moment that was as painful as it was loving.

Miriam broke the gaze. She tugged at her tank top and tried to collect herself.

She turned to Kelly: "Your name is . . . ?"

"I'm Kelly Banis."

"Kelly, have you ever known someone you loved so completely, and respected from the soles of your shoes to the summit of your knowledge, and yet argued with at every turn? Have you ever known someone like that?"

Kelly took a long time to answer.

Jacob, who thought he knew everything there was to know about Kelly, found himself watching her face, waiting for the answer. Part of him believed that she might actually be thinking of him. The two of them had certainly burned up that summer twenty years earlier. She'd told him she loved him then, and he, at seventeen, between her legs, had told her he loved her, too. He'd believed it without reservation, right down to his core.

But in the years that followed, Kelly Jackson had gone on to earn the equivalent of a doctoral degree in botany. Arbella didn't have anything like a college, but she'd first mastered the skills of the amateur gardeners—did that as a child, in fact—and then went on to study under, and in time, most said, surpassed the knowledge of the man who would become her husband, Dr. Barry Banis, former professor of botany at the University of

Arkansas. She'd distinguished herself as the best and brightest mind of her generation, and when brilliant men like Barry Banis started turning their affections her way, boys like Jacob started to fade into memory.

But she said nothing. Kelly simply closed her eyes and nodded.

And whatever that meant was a mystery to Jacob.

"I see that you have," Miriam said. "Well, then, you know where I'm coming from when I tell you that I will look through every word of this. It'll probably make me mad as hell, but then, that was always Alfred's special gift." She turned to Kelly. "Have you read through this, Kelly?"

"I have. Some of it's a bit beyond my reach. I'm a botanist. But what I could grasp sounded pretty scary."

"Scary?" the man with the skinny face said. He got in close to Kelly, too close for her comfort, though he didn't seem to notice. "Did you say scary? It's not scary when it powers your aerofluyts or lights your city, is it? Don't tell me you're one of those Triune nut jobs."

Kelly backed away from him.

Jacob sat up on the cot. His head felt like it was about to burst open, but he figured he could still haul himself to his feet if the guy was going to get in Kelly's face again.

"Stu, stop it," Miriam said. "Calm down."

"I'm sorry," the man said, suddenly looking sheepish. "Was I doing it again?"

"Yes, you're doing it again. Back up. Give the poor girl some space."

"Sorry," the man said to Kelly. "I wish people would just tell me when I'm being a jerk. It's hard sometimes for me to know."

"You're being a jerk, Stu," Miriam said. "Now give her some space."

Stu did as he was told.

Miriam smiled at Kelly. "I'm sorry about that. This is Stu and Juliette Huffman, my leading researchers. It may not seem like it, but I can assure you they're both quite brilliant."

"It's alright," Kelly said, though she still looked a little doubtfully at Stu.

"We build morphic field generators here," said Miriam. "As you can imagine, the Triune Movement gets discussed quite a bit around here."

"There's no discussion," Stu said. "It's nothing but a bunch of alarmist nonsense."

"I don't think it can be dismissed that easily," Juliette said.

"Don't even start," Stu said.

"I'll start with you if I want to, mister. You can't dismiss it that easily. You know you can't."

"The triune brain was dismissed as hogwash a hundred and fifty years ago," Stu said. "I don't see why we have to keep dragging it out again. Nobody seriously believes that."

"I'm not so sure about that."

"Great!" Stu said, throwing his hands into the air. "My own wife, a Triune nut job. Next you'll be dragging out phrenology as a basis for zombie behavior."

"Don't be so dismissive with me. You know you can't explain why the shepherding runs failed to turn away the herd. Or have you come up with a magical explanation for that, too?"

"You're the one who's going to need a magical explanation if you want to show how there's any possible way a morphic circuit could form between the basal ganglia and the limbic system. That just doesn't happen. There's no commonality to act as a circuit bridge."

"You two," Miriam said. "Please. You give me a headache." Miriam turned to Kelly and rolled her eyes with a smile. "It's like this all day long, every day with these two."

"It's okay," Kelly said. "It's fascinating. But Stu, earlier you called me a Triune nut job. What is that?"

"What do you mean?" Stu said.

"What's a Triune nut job?"

"Have you never heard that term before?" Miriam asked. "Triune, I mean. Not the nut job part. That's just Stu being a jerk again."

"I read mention of it in those journals, but . . ."

"Aunt Miriam, they're not part of Temple society," said Chelsea.

"Really?" Miriam said, raising an eyebrow. "Where are you from?"

Chelsea spent the next twenty minutes describing the wreck of the *Darwin* and everything she'd been through after that. She told her about being beaten and raped in the Slaver caravans and how her brother, Chris, had turned on her. She included everything, right up to the moment when Miriam had rescued them.

Everything except Nick.

Jacob noticed she left that part out.

"Oh child," Miriam said. She took her niece's head in her hands and hugged her to her breast. "These men, do you know who they were working for?"

"No," Chelsea said. "They didn't say. They just wanted Daddy's notebooks."

Miriam shook her head. "That's not good."

"Wait," Kelly said. "I'm still confused. What is a triune brain, and does it have something to do with those men who were trying to kill us?"

"I think it does," Miriam said. "Okay, I'll run it down for you. You know that the morphic field generators are the basis of our technology, right?"

Kelly nodded.

"Okay, well, for years before the outbreak, morphic fields were used solely as a power source. The U.S. military developed it in the 2060s as a cheaper and safer replacement for nuclear power. As a form of electromagnetic energy, they have the power to make aerofluyts fly and light cities. Unfortunately, the outbreak kept the technology from reaching around the world. But that's when we discovered that morphic fields had peculiar effects on zombies. It was called the shepherding effect. Modulate a morphic field a given way, and you could make a zombie go anywhere you wanted it to go. We've used it for years to guide the bigger herds away from developing communities like your home of Arbella."

"You do that?" Kelly asked.

"Is that why we've never seen these aerofluyts before now?" Jacob asked. He'd risen from the cot and was standing on shaky legs.

"Jacob," Kelly said. "Get back in bed."

"No, no," he said. "I'm fine. And I want to hear this. Is that why we've never seen the aerofluyts before now?"

Miriam nodded. "They have carefully controlled flight paths that keep them away from the established communities. The caravans, like the one you described,

Chelsea, see them sometimes, but that can't be helped. The regular communities, though, those are off-limits."

Kelly waved her hand in the air like she wanted to dismiss all that. "What about the triune brain? You were telling me about that."

"Yes," Miriam said. "So for years we've relied on morphic field technology. But about fifteen years ago some of our medical community started noticing a simultaneous rise in children born with autism and a rapid rise in Alzheimer's cases in people in their middle age. Both trends are accelerating, unfortunately. Some of those same researchers went back to the triune brain theory, which was first developed by a neuroscientist named Paul D. MacLean back in the 1960s.

"His idea was that the human brain was divided into three parts. You had the primitive reptilian core, the basal ganglia, which, incidentally, is the only part of the brain to still show signs of function in reanimates. Paired with that is the paleomammalian complex, or the limbic system, which consists of a number of parts of the brain and regulates things like emotion, certain types of behaviors, and how motivated a person can be. The third part of the brain is the neomammalian complex, which is only present in humans and gives us the power of speech and other higher forms of thought."

"Okay," Kelly said. "I got that. But how does that have anything to do with zombies?"

"MacLean's theory was thrown out in the late twentieth century and replaced with more involved theories of how the brain functions," Miriam said. "But zombies changed all that. As soon as people started studying reanimates, we learned that the higher cognitive functions of the brain were nonexistent. Anybody who's ever watched a zombie try to work its way past a simple obstacle can tell you that. Researchers found that there was limited activity in the hypothalamus, cingulate cortex, and the amygdalae portions of the brain—all part of MacLean's paleomammalian complex, by the way—but in the main, only the reptilian part—actually, that's a misnomer, because the basal ganglia is present in all vertebrates and therefore probably dates to the common ancestor of all vertebrates, long before reptiles—but anyway, only the basal ganglia showed any considerable signs of activity in reanimates. MacLean's model of the brain seemed to explain what was going on with the reanimates, and so the model of the triune brain was dusted off and revamped."

"And calling someone a Triune means what?" Kelly asked.

Miriam frowned deeply. "It means that a person is a follower of the Triune Theory. In most of the scientific community, it's an insult. Like calling someone a Luddite, if you know that term."

Kelly shook her head.

"It's not important," Miriam said.

"It means that believers in that tripe haven't got a lick of common sense," Stu said.

"Will you please put a fucking sock in it?" Miriam said.

The whole room went quiet.

"Please," she said. "Just for a minute." Miriam motioned to the suits along the side wall. "Stu, will you and Juliette please go make the battle suits ready? Please. I got a quick look at what we're dealing with down there on the ground level, and I think we're going to need them."

"Yes, of course," Stu said.

He shrank away without another word, and Juliette followed right behind him.

"I'm sorry," Miriam said. "But as you can probably see, this issue has sharply divided Temple society."

"Yeah, I can see that," Kelly said.

"Here's the thing. When the first studies were done on zombies and the triune brain model, researchers found that the morphic fields acted directly on the basal ganglia. That formed the basis for our shepherding strategies, which we used to control the movements of the larger herds."

"But . . . ?"

Miriam smiled. "You caught that. Good. Well, the problem, as I mentioned, was that no one seemed to know what to make of the limited activity still present in the limbic system. It didn't seem to influence zombie behavior in any way, but it couldn't be explained away, either. It still hasn't. That's where the Triunes come in.

"My brother, Alfred, started out as a neurosurgeon. People used to tell me all the time that he was the most brilliant man they'd ever met, and I would always have to agree. It pained me to admit it, because Alfred could be a real prick about it, but they were right. He was brilliant. Freakishly smart, actually. And, like most of the scientific community, when he first heard the Triune Theory that morphic fields were somehow changing the zombie brain by acting on the limbic system, he dismissed it as sloppy reasoning."

"Yeah," Kelly said, "but the brain is complex. I've read stories about people who suffered terrible head trauma, who nonetheless relearned things like language and how to walk. The different parts of the brain overlap and can even change function, can't they?"

Miriam nodded. "Absolutely. Spoken like a true believer in the Triune Theory, by the way. It was that same line of thinking that led my brother to change his thoughts on the Triune Theory. About ten years ago, he flipped to the other side. He converted, if you will. He even sent me a note one day saying that he had become the Paul to MacLean's Triune Church. I didn't even know what he was talking about at the time, but he began speaking out publicly against morphic field technology. He claimed it was responsible for the increased incidence of autism and the rise in cases of the early onset of Alzheimer's. I don't know if you've had a girlfriend start a new diet and she gets all weird about it, and it's all you hear from her, but that's what he was like in those days. I couldn't have a conversation with him that didn't turn into a debate on morphic field technology. It put a rift in our family that never healed. He made a lot of enemies in the public sphere, as well. The same people who used to tell me how brilliant he was started calling him a crackpot."

"Why? Because he was saying that the morphic field generators were working on living brains the same way they did on the zombies?"

"Essentially, yes. You have a better grasp on this than you think you do, young lady. Alfred's main idea was that the living person's brain was not all that different from the zombie brain. Take away the neomammalian complex and you have, essentially, a zombie brain. His idea was that our constant exposure to morphic fields was somehow damaging our brains."

"Which should be easy to prove, right?"

"You would think, but no one ever could. The main problem is that morphic fields obey the laws of electromagnetism. If there was truly something to the Triune Theory, then there should have been a viable circuit working within the brain, two poles with the circuit going between them, right? But nobody, including my brilliant brain surgeon brother, could ever find that second pole. And that's why the theory has split our society the way it has. Half the population thinks this technology is just fine. The other half thinks that it is responsible for killing us all. If Alfred's theories turn out to be true, a lot of people will stand to lose an awful lot of money, not to mention their professional reputations. You can see why he made enemies."

Kelly pointed to the notebooks. "Could I show you something I saw in there? Please? I think your brother may have found that second pole."

The two women carried the notebooks off to a far corner of the room, leaving Jacob standing there.

Which was just as well. He hadn't followed half of their conversation. Hell, he hadn't even understood that much of it. As soon as Kelly started in on her science stuff he just tuned it out. He'd learned enough of it to get through school, but as far as he was concerned, that was the end of his involvement with the subject. Anyway, whatever he actually needed to know, Kelly would dumb down for him later.

What really interested him were the space suits parked along the side wall. No, not space suits, he reminded himself. Miriam had called them battle suits, and after seeing her use the suit downstairs, he wondered why the term hadn't occurred to him already.

"Did you guys build these?" he asked Stu and Juliette.

Stu glanced back over his shoulder at him. "No, these are antiques. We just keep them running."

"Antiques? They look pretty impressive to me."

"They're relics from the outbreak. They used to outfit every soldier with one of these."

"An army of these?"

"That's what I'm told. Whole hell of a lot of good it did them, though."

Jacob could hardly imagine that. If one of these things could level the crowd he'd faced downstairs, an army of them must have been able to make short work of a herd.

Even a huge one.

With a phalanx of battle suits taking the field, the zombies should have been rolled back into oblivion.

"The early military versions weren't like this," Stu said, almost as though he could read Jacob's thoughts on his face. "We've made a few improvements."

And despite the fact that Stu's pride was still smarting from the send-off Miriam had given him, he was obviously a man proud of his work. Weird little fellow that he was, Jacob felt a sort of kinship with him at that moment. He was a fellow tinkerer.

Jacob leaned closer. "Show me," he said.

"Look here," Stu said, pointing to the bib that covered the front of the suit. "The suit itself is two-centimeter-thick Kevlar armor. By itself, it'll stop everything up to and including a fifty-caliber round. But we've added this." Stu thumped the bib proudly. "Five centimeters of Kevlar, micro-grafted to the base plate. You couldn't punch through this with a truck. And don't even get me started on the suit's weapon's systems."

"I saw the gun she was firing," Jacob said. He pulled his pistol from the small of his back. "Does it use the same ammunition as this? The same compressed-air cartridges?"

Stu stared at the weapon for a long moment, and then traded a look with Juliette. "Where did you get that?" he asked.

"I took it off one of the men who attacked us today. I'm out of ammo, though."

"We've got my ammunition," Stu said. He reached for the weapon. "May I?" he said.

"Yeah, sure."

Jacob handed it over to him.

Stu turned the weapon over in his hands and whistled. He looked over at Juliette. "This is a real Glock."

"No," Jacob said. "I have a bunch of Glocks back home. There's no logo on it, no serial number."

"This is a Glock," Stu said again. "A Glock 90. You have any idea how rare this is? These aren't even available for lab testing. From what I was told, they were made especially for the Austrian Auftragskillers. How did you say you got this?"

"We were attacked earlier this morning. One of the men who attacked us had this on him."

"And you took it from him?"

"Yes."

"Just took it from him? Just like that?"

"We fought," Jacob said. "I shot him in the head with it."

Stu swallowed the lump in his throat and then handed the weapon back to Jacob. "We have ammunition for that. It uses the same round as the mini gun here. I'll get you some."

He went over to a nearby workbench and brought back a green metal box of ammunition. "I don't know how many magazines you have," Stu said, "but I think that should be enough."

"It's plenty," Jacob said. "Thanks."

He ejected the magazine from his weapon and studied it. The design, while sleek and streamlined, wasn't anything he hadn't seen before, and it took him back to his school days, when he got his first lessons in firearms. "This," his instructor had said, holding up a battered-looking service pistol with a blue barrel and walnut grips, "is a Colt 1911, so named for the year it first entered production. It was one of the first semiautomatic handguns ever made. For those of you who don't know shit about math, that was more than two hundred years ago. But you will find that this weapon is no different from any of the other weapons you will be working with in this course. It served the U.S. military faithfully through four wars. Its design has been tweaked, but it has never been improved upon. Learn this now, you lunkheads, perfection was found early in the handgun, and it's hard to do better than perfection."

Jacob smiled at the memory as he thumbed the first compressed-air round into the magazine. Though he'd never loaded one of these weapons before, and indeed, had never even seen one before today, it still worked almost exactly like the Colt 1911 he'd fired for the first time that day, so many years earlier. Truly, it was hard to do better than perfection.

Once it was loaded, he slapped the magazine back into his pistol.

"That is a good gun," he said. "Now, tell me more about that battle suit. I saw when you took it off of her it made a hissing sound. Is it pressurized?"

Stu swallowed another lump in his throat.

His gaze hadn't left the pistol in Jacob's hand.

"Stu?" Jacob said.

"Yeah," Stu said. "It's pressurized. On the surface it recycles and filters air, but when submerged it can sustain the wearer for up to three hours on its stored air and carbon dioxide filters."

Jacob was about to respond when he felt a shudder go through the floor.

He stood up, weapon at the ready.

"What is it, Jacob?" Kelly said.

"Didn't you feel that?"

"Feel what?"

"That bump."

Beside Kelly, Miriam stood up and closed her eyes, straining her senses against the quiet. "The zombies down below," she finally said. "They must be trying to get through the screen. You don't have to worry about it. I sealed it."

"No," Jacob said. "That came from below us."

"That's impossible," Miriam said. "There's nothing below us."

"There is now."

Jacob listened to the sounds of the building, the mechanical groan of the air-conditioning, the wind curling around the balconies. But something didn't seem right. Ten years of working in Arbella's constabulary had taught him to trust his instincts. He'd learned how to recognize that sensation when the hairs stood up on the back of his neck.

"Clear the doorway," he said. He brought his pistol up and squared off on the door. "Get back," he said. "Get away from the door."

Chelsea looked like she had no idea what he was

talking about, but Kelly directed the girl out of Jacob's way.

The next instant the door crashed open. Four men in dark black body armor rushed through the door, all of them armed with rifles. They came through the door using a technique that Jacob had learned during his early days at the constabulary. It was called a dynamic entry. They hit the doorway hard and fast and then rolled out along the walls, spacing out so that they maximized muzzle coverage over the entire room. Jacob had done the same entry himself back in Arbella when he and his fellow deputies had gone in after Old Man Richards the night he threatened to slash his wife's throat.

Jacob knew what to expect, and how to beat it.

He ran to the wall to his right, keeping low and screening himself behind the furniture. The armored men were caught by surprise. They tried to track Jacob with their weapons, but he was faster. He squeezed off two quick rounds, striking the men along the right side of the room squarely in the chest.

It was much like the *El Presidente* exercise he'd learned back in school.

A single shooter confronted by multiple attackers is statistically more likely to survive the assault if he first plants a round in each attacker, then doubles back to finish off the wounded.

Stay still, and you're guaranteed to die.

Take the time to double-tap, and again, you're guaranteed to die.

The only way to live was to move fast and shoot fast, one target one round. Put the enemy back on their heels, and then readjust to the situation.

That's what Jacob did. He put a round to the chest

into both of the men who went to the right side of the room, then ducked back behind the furniture and came up with another two shots center mass into the chests of the two men on the opposite side of the room.

Only then did he stop to look at the damage he'd caused.

Or, rather, hadn't.

All four men were still on their feet, untouched.

Jacob raised his pistol again and shot two rounds into the helmeted figure closest to him. Both shots hit the man's faceplate and exploded harmlessly. The man rocked back on his heels, but aside from the shock of the explosion, was none the worse for wear.

"Get him," a man's voice said from the doorway.

One of the armored men ran at him. Jacob tried to shoot him, but he wasn't fast enough. The armored man tackled him to the ground. The others piled on soon after. Jacob felt knees and fists smashing into his face, and groping hands trying to pull his arms behind his back.

He twisted and kicked.

He'd been taught that you fight with everything you have. You never give them an inch. He even tried to bite one of the men who got his gloved hands too close.

But there was little he could do.

Trying to bite got him a fist in the mouth.

They finally got his hands pulled his back. He struggled again, trying to get his hands as far apart as possible, but they held him fast.

The next instant he felt something like hot wax pouring over his wrists.

He kept the struggle up, but the waxy substance hardened before he could break loose.

"What the hell are you doing?" he yelled. "Let me go."

A man walked by him. Jacob saw a flash of boots, but nothing else. When he tried to look up, one of the armored men pushed his face to the floor.

"If he speaks up again, take him out of here," one of the men said.

Jacob recognized the voice. He shook his head free until he could see across the room, and just as he suspected, he saw Lester Brooks.

Brooks seemed to know exactly what he wanted, for he crossed straight to Miriam and put a hand on her shoulder. "I am so glad you're safe," he said. "I was worried sick."

Miriam didn't seem to know what to do. "What is going on here?" she demanded. "Let him up. Why are they hurting him?"

"They're arresting him," Brooks said. He pointed to Kelly and Chelsea. "And these two also."

"Arrest? Are you insane? That's my niece."

"I know exactly who she is. That's why we were able to track them here."

"But why are you arresting her?"

"For murder. She and her friends here killed seven men this morning back in Temple. The Council has issued arrest warrants for all three of them."

Jacob let his face sink to the floor.

CHAPTER 12

"Murder?" Miriam said. "My niece is wanted for murder? I don't believe that for a second."

"There's video," Brooks said.

"Okay, well then, let's see it."

"It's not going to work that way," Brooks said. "And it's not up for discussion. If you'd like, you can watch the video contained in the affidavit once we're underway, but she and her friends have to come with us right now. And you do, too."

"Me? Why? Am I wanted for murder, too?"

"No, Miriam," Brooks said. "Please, don't be like that."

"You're trying to take my niece in for murder, Les. She's just come back into my life after seven years, and you storm in here with a goon squad and tell me you're taking her away. How am I supposed to be, Les? Tell me, how am I supposed to be?"

Even with one of the armored goons digging a knee into his back, Jacob could tell Brooks was making an effort to treat Miriam with kid gloves. Jacob didn't have Kelly's aptitude for math and science, but he could read people very well, and he could see that Miriam and Brooks were an iceberg, with most of what mattered below the surface.

Chelsea stepped from behind a desk and jabbed a finger in Brooks's chest. "We didn't murder anybody. We were attacked! All we did was defend ourselves."

Three of the armored men moved toward her, but Brooks put up a hand for them to stay back.

"You're lying," Chelsea said. "You know you are. All we did is defend ourselves. Why don't you ask who sent those men? Huh? Why aren't you doing that? Or is it because you already know who sent them?"

Brooks had already turned away from her, but when he heard that, he spun back around and "Excuse me?" he said. "Young lady, I don't think I like what you're suggesting."

"Well then, maybe you shouldn't have sent people to kill us."

"Chelsea!" Miriam said. "That is enough!"

Brooks put a hand on the older woman's shoulder. "Miriam, it's okay. She's mad, and lashing out at me because I'm the logical target here. We'll get all this sorted out back in Temple."

"You're framing my father, you fucking bastard!" Chelsea said.

"Chelsea, I'm not doing anything of the sort."

"Liar! You fucking liar!" Chelsea lashed out at him with the hardest kick she could muster. Brooks ducked to one side, but she still landed a glancing blow to his hip. "You are lying!"

Brooks backed away and motioned to his men. Three of the men moved on Chelsea. They grabbed her and pulled her back, but not before she got in one last parting kick, catching Brooks in the knee and making him stumble.

"I won't let you destroy my daddy's name," she said. She was so mad spittle was flying from her mouth. "I won't let that happen!"

"Young lady," he said, "you need to calm yourself down right now. It's only out of respect for your family that I'm not having you shackled."

"Respect?" Chelsea shouted. "Respect? You dare talk about respect around me? You're trying everything you can to ruin my daddy's reputation. You lied about him. He didn't cause the wreck of the *Darwin*. You did!"

Brooks let out a frustrated sigh. "How is that even possible? I wasn't onboard the *Darwin* when it crashed," Brooks said. "This isn't getting us anywhere. Take them to the ship."

Chelsea's only response was to spit at Brooks, a futile gesture that didn't even reach his shoes.

"Get them out of here," Brooks said.

His men pulled Chelsea toward the door. One of the men came over to where Jacob was still facedown on the ground and helped his partner pull Jacob to his feet.

"Les, you can't do this," Miriam said.

"Miriam, we have to. They have to answer for their actions. And I have to get you out of here."

"You're not taking me anywhere."

"Miriam, please, don't be like this. We don't have much time."

"Time for what?"

"Have you been outside?" Brooks asked. "Have you been watching the news feed?"

"I was on the street level thirty minutes ago," she said.

"Then you saw the zombies."

"A few, yes. Nothing our defenses can't handle."

"Miriam, no. You're about to get hit with the leading edge of the herd. The defenses in this building were never meant to handle anything like what's coming. We have to get you out of here, and we have to do it fast. We've been tracking the herd and they're already here."

"And what if I don't want to go?"

"Miriam, please. I came here to get you."

"I thought you came here to arrest my niece."

Brooks looked like he was holding on to his patience with both hands, and Jacob wondered exactly what the deal was between the two of them. In his experience, men didn't check themselves like Brooks was doing unless the lady in question meant something special.

"I didn't have to come here," Brooks said.

"Well, I wish you hadn't."

Again, Brooks stopped himself from barking at her. "I didn't have to come here," he started again. "But when I heard that you were here, I knew you'd stay at your post. I've seen the migration projections. It's not safe here. Please, Miriam, come with me."

"Dr. Brooks."

It was a man's voice.

Jacob turned to the doorway and saw the same young man who had insulted the Arbella Code in the council meeting earlier that morning. Like the others, he was wearing black body armor, but he carried his helmet under his arm. From the look of his carefully spiked and styled sandy brown hair, it was obvious he hadn't put the helmet on yet.

"Oh yes," Brooks said. He turned to Miriam. "Your niece was in possession of three journals. Where are they?"

"Why do you want the journals?" Miriam asked. She'd been angry, but now her face colored with suspicion.

"They're evidence," Brooks said.

"A dissertation on the Triune Theory is evidence in a murder trial? Seriously? Les, what in the hell is going on here? What are you playing at?"

"We're not playing at anything," the young man said. "Now, where are the journals? Quickly, we don't have time to waste."

Miriam looked from the young man to Lester Brooks, her face simmering with rage. "You're Jordan Anson?" she said. "I've heard of you. What are you doing here?"

Anson didn't answer.

"Les, what's going on here? Why is he here?"

"Miriam, please," Brooks said, looking like a man who'd just taken a bite of something nasty. "Where are the journals?"

Miriam crossed her arms over her chest and let out an angry huff.

Brooks said nothing, simply waited.

Finally Miriam nodded toward a workbench on the opposite side. Brooks followed her gaze, then went over to the satchel resting there. He opened it, pulled out the journals, thumbed through them, then stuffed them back inside.

Jacob watched him flip through the journals. He was about to turn his attention back to Jordan Anson when he saw Brooks pause and focus his attention on the blue light above the table. Some people made lousy poker players, and Jacob tell from Brooks's reaction to the blue light that he was one of them. He'd seen something he didn't like.

"You have them?" Anson said.

Brooks turned away from the table with the satchel clutched in his hand. "They're all here."

"Good." Anson nodded to the men holding Jacob. "Let's get out of here."

They started to lead Jacob away, but as he passed Anson, Jacob shook away the hands that held him. "I remember you. You were at the Council hearing this morning. You didn't say your name. Who are you?"

The man looked about thirty-five. From his build he obviously took care of himself. Was probably a runner, Jacob thought. He was tall and slender, even in the body armor, with a handsome, almond-shaped face and the bearing of a man long accustomed to being in charge.

The look he turned on Jacob, though, was one of abject disgust.

"Get him out of here," he said.

The men pushed Jacob toward the door.

As they struggled to push Jacob to the door, something crashed far below them. Footfalls on the stairs and a bloodcurdling chorus of moans followed soon after.

"They've busted through the defenses," Jacob said to Anson. He turned to the guard at his left and said, "Get me out of these cuffs, will you?"

"Be quiet," the man said.

"Come on, man," Jacob said. "Things are about to get nasty. Get me out of these cuffs."

Anson grabbed the man to Jacob's left and pushed

him toward the door. "Check that. Make sure we have a safe way out of here." He turned to face Brooks. "We need to leave right now."

"Agreed," Brooks said. "Miriam, you and your staff, come with me please."

Miriam looked as though she was still in the mood for a fight, but at that moment the armored man at the doorway started firing down the stairs.

"They're coming," he yelled. "Let's move it out!"

Jacob got pushed toward the door. The others were following along behind him. He'd made it halfway across the room when the armored man at the doorway fell back into the room beneath a wave of the undead. Several stopped to tear into the man's armor, but most rushed past him, flooding into the room.

The guard who'd been holding Jacob in place let go of him and turned his rifle on the advancing crowd. He dropped the first three zombies to work their way through the furniture, but he was a slow and deliberate shooter. Jacob screamed at the man to move and shoot, but he stood his ground and took careful shots.

All the while the zombies flooded into the room.

Two dead men managed to make their way around the outside of the room and charged at Jacob. He saw them coming and looked around for a way to escape. With his hands secured behind his back, there was little he could to fight them off. Instead, he saw a wheeled chair at one of the desks nearest him. He maneuvered it out of the desk well, and then kicked it into the path of the charging zombie.

The zombie barely noticed it. It charged forward, hit the chair, and tumbled over the top. It ended up on the floor, on its back, unable to figure out how it got that way.

But Jacob didn't have a chance to engage the zombie further.

The second zombie was coming around the desk, snarling and snapping like a wild animal. Jacob kicked the desk and sent it skidding into the zombie's way. It connected with the zombie's leg and knocked it off balance.

It was enough to give Jacob room to run.

The zombies were pouring through the doorway so fast he couldn't even count them. He rolled over one of the desks just in time to avoid another of the zombies and landed next to one of Brooks's men. The man was shooting just like his partners, standing his ground and taking slow, deliberate shots.

Jacob barrel-rolled over another desk just as a fresh wave of zombies closed in around him. He came up behind the man in the body armor, and in that moment he knew he wasn't going to be a prisoner anymore.

Fuck these guys.

He kicked the man between his shoulder blades and sent him tumbling into the advancing zombie wave. They knocked him to the ground, and as he screamed, they tore through his body armor and started to dig into the flesh beneath.

Kelly, Chelsea, Miriam, and Brooks were standing near the back of the room. Jacob ran for them, planted his shoulder against Kelly's chest, and pushed her back.

"Stu!" he yelled. "Load up the suit."

Stu and Juliette were huddled in each other's arms near the battle suits.

Neither moved.

Jacob lowered his shoulder and rammed Stu in the chest, pushing him back against the suit Miriam had used to rescue him.

"Grab that magazine," he yelled. "Load that weapon. Hurry!"

Stu looked at the battle suit and shook his head. "I don't . . ."

"Load the weapon!"

The command was enough to trip something inside of Stu. He understood. He grabbed one of the rifle magazines and jammed it into the battle suit's built-in mini gun. Then he wrapped his arm around the suit's arm and maneuvered it like it was a fire hose. He turned it on the advancing horde and started to fire. There was very little noise, just a continuous muffled popping sound as the mini gun leveled the zombies filtering through the room.

But even as the mini gun cleared the zombies already inside the room, Lester Brooks was forcing his way toward to the door. He pulled Miriam along with him as he shot the zombies charging him, and in that moment Jacob knew the man would leave the rest of them behind without reservation.

"Drag it with us," Jacob said. "We have to hit the door."

"Drag it . . . ?"

"Come on," Jacob said. "I can't use my hands. Pull the suit out of its cradle and let's hit the door. Move!"

Stu and Juliette moved in perfect unison, just like Jacob hoped they would. They pulled the suit down from its rack and, while Juliette pulled it along, Stu aimed it at the zombies filing through the door.

In seconds they cut a path through the dead.

They made it to the door a moment later. Brooks and Miriam were already heading up the stairs. Jordan Anson was already a level above them. He met Jacob's gaze with a *fuck you* stare that left little room for interpretation.

Jacob returned the look. Beside him, Stu, Juliette, Kelly, and Chelsea all filed through the door. Jacob kept pace right behind them as they all made their way to the roof access.

He hit the roof access doorway right behind Kelly. Night had fallen since they'd been in Miriam's office, and the hot, dry desert air hit his throat like an electrical shock.

Ahead of him was the shuttle Dr. Brooks and his team had flown in on.

The zombies had been gaining on them while they were on the stairs, and now they flooded through the doorway. With his hands behind his back, Jacob was almost defenseless. He met the first zombie through the door with a hard kick to the chest, knocking it down, but he was unable to twist and dodge the one right behind it. The zombie lunged and managed to wrap its fingers into Jacob's shirt. Jacob backpedaled as fast as he could, twisting one way and then the other in an attempt to shake the zombie loose, but it didn't work. The thing held tight, even though it lost its balance and sank to its knees.

The weight pulled Jacob down and he felt himself losing the struggle to stay upright. He knew if he fell he'd die right there. They would swarm him and devour him in seconds.

The zombie was struggling, trying to pull Jacob toward its reeking mouth. Jacob did the only thing he could and head-butted the zombie, knocking it backward hard enough to dislodge its fingers from his shirt.

The zombie fell into the wall at the edge of the roof, and Jacob ran at him. He lowered his shoulder and hit the zombie square in the chest, knocking him back again so that the dead man went over the side, tumbling to his second death.

Three more, then eight more, then fifteen came surging through the door.

He started to backpedal again, only this time it wasn't a zombie that slowed him down. Lester Brooks was right behind him. He grabbed Jacob by the shoulder and pulled him out of the way. Then he stepped into the spot where Jacob had just stood, leveled his pistol at the crowd of snarling dead surging out of the doorway, and started firing.

The three closest to him sank silently to the ground, their heads ruptured by the compressed air and leaking down their backs. Brooks ignored them. More were coming up the stairs every second.

Jacob had been taught to shoot a handgun with two hands. Feet together, shoulder-width apart, both hands on the weapon straight out in front the chest, so that the body formed a triangle.

But Brooks fired one-handed. He had his shoulders bladed toward the onrushing zombies, weapon in the right hand, extended toward the target.

Jacob had been taught that the accuracy of a two-handed stance was far better than that of a single-handed stance, and he'd known older shooters back in Arbella who insisted on using just one hand. They never shot as well as those who used the two-handed Weaver stance, like Jacob.

Brooks didn't seem to have any trouble with accuracy, though. He scored one head shot after another, and didn't miss once.

"Get to the shuttle!" Brooks said to him. "Move. I'll cover you."

Jacob didn't have to be told twice. He ran for the shuttle. It was a hulking aircraft shaped like a wedge, with thick, stubby wings sloping off the aircraft's spine like a man's shoulders. Underneath each wing was a fat, roaring engine, and even as he sprinted for the open doorway near the front of the shuttle, Jacob got the sense that this airship, even more so than the freighter upon which he'd hitched a ride earlier that day, was built for power and speed. The doorway that led inside was standing open. Kelly and Chelsea had just slipped inside. Jordan Anson was in the doorway, waving at Lester Brooks to hurry.

Jacob stopped in the doorway long enough to watch Brooks drop four more zombies. Then the older man turned and ran for the shuttle.

Jacob hustled inside. There was very little light, but enough that he could see Kelly strapping herself into a couch along the far wall.

"Jacob," she called out. "Over here!"

He dropped onto the couch beside her and she helped him get strapped in.

Brooks scrambled aboard a moment later, and in the seconds it took for the door to draw up and close, Jacob saw the roof filling with the undead.

They ran at the shuttle and tried to climb its hull, looking for a way in. Through the small port windows above the couch on the opposite wall, Jacob could see dead men and women beating against the hull.

"Got everybody," Brooks yelled toward the front of the shuttle.

The pilot, the only one of the goon squad to survive the retreat to the roof, gave Brooks a big thumbs-up. Then he turned to the controls and powered up the shuttle's massive engines. The shuttle's engines strained loudly as it fought to gain the air, but the zombies piling on made the craft rock and shudder. Whether to try to shake off the zombies, or simply to regain control of the rising aircraft, Jacob couldn't tell, but the pilot rotated the shuttle, swinging one wing over the edge of the roof.

Jacob found himself looking out the window, six stories down, with zombies slipping off the craft and tumbling to the street far below. A terrible sense of vertigo overwhelmed him, and all he wanted to do was shrink into himself and hold on for dear life.

The next instant the aircraft rotated back the other way, carrying them over the roof. The view was no better there. Hundreds of zombies crowded the roof, all of them rushing toward the shuttle. As Jacob watched, the huge engine on the opposite wing swept through the crowd. It swept through the zombie masses like a giant maw, scooping up bodies until the sheer mass of the dead clogged the engine. It shuddered and smoked, coughing so violently that it shook the aircraft.

The next instant, it exploded. The window Jacob had been looking through disappeared in a fireball, and when the flames cleared, nothing was left but a hole in the side of the ship and tangled, smoking metal.

Beyond, burnt and broken bodies littered the rooftop. A few were still moving, even as their hair and clothes were engulfed in fire.

From the front of the aircraft, Jacob heard Brooks yelling at the pilot. "Put us back down on the roof!"

"I can't," the pilot screamed. "I can't stop the rotation."

The spinning craft rocked again over the side of the roof, and Jacob felt his stomach rise into his throat.

"We're going over!" Kelly screamed. "Oh God, oh God, oh God!"

Jacob could see the ground rushing up at them through the hole in the fuselage. But the craft continued to spin. Things were happening so fast he could barely process it all. The view outside the hole turned to brick and cement as they spun into the side of the building, smashing into it with so much force it took his breath away.

Amid the screams of the passengers, the aircraft continued to spiral down to the ground, hitting hard as it slid across the street in a chorus of shrieking and moaning metal.

The whole world seemed to roll. Jacob felt like a piece of driftwood caught in the waves, completely out of control, unable to hold on to anything.

He was jerked so violently against his restraints that he blacked out.

When he came to, dizzy and disoriented, he was choking on smoke.

From somewhere, an angry Klaxon whined.

CHAPTER 13

Kelly was gone. During the crash, a huge strut had collapsed and impaled itself through the seat where Kelly had been just moments before. Jacob couldn't hold back the panic.

"Kelly?" Jacob said. He tried to see through the smoke, but it was too thick. He could barely breathe. He hacked and coughed as his eyes filled with burning tears. "Kelly? Where are you?"

"Jacob, here!"

"Where are you? I can't see you."

Suddenly she was there, stepping out of the smoke, ducking under the strut that would have killed her had she still been in her seat. "I'm here," she said. "Are you okay? Is anything broken?"

"I don't know. I can't feel my arms."

"Damn," she said. "It's those cuffs they put you in." She looked to the front of the shuttle, where the smoke was starting to clear. The front of the ship looked to have taken most of the hit of the impact. There was little ahead of them but twisted metal and the broken body of the pilot leaning out of his seat.

Kelly took a few steps that way.

"Where are you going?" he asked her.

"Stay still."

Jacob shook against his restraints. "Is that a joke?"

"I'm going to try to get you out of those cuffs."

She pulled her way through the wreckage, toward the pilot. She pushed his body out of the chair and ran her hands over his gun belt. A moment later she held up a silver disk about the size of a coin.

"Got it!" she said.

"Get his gun, too."

"Oh, right."

Kelly turned the pilot's corpse over and wrestled with the built-in retention safeties in the holster, but eventually managed to pull the weapon. She held it up for Jacob to see.

"Kelly! Heads up!"

She glanced down at the pilot's corpse. The man's face had been burned away. There was smoke coming from under his helmet. But he was still moving. He pulled himself from the chair and somehow got to his feet. His head rocked back and lolled on his shoulders. But then he saw Kelly and he staggered toward her.

"Shoot him!" Jacob yelled.

Kelly was terrified. She backed away from the dead pilot, shaking her head in disbelief.

"Kelly, shoot him!"

She raised the gun in both hands, just like she'd been taught, and fired.

The shot was low.

It hit the man in the chest and exploded harmlessly off his body armor.

The zombie didn't even notice the shot. He staggered forward again, hands outstretched and grabbing for her.

"Kelly, shoot him in the head!"

"I'm trying," she said.

The zombie fell forward, its mangled hands falling on her shoulders.

Kelly screamed and fell back, but the touch of those dead hands on her skin clicked something inside her. She steadied herself, aimed the pistol at the man's chin, the only part visible through his cracked helmet, and shot him.

The resulting blast tore the man's neck in two, and his helmeted head slid off his body and clanked to the floor.

"I did it!" she said.

"Yes, you did. Now get me out of these cuffs."

She made her way back to him, undid his harness, and then pushed him forward so she could see his hands. "I don't know what this stuff is," she said. "It looks like wax, or melted plastic."

"Just get it off me."

"Okay, okay."

Kelly took the metal disk from her pocket and leaned over Jacob's back.

"Stop!" Brooks yelled from the other side of the shuttle. He'd been caught up in the explosion that damaged that side of the shuttle, and was trapped beneath a tangle of wires and metal pipes. But he was pulling himself loose, bit by bit. "Don't you touch him. That man is under arrest."

He got an arm free and pulled his pistol. He pointed it right at Kelly's head.

"I mean it. Do not release him."

Kelly stared at the pistol, but she didn't flinch. "You're not going to shoot me," she said. "And there are zombies closing in on us. I will not leave him defenseless."

The next thing Jacob knew, she'd leaned over his back and touched the metal disk to the handcuffs. In seconds, they turned to a warm liquid and ran off his skin, leaving his hands free to move. He stood up, rubbing his wrists.

"Stop where you're at!" Brooks said. He turned his pistol to cover Jacob.

Jacob took the pistol from Kelly and slid it into the back of his pants. Then he reached down and grabbed a flat piece of sheet metal that the explosion had ripped from the wall. He held it up in front of him and rushed toward Brooks.

Brooks popped off three rounds, but they didn't penetrate the sheet metal. They just exploded harmlessly off of it.

Jacob pressed the sheet metal into Brooks's face, pinning him and his weapon hand against the debris. He reached around the sheet metal shield and found Brooks's gun. He twisted it and bent the man's hand backward until Brooks couldn't hold it anymore and released the weapon.

Jacob got back to his feet and held up the weapon for Brooks to see. "You won't be needing this anymore."

Only then did Jacob throw away the sheet metal.

"You've got him," Chelsea said. She and her aunt and Stu and Juliette came forward from the rear of the aircraft. They were covered in dust, and Stu's forehead had a nasty cut on it. Seven or eight stitches easy to put that together, Jacob thought.

Chelsea gave Jacob a shove.

"What are you waiting for?" she said. "Kill the son of a bitch."

"Jacob, no!" Miriam shouted. "For God's sake, no."

"Relax," Jacob said. "I'm not going to be killing anybody." He motioned to Stu and Juliette. "Can you two help him out of there, please?"

"I won't be anybody's hostage," Brooks said. "If that's what you have in mind, you can just kill me now, because if not, I'll kill you as soon as I can."

"You know," Jacob said, "for a doctor you're pretty fucking stupid. I'm not interested in hostages. I'm interested in getting out of here."

"Then give me back my weapon."

"That's not gonna happen, either," Jacob said. "You've already shown me you can't be trusted."

"I thought you said I wasn't a hostage."

"You're not."

Jacob walked to the jagged hole in the side of the aircraft. It was big enough they could all just walk right out into the El Paso night. The streetlights were on. In their glow, Jacob could see hundreds of bodies scattered around the wreckage. A man nearest them was missing everything from his waist up. Still another was as crispy and black as a burned sheet of paper. But farther off, in the distance, he could see thicker crowds of zombies gathering, coming closer. He gauged their rate of progress down the street and figured he and the others had a minute, maybe forty-five seconds, before things got hot again. Jacob got Brooks's attention and nodded toward the oncoming ground.

"You're not a hostage," Jacob said, turning back to Brooks. "You're free to go. In fact, I recommend you go that way."

Brooks just stared at him.

"Wait a minute," Kelly said. "Where's his friend, the white guy with the attitude?"

"I think he's dead," Stu said. "Right after the crash, I saw him outside on the road. A zombie was trying to dig into his body armor."

"Okay," Jacob said. "So where do we go from here? We're about to have a whole lot of company. Miriam, can you get us out here?"

The older woman nodded. "I think so. There's a machine shop not far from here. If we can get there, we can take a tunnel over to the armory."

"That's no good," Jacob said. "The tunnels are compromised."

"Not this one," Miriam answered. "It's a dedicated tunnel, dating back to when the U.S. military ran this place. It connects the machine shop to the armory without any other access points."

"And what's in the armory?"

"We need a way out of here, right?"

"Yeah."

"We store the armored personnel carriers that go into the aerofluyts there. If we can make it to one of those, we drive our way out of here."

"She's right," Brooks said. "We could do that."

"Okay," Jacob said. "Alright, that sounds good. Which way do we go to get to this machine shop?"

Miriam ducked under the tangled debris hanging from the ceiling and looked out to the street. "Oh my," she said. "They're so close." She pointed toward the front of the aircraft. "It's that way, about four blocks."

"Alright, then," Jacob said. He looked around the wreckage. "Everybody ready to move?"

The others nodded.

"Okay, then. Let's do this."

CHAPTER 14

Jacob took the lead running out into the street.

The others filed out behind him, moving toward the front of the downed aircraft. "Let's go, let's go!" he said. "Miriam, show us the way."

Several of the faster zombies had already closed the distance between them, and Jacob ran out to intercept. Any of them that got too close, he popped with a head shot, dropping them to the street to lie among the dead left behind from the aircraft's swirling crash. They were easy when they came by ones and twos. He could let them come to him, putting them down with carefully aimed head shots. But beyond the fast movers there were thousands more. The army of the undead was so vast their feet made his teeth vibrate.

"Let's go," he said again. "Come on, everybody, move it!"

Kelly and Chelsea; Stu, Juliette, and Miriam; and finally Brooks: The group filed out of the downed aircraft and ran toward the machine shop at the end of the street.

Glancing ahead, Jacob's confidence wavered.

Miriam had said it was only four blocks down the road. He could see now that it was much farther. Ten blocks at least.

Still, he waved them on, directing them down the street.

Turning to his right, he could see huge masses of zombies coming their way. They weren't seeing the techs and hospital staff anymore. The zombies they were dealing with now were from the main body of the Great Texas Herd. They were filthy and starved-looking, most of them so rotten and deteriorated that they seemed ready to fall apart.

And yet their moaning filled up the night. It echoed off the buildings like voices down a canyon, so loud it seemed to shake the guts inside him.

The two pistols that he carried would never be enough for that.

Jacob glanced over his shoulder and saw Lester Brooks staring at him. Jacob had developed a hatred for the man over the last few days, what with his talk of how great the world would be without cops, and those feelings of disgust were only augmented by the betrayal he'd seen from the man during the Council meeting. Brooks was, in his mind, the kind of man who wouldn't hesitate to stab a friend in the back.

But in that moment he could not deny the strength within the man. A backstabbing asshole though he may be, he was no coward. His gaze moved from Jacob, to the approaching herd, and back to Jacob with a fierce intensity that seemed earned, rather than affected.

"Behind you," Brooks said.

Jacob turned, and sure enough, four dead things were close enough to touch him. He landed head shots on each, but when he turned back to thank Brooks, he was already trotting away behind the others.

Jacob took a moment to study the street. He and the others had a straight shot to the machine shop. It was a low, decrepit two-story building with boarded-up windows and graffiti scrawled all across its ground floor. At the jogging pace they were setting, he bet they could make it in ten minutes.

Looking to the west, he saw the main body of the Great Texas Herd zeroing in on their location, attracted no doubt by the noise of the crash. They'd certainly scarred the side of the building. Even at a glance, Jacob could track the course their aircraft had taken as it rotated down the side of the building. The face of the building was ruined.

And that was no doubt going to get worse as the main body of the herd advanced into town. Jacob had never seen a zombie herd so large. They kicked up enough dust to blot out the stars, and their moaning really did shake him to the core.

"Jacob!"

It was Kelly. Jacob turned back to the main street. Kelly and the others were running toward the machine shop, but there were fast-moving zombies filtering through the buildings ahead of them.

Jacob had thought the herd would be homogenous within its main body. There would be fast movers, the more recently turned, among the leading numbers, but they would be few and far between. The main portion, the overriding majority, would be slow-moving zombies in an advanced state of decay.

He saw now that he was wrong.

A few fast movers had already made their way into El Paso. They'd managed to charge into Miriam Sayers's lab and kill three of Lester Brooks's hired goons. They'd even managed to wreck an aircraft.

But Jacob had thought he'd seen the last of them.

He told himself they could do this because he'd wanted to believe they could make it. But he saw now that he had misjudged the herd. They were anything but homogenous. They were pouring around the sides of the buildings ahead of him in droves, some of them even sprinting toward Kelly and the others.

Jacob picked Kelly out of the crowd. She was close to the machine shop's main entrance, with Chelsea and the others coming up fast behind her. As the group reached the main entranceway, they started to work on the wooden boards that had been put in place over the doors and windows, peeling them away with their bare hands.

Jacob sprinted their way, turning on every bit of speed he had.

His ribs were burning again as he reached the machine shop, but he couldn't help that. The fast movers were pouring into the street, surrounding Kelly and the others faster than he could count their numbers.

Glancing back over his shoulder, he saw Kelly and the others running down a short alleyway to the entrance of the machine shop. There were several openings down the length of the alley, but they were sealed with hurricane fencing. Kelly reached the main entrance to the shop and turned to Jacob.

"It's boarded up tight," she called to him.

"Can you get it open?"

"How?"

"Find something to pry it open."

"With what?" she said.

"Anything, Kelly. It's a fucking machine shop. There's bound to be something. Stu, you guys figure it out."

"It's gonna take us a few minutes," Stu said.

"Roger that," Jacob said. "Just find a way. I'll cover this."

He turned back to the street. The main road ahead of him was already filling up with zombies. Too many to count, but it looked like at least a hundred of them. All of them fast movers. There were two smaller streets, more like alleys, like the one he was guarding, to his left, and three larger cross streets to his right. Most of the zombies were coming from that direction.

Jacob ejected the magazine from his gun and inspected it. It looked full. He had another magazine in his pocket that he'd loaded up back at Miriam's lab, as well as Lester Brooks's pistol tucked into the back of his pants. That gave him roughly two hundred and forty rounds. And there were more zombies pouring into the street with every passing second.

This was going to be tricky.

Because of the gun's limited range, he had to wait for the zombies to get in close. With a handgun like this, long-range shots were a waste of ammunition. He wished he had his Ruger 10-22 again. With a rifle, he'd already be dropping the dead. But then, if it was as easy as wishing, he'd be back in Arbella with a couple of naked girls in his bed helping him to forget all about the rest of the world.

And of course, nothing was ever that easy.

He slapped the magazine back into the gun's receiver, then stepped into the street and turned to face the nearest cluster of zombies.

He let two come right up on him before he fired.

Both sank to the pavement, only to make way for the ten behind them. He'd always been taught that the only way to survive an encounter with a large number of the undead was to move and shoot. Never stop moving. Stand still and you'd get overwhelmed in no time.

But Jacob didn't have that luxury. He could fall back a little, but he couldn't leave the natural choke point of the head of the alleyway. It was the only way to give Kelly and the others the time they needed and still keep as much control as he could over the course of the fight.

He readjusted his grip on the pistol and started firing. The head shots came easily when he was just dealing with small groups. Because he was getting the fastest zombies in the herd first, they were more spaced out, coming at him in smaller groups. He could pop one, adjust his aim on the next one, and gently squeeze off another shot. He was even able to glance over his shoulder and keep tabs on the three zombies closing in on him from the left.

Soon a berm of bodies formed around him, and the zombies closing in had to step through and over the obstacles.

That slowed them down a little, but not enough to keep up the easy pace.

Their numbers continued to swell, crowding into the street, and as the ring of broken and rotted faces closed tighter around him, his shots got sloppier.

Two zombies climbed over the mound of bodies and reached for him. Jacob landed two head shots, but a third zombie came up right behind them and closed the distance too quickly. Jacob shot her, but he only hit her left arm. The explosion severed the arm and spun her around, but it didn't put her down, and when she came at him a second time, her face and hair were spattered with her own gore.

With her remaining arm she grabbed at his face. Jacob got the gun under her chin and fired, leaving another headless corpse.

Another zombie fell on him from the left, pulling his weapon off target just as he was about to fire. Jacob fumbled with the gun, but he was off balance, and when the zombie fell on him, arms flailing and teeth snapping, Jacob went down.

He rolled as soon as he hit the ground. The zombie came down on top of him, and as she opened her mouth to tear into him, Jacob got the fetid odor of rotting meat square in the face. He turned his head to one side and shoved the zombie, rolling in the same direction to get her off him. The zombie tumbled away and rolled into a forest of rotting legs. Jacob was still on his hands and knees, though, and had to crawl away, fighting the whole time to get back on his feet.

Turning, he found himself a few meters inside the alley. He redoubled his efforts, firing more for speed than accuracy. He burned through his last few rounds, ejected the empty magazine, and slapped in a new. He immediately went back to firing, putting as many rounds as he could into the crowd.

And then he felt hands at his back.

He let out a startled gasp and tried to spin away again, but a strong hand held him in place. "Give me the other gun," Lester Brooks said.

Before Jacob could react, Brooks reached behind

him and pulled the pistol himself. Brooks didn't say another word. He just turned toward the street and started shooting one-handed into the crowd.

Jacob got shoulder to shoulder with Brooks, and between the two of them they managed to slow up the herd's advance.

But they couldn't stop it.

"How's it going?" Jacob yelled over his shoulder.

"Almost there," Kelly answered.

"Hurry it up!"

He checked the ammunition tracker on the side of the weapon's receiver. Nine rounds left.

"I'm almost out," he said to Brooks.

"Fall back then. I'll cover you."

Jacob took a few steps back. He went to the right side of the alleyway in order to open up a lane of fire that didn't include Brooks and shot two more zombies.

"Go!" Brooks said. "I'm right behind you."

From behind them, Kelly let out a cheer. "We got it, Jacob!"

"That's the cue," Brooks said.

Both men turned and sprinted down the alley, leaving the herd to push their way in behind them. Jacob reached the window that Kelly and the others had managed to pry open and started helping Chelsea, Miriam, and Juliette climb through. Kelly went next, then Stu. They both turned as soon as they were inside and helped Jacob get inside. Brooks got to them moments later.

Behind him, the alley was choked with the dead, and they were getting closer.

"Help me get him up here," Jacob said.

He tossed his weapon aside and reached for Brooks. Stu got next to him, and together they grabbed Brooks and pulled him inside. The three of them landed in a heap on the floor.

"Get that board back in place!" Jacob yelled.

Kelly, Chelsea, and Juliette grabbed the handle on the inside of the plywood window covering and slid it back into its grooves on the windowsill just as the crowd reached the building.

Moans filled the air as the zombies sensed living meat just out of reach. They slapped on the walls and on the plywood covering the windows and doors, sending pounding echoes through the building.

Chapter 15

Jacob climbed to his feet. The ribs on his right side were screaming at him. He put a hand against them and tried to master the pain, but he felt like he was going to black out again. His vision turned soupy at the edges and he felt himself starting to drift.

But then he saw his gun on the floor at Lester Brooks's feet and that cleared his head fast.

Brooks saw him looking at it, but said nothing.

"Give me my gun," Jacob said.

"You're still under arrest," Brooks said.

"Oh my God," Miriam said. "Are we really doing this again? Les, you can't arrest him now. Those things are crawling all over the place out there."

"I'm not putting a gun in his hand again. He's a murderer."

"I'm the murderer?" Jacob said. "You're the one who sent those men after us in the first place."

"I did?" Brooks said. "Mr. Carlton, I did nothing of the sort."

"Liar."

"You know, for a policeman, you sure throw around a lot of unsubstantiated accusations. That's one of the reasons why we did away with your kind."

"You honestly deny sending those men to kill us?" Chelsea said. "You tried to wreck my father's reputation, and then you tried to kill me. How can you stand there and deny it?"

"I can deny it because I have never once raised a finger to hurt you, Chelsea. And, as for your father, well, he was a grown man who made his own decisions."

"Liar!"

"Chelsea," Miriam said. "Please. He's right. You can't go around saying stuff like that without proof. He's a member of the Council."

"That may be," Jacob said, "but he's not above the law. You want proof? Okay, all those techs down in the tunnel. They were gassed to death."

"What are you talking about?" Brooks said. "Who was gassed?"

"The people down in the safe areas beneath the base," Kelly said. "I examined several of them. None of them had any injuries, but they all showed signs of cyanosis around the mouth. They were asphyxiated by some sort of lethal gas."

"That's outrageous," Brooks said. He tried to appear unflustered, but something had rattled him. "And even if that is the case, which I seriously doubt, maybe there was a gas leak somewhere. This is an old facility. A lot of things are falling apart."

"I doubt it," Kelly said.

"And this is proof somehow that I sent a mysterious

group of mercenaries to have Chelsea killed? I don't see how one thing connects to another, and frankly, if this is what passes for proof in your mind, Mr. Carlton, it's little wonder you executed an innocent man."

Jacob stiffened, but refused to take the bait. "When your men failed to kill her in Temple, you tracked us here. You knew where we'd be going, that Miriam was the only person who could help her. And at the same time, you had the people down in the tunnels gassed so that the reanimates would be waiting for us when we got off the train."

Brooks shook his head. "I don't even know where to begin. You're crazy. All three of you."

"And you, Dr. Brooks, are a fucking bastard. By the way, Dr. Sayers has read the contents of the notebooks you stole from us. What will you do with her now? Will you have her killed, or simply thrown in jail on more made-up charges?"

"That's enough," Miriam said. She turned to Chelsea. "Child, you and your friends are way off base here. Les didn't kill anybody. He's a good man."

"He's a monster!" Chelsea said. "Aunt Miriam, how can you defend him like this? He's trying to ruin our family name."

"No, child, he's not."

"There's one other thing you haven't heard yet," Jacob said.

"I can't wait," Lester said.

"When we got off the train, we found the station's defenses had been sabotaged. Key gates between the common areas and the concourse had been damaged."

"Damaged how?"

"Nothing obvious. Gates were jammed. Locks not

engaged. It was nothing that would show up later during inspections, but it was enough to allow the zombies down in the concourse to intercept us."

Brooks scoffed at him. "These mercenaries you imagine me having at my beck and call, I suppose they were so fast and so talented that they were able to do all of this and still avoid the zombies down in the concourse. That's a pretty impressive team of soldiers, Mr. Carlton."

"Actually, no. They didn't make it out without incident. While we were down there, we found five zombies that had been put down with bullets to the head."

"That is the usual way to put down a zombie, I believe."

"Yes, but these five were put down by bullets. I mean real bullets. Like from a rifle."

"That's not possible," Miriam said. "There are no guns in Temple society."

"Maybe not in the general population, but there are plenty onboard the aerofluyts. I know that for a fact. I've used them before. So, tell me, Dr. Brooks, if there are no guns here, then where did those come from?"

"I have no idea. How do I even know you're telling the truth about any of this?"

Jacob shrugged. "If you ask me, it seems like you tried to cover all your bases. Between the zombies and the warrant you keep talking about, you probably figured Chelsea was done for. If the zombies didn't kill her, you could always gag her with political corruption. Maybe that's why your society got rid of cops, huh? Makes it easier to break the rules."

"I think this has gone on long enough," Brooks said.

Before Jacob had a chance to answer, one of the boards on the opposite side of the shop snapped. Stu ran toward the sound and gave it a quick once-over. "Okay," he said as he ran back to the others, "we need to find that tunnel right now. That's thing's not gonna hold."

No sooner had the words left his mouth than the plywood covering the window shattered and a tangle of bloody hands and gray arms came through the window. The noise from the street went up to a roar as more windows snapped and gave way.

"Where did you say that tunnel was again?" Kelly said to Miriam.

"This way."

She led them to the back of the shop. The walls were all red brick on the inside, and Jacob got the sense that he was looking at a much older building, which had been built on to so many times over the years that the original structure had become merely an interior portion of the newer, larger building. It was the red brick that did it. It looked old and pocked, and the mortar between the bricks sloppily applied.

While he was examining that, the wall to his right ended. Or at least the top of it did. The bottom half continued on another ten feet or so and became part of a short maze, like he'd seen in the ruins of slaughter yards.

"What is this?" Jacob asked.

"It's right through here," Miriam said, leading through the maze. It ended at a flight of stairs leading down into darkness.

"The tunnel's down there?" Jacob said.

"Yes. Is something wrong?"

"It's smaller than I expected," Jacob said. He swallowed a knot in his throat, thinking about being hemmed in by the walls of the tunnel.

"Seriously?" she said. "You're claustrophobic?"

Jacob nodded toward the tunnel. "It's okay," he said. "That beats the zombies any day."

"Here, get out of the way," Brooks said.

He started down the stairs, but stopped on the third one. He touched something on his left shoulder, and an intensely bright blue light lit up the tunnel. Jacob ducked down so he could see what was ahead. The walls were caked with dust. Spiderwebs hung from the corners where the walls met the ceiling. It went on for a long ways.

"Let's move out," Brooks said. "Mr. Carlton, you're out front, if you please."

Chapter 16

"I don't understand why these tunnels are here," Kelly said as they made their way through the dusty passageway. "I mean, the mass transit system I can understand. I read in a history book about cities that had whole networks of trains underground. But what about tunnels like this?"

Jacob was sneezing from the dust and feeling almost sick to his stomach from the closeness of the walls and the low ceiling, but that got his attention. He'd been wondering the same thing, and the meager explanations that Chelsea had been able to provide had left him more curious than anything else.

Plus, listening to the answer would help to take his mind off the claustrophobia.

At least he hoped it would.

"Some of them are older than the city," Miriam said. "Dug by Native American tribes hundreds of years ago. But the real birth of the tunnel system happened in the late eighteen hundreds, when the Chinese came here.

They were hired workers for the railroad, and when the project was completed here in El Paso, and they weren't needed anymore, the railroad fired them. After that, there were so many Chinese immigrants across the country that the U.S. government passed a law prohibiting any future Chinese immigration. The Chinese already in the country could stay, but if they left the country for any reason, they weren't allowed back in. And, of course, the people of El Paso being who they were, they started digging tunnels to help smuggle Chinese illegals into the country. Most of the tunnel system around the river was created for that. There's an equally large, though not as extensively mapped or renovated, tunnel on the Ciudad Juarez side of the river."

"That's pretty cool," Kelly said.

"Yeah, but that's only part of the story," Miriam said. "In the middle of the twentieth century, the tunnels were taken over by drug smugglers and human traffickers. Cartel drug money paid for huge renovations to the tunnels, expanding them, creating a lot of the pedestrian throughways we still use today.

"At the same time, a lot of private citizens in El Paso dug their own personal tunnels. I don't know, I guess it was the popular thing to do. Just south of here there are a number of personal tunnels, sort of like this one, that connect homes owned by the same family, or a family's home to the business that they owned down the street. We've mapped a good many of them, but few have been explored."

"So, who built all the tunnels we've seen under the airport and around here? Did Temple society do that?"

"Some of it, though not nearly as much as you might think. A good part of all this was built by the U.S. military at the end of the twentieth century. Those military tunnels were big-time. Almost all of them were large enough to move heavy machinery underground, and almost all of them were professionally engineered for heavy loads. Most of our Tube system was adapted from what the military had already put in place."

"Wow, this is just staggering," Kelly said.

"Nothing like this in Arbella, eh?"

Kelly laughed. "We don't even have electric lights. Or, well, sometimes we do, but that's only when there's fuel for the generators, and that doesn't happen very often. Most of the time, all we have is candlelight."

"That actually sounds kind of nice," Miriam said. "Sometimes I think I'd like living life that way."

"We should switch lives then."

"Okay," Miriam said. "Done! And look, we're here!"

Ahead of them was a flight of stairs leading up to metal door. Jacob trotted up to it and gave it a push. "It's locked," he said. "We'll have to pry it open."

"That shouldn't be necessary," Miriam said. "This is one of the technology-sensitive parts of the base. Let Juliette try it."

Juliette climbed up the stairs. In the blue light of Brooks's torch, her pasty white skin took on an unnatural glow. "Excuse me," she said, and stepped around Jacob. She pressed on the door handle and it clicked open.

Jacob caught the door in surprise. "How did you do that?"

Juliette tapped a small metal disk clipped to her belt. "It codes my access privileges to the door so I can get in wherever I need to go. It's like a key, basically."

Then she stepped through the door.

When they were all inside, Jacob turned and closed the door. He found Miriam and said, "How many of the technicians and hospital staff we saw earlier would have a coding key like that?"

Miriam shrugged. "I don't know. It would depend on their rank, I guess. Or perhaps the nature of their duties."

"But some of them?"

"Yes, probably."

"Okay, we need to barricade this door. Most of the zombies I saw over at the machine shop were part of the herd, but we can't take a chance that some of the technicians will be among the ones pounding on this door in a few minutes."

"Yeah, he's right about that," Stu said. "They'll be down that hall any minute now."

"Fine," Brooks said. "Go ahead. Do whatever you need to do."

Jacob didn't like Brooks's tone, but that was no problem. He'd only known Brooks for a few weeks, but that was long enough for him to form an opinion of the man. He was intelligent and charismatic, of that there was no question, but he was also arrogant. Jacob suspected that the man lacked any real sense of empathy, and that whatever lip service he paid to that, as he'd done in Jacob's hospital room the day he tried to prep him for the hearing, was an act. His real motivation, like that of most politicians, was nothing more than self-aggrandizement. It made Jacob wonder if Temple wouldn't have been better off banning politicians rather than policemen.

But it didn't matter, for Brooks was a politician. Tactics were not his thing. He stood off to one side, his pistol pointed toward the ceiling, looking bored.

He didn't even flinch when Jacob found a heavy metal bar and picked it up to test the heft of it.

"This'll do," Jacob said. "I think we can Katy bar the door with this."

Jacob stepped a little to Brooks's right. The man was still letting his boredom get the best of him, and Jacob had to telegraph his next move to get Brooks to engage.

Jacob raised the bar over his head in an unmistakably hostile gesture. Only then did Brooks react. He took a step back and tried to bring the gun up to Jacob, but he was too slow. Jacob sidestepped again and brought the metal bar down on Brooks's wrist, sending the gun clattering to the floor.

Brooks went down, too, groaning in pain as he clamped his other hand on his injured wrist.

"What are you doing?" Miriam yelled. "Stop!"

Jacob threw the metal pole over near the door. "Relax," he said. "I'm not going to kill him."

He reached down and picked up Brooks's gun. Then fished through the man's pockets and came up with five more magazines, Jacob's almost empty pistol, and a pocketknife.

He looked up at Miriam and smiled. "I just don't like being the one without the gun."

CHAPTER 17

"Alright," Jacob said, pointing the weapon at Brooks. "Everybody up. Let's get what we came for."

"I'm not going anywhere with you," Brooks said, still holding his wrist. "Go ahead, shoot me. Prove to everybody here that you're nothing but a killer."

"I don't want to shoot you," Jacob said. "I just want to—"

"Now who's lying?" Brooks said. "I can see it in your eyes. It's what you live for, isn't it? Does it help if you think of me as that innocent man you killed back in your hometown? No? How about Nick? That was his name, right? Your friend whom you murdered in the name of justice?"

"Just get up," Jacob said. "You're not worth arguing with."

"Why? Am I an ugly reminder of your hypocrisy?"

"You have no right to call anybody a hypocrite."

"But I'm doing it, Jacob. I'm calling you out. I'm calling you—"

"Oh, for fuck's sake, will you two stop it!" Miriam roared. "Stop it! Enough already. Look at him, Jacob. You broke his arm."

"Okay," Jacob said. "Help him, then. We need to locate those armored personnel carriers and get out of here."

Miriam helped Brooks to his feet, and in that moment, Jacob saw exactly what he already suspected to be true. The two of them had shared something in the past. Exactly what he wasn't sure, but it was pretty clear there were strong feelings there. She held Brooks's hand like one long-accustomed to his tenderness, like a lover. He had no idea what sort of past they'd had since then. Some kind of breakup or separation, probably. After all, they worked in different parts of the world. But he had come back for her. Whatever other motivations he had had, he'd been very clear on that point. He'd come back to get her. Would Jacob have done any different for Kelly?

He didn't answer the question because there was no need.

He knew the answer in his heart.

And so they moved out, making their way through the arsenal building with Stu and Juliette in the lead. Jacob had hoped that a building called an arsenal would include all the weapons he would ever need, but after moving through just a few rooms, he started to have his doubts.

The place looked more like a laboratory than a weapons cache.

Every door he passed led to an office.

Nothing but computers and books.

"Where are the personnel carriers?" Jacob finally said.

"There's a bay at the other end of the building," Stu said. "There should be four or five of them there. We can take our pick."

"Should be?"

"Yeah."

"Fuck," Jacob muttered. If there was one thing he'd learned to hate, it was the phrase "should be."

Stu led them straight to the observation deck overlooking the vehicle bay.

Which was completely empty.

"Uh, Stu . . . ?"

"I don't understand," Stu said. "They should be here. This is where we keep them. I don't get it."

"That's because you build aerofluyts," Brooks said. "You don't fly them. Look out that window. Can you see them?"

Stu went to the windows on the far wall. North El Paso was dark, lit only by starlight. But there was enough ambient light from the giant hangars off to the west to illuminate the three aerofluyts out on the flight line.

"Yes," Stu said.

"Which ones are they?"

"There's three," Stu said. "The one closest to us is the *Einstein*. It's being scrapped right now. Next to that is the *Maxwell*. It's still eighteen months from completion. The far one is the *Archimedes*. That's the one that's getting ready for its maiden voyage."

"Then that's where you'll find the armored personnel carriers. Last on, last off, that's the procedure."

Jacob took a step forward. "You knew that, and you let us come here anyway?"

"Yes."

"Why?"

"Why do you need to know?"

"Because I have every intention of getting out of this alive. And if some knuckleheaded motherfucker is trying to keep me from doing that, I need to know who he is. Now, what's your malfunction, asshole? Why didn't you say anything?"

Brooks sighed, then reached into one of the folds of his body armor and came up with a small black rectangular device about the size of a matchbook. "I called for extraction before we left the machine shop. This area is too hot right now for that, but I have a crew standing by to get us out of here. They should be here in sixteen hours."

"Are these the same crew that tried to kill us earlier?" Jacob said.

Brooks just stared at him.

"Why so long?" Jacob said. "It only took us forty-five minutes on a freighter to get here."

"Yes, before the lockdown went critical. El Paso is currently dead center for the Great Texas Herd. We have the largest concentration of zombies in the entire world surrounding us as we speak. Nothing's going to happen until the herd passes us by."

"Great. So we're fucked."

"No, we're in one of the most secure facilities in El Paso. We have help on the way, and the herd has absolutely no idea that we're in here. As long as we keep our heads down and the noise low, we have no reason to worry. We simply wait for my crews to extract us."

"And haul us before another sham of a hearing for crimes we didn't commit?" Jacob asked.

"Tell me your plan," Brooks said. "I'd love to hear it."

Chapter 18

They weren't going anywhere anytime soon.

As much as Jacob hated to admit it, he knew it was true. There were no tunnels leading to the aerofluyt yards. No safe passage. That left surface-level travel, which wasn't an option. It galled Jacob, but Brooks was right. They were dead in the middle of the greatest concentration of zombies on the entire planet. Going outside, even though the zombies didn't know they were there, would be suicide.

Here in the arsenal, they were safe. At least for the time being. The zombies had no way of knowing they were in here, and as long as they didn't make a whole bunch of noise or flick the lights on and off, that wouldn't change.

Zombies were creatures of opportunity. They attacked only when prey made itself available. If they didn't know it was there, they didn't go out of their way to investigate. That was why the hurricane fences that were so prevalent in El Paso were so effective. Without a reason, zombies didn't press defenses. The trick was to stay out of sight.

And they were out of sight.

"I think you guys should get some sleep," Jacob said to Kelly.

"What? Are you kidding? Now?"

"Yeah." He motioned toward a lab behind her. "They've got cots back there."

"Jacob, those are autopsy tables."

"Oh," he said. "Well, they're better than sleeping on the floor, right?"

She curled her lips in disgust. "Uh, no, not really."

"Okay, well, it's the best I got. Look," he said, "I need you to help me with this. I don't trust Brooks as far as I can throw him, but his extraction team is the best bet we've got right now."

"What about the personnel transports? I thought that was the whole reason we came here."

"It was. But can we really make it all the way to the *Archimedes*? Did you see how far away it was? That's like two kilometers, easy. And that across open country. The herd would swarm us in no time."

"Jacob, we can't trust him."

"I know that. The man's a snake. He's a liar and a hypocrite. But for right now, his extraction team is the only way I see us getting out of here alive."

Kelly didn't look at all convinced. "So, what's your plan?"

"For right now? I watch Brooks while you guys get some sleep."

"You need it more than we do. My God, Jacob, you've nearly passed out twice in the last two hours. You're exhausted."

"And hungry, too. But right now, I'm the only one

that Brooks fears enough to not take a gun from. I can hold him at bay. Take the six hours. Get some sleep. See if you can get Chelsea and Miriam to join you. Brooks is probably as tired as we are. He can't watch us forever. By the time he falls asleep, I'll be ready to hand the watch over to you. We'll be rested; he won't be."

Kelly took a long time to think about it, but she finally nodded. "Okay," she said. "Alright, that makes sense. You'll wake me up in six hours?"

Jacob looked over at a digital clock on the wall.

It read 3:43 a.m.

Jacob did the math in his head and calculated the time to sunrise. Things would change after sunrise. They'd be able to see the field outside their windows. They'd be able to see how bad things really were.

But Jacob found it hard to concentrate on that. Looking at Kelly's face, he remembered why he'd found her so beautiful all those years ago. There had come a dawn, in their teens, when he'd woken on a bed of cool grass on the banks of the Mississippi with Kelly's bare breast cupped in his hand. Things had been so easy in those days, so centered around the natural gravity of two teenagers in love.

He laughed to himself. God, they'd fucked like rabbits that summer.

But now, even something as simple as calculating the time to wake up seemed complicated by the jealousy and the anger and the rest of the emotional baggage that had built up since then.

"At nine forty-three," he said. "That'll give me time to watch the sunrise before I go to sleep."

"And what will you be thinking?" she said.

"What?"

"During sunrise," she said. "What will you be thinking?"

He knew the answer without hesitation. He'd be thinking of that morning, a June morning on the banks of the Mississippi, after their first time together.

The first time for both of them.

It was the first time in twenty years that she'd acknowledged the memory, that she'd called him out on it.

"I'll be thinking of the river," he said.

She smiled, but said nothing.

She went over to Chelsea and Miriam and the three women talked for a few moments, then went off to sleep on the autopsy tables.

Brooks had been half-listening to the conversation, and he looked disgusted. With a shake of his head and an angry huff, he walked to the far side of the lab, took a small tablet from one of the pockets of his body armor, and sat down to read.

Jacob watched him go, careful to keep an eye on him.

He'd met men he disliked before, but he couldn't remember ever hating a man the way he hated Brooks. He was ashamed to say it, but he kind of wished he'd smashed the man's head back when he disarmed him. It had certainly taken effort to hold back.

He turned to Stu and Juliette. "You two could get some sleep, too, if you wanted."

The couple glanced at each other, then Stu shook his. He had a conspiratorial look on his face that made Jacob lower his voice to a whisper. "What's going on?"

Stu looked over at Brooks, then nodded toward a corner of the lab and indicated for Jacob to follow.

"We've been talking about what you said, about the people getting gassed down in the concourse."

"Yeah?"

"You really did see bullet wounds on those corpses down there? You're sure about that?"

A sudden memory of Jerry Greider's execution played in his mind, how he'd been trembling so badly he flubbed the kill shot and put a black, muddy hole where the man's eye had been. He remembered it all, right down to the burn ring that had replaced the man's eyebrow.

Right down to the gentle sobbing of the man's widow.

"I'm sure," he said.

Stu glanced over at Brooks and sighed, like he was committing himself to treason.

He let out a deep breath.

"Alright," he said. "We talked this over, and we don't think there's any way that this will end well if we let Brooks's people extract us. Brooks is a powerful man, and he's built a fortune off of morphic field technology. I don't . . . entirely buy the Triune stuff that Dr. Sayer's brother preached, but—"

"Don't say 'preached,'" Juliette said. "It's dismissive."

Stu took another deep breath. Evidently, for the first time, his inner *you're being a jackass* filter was working.

He started again. "I think there are problems with the Triune Theory, but I looked at a few pages of Dr. Walker's notebooks, and there is some compelling evidence there."

"I knew it!" Juliette said.

"Stop . . ." Stu bit his lip. "At least," he said, starting yet again, "there are some things there that I can't refute without proper testing. That's not possible under the present circumstances, though, and I think that his theories deserve serious consideration. That won't happen if his theories are squashed by the Council."

"Okay," Jacob said. He glanced back over his shoulder at Brooks. The man was lost in whatever he was reading. "So, what does that mean?"

"We have to find another way out of here. If we leave with his extraction team, we can pretty much count on any evidence supporting Dr. Walker's theories being lost." Stu shook his head angrily. "The man should have put his findings on the servers. We wouldn't even be having this conversation."

"That's not the way he worked," Juliette said. "Miriam told us that a dozen times."

"I know," he said. "It's just frustrating."

"Okay," Jacob said. These two frustrated the hell out of him with their back-and-forth, but he liked the direction they were headed. "So, do you have a plan?"

"Yes," Stu said. "We want to go get one of the personnel transports from the *Einstein*. They're still aboard. They're awaiting refit and retooling, but they can at least get us over to the *Archimedes*. From there, we can take one of the new ones. It could get us through anything."

"And how are you going to do that?"

"What?"

"Get over to the *Einstein*. You've seen what it looks like out there. There are zombies everywhere."

Stu nodded like he'd already considered that. "They'll be clustered around the machine shop."

"All hundred million of them?"

"No, of course not. But the ones we saw were only the first wave. They saw us around the machine shop, and that's where they'll focus."

"You're betting your lives on that?" Jacob said. "I thought you people were supposed to be smart and shit."

Stu sighed again. "The odds are in our favor if we leave right now," he said. "We have the cover of night, and we have the fact that they don't know we're here. If Juliette and I move quickly, and quietly, we can reach the *Einstein* without attracting any attention."

"Uh," Jacob said. "I don't know. That sounds like an awful lot of variables. The *Einstein* is what, half a kilometer away? That's a long way to go if you're dodging a hundred million zombies."

"It won't be that many," Stu said.

"You hope, anyway."

"Yes, of course."

Jacob shook his head. "I think it's crazy."

"But is it better than the alternative? After what we've seen, do you really think you'll get a fair trial? Do you really think Dr. Walker's evidence will reach the scientific community? I have to tell you, if what you say is true, all of us are probably on some hit list somewhere."

"He's right," Juliette said. "We've all heard at least some of the evidence. I'm sure they'd rather see us dead than hear us asking questions at the conferences."

They had a point, Jacob admitted to himself. Their plan sounded like suicide to him, but it was better than anything he'd been able to come up with. If they succeeded, they'd be able to get out of here on their own. They'd be able to get home. And Chelsea would be able to argue her father's case.

"Okay," he said. "If you want to . . ."

"We do," Juliette said. "Right, baby?"

Stu took her hand. "That's right."

"What do you need?"

"Nothing," Stu said. "We'll leave right now."

Jacob really had nothing to say. He hated himself for being such a self-centered dick about it, but if they died, he was right back where he started. And if they succeeded, well, if they succeeded, he and Kelly could be in a position to put Temple and all its craziness in the past. The chance alone made it worth it. "Alright." He nodded at Juliette. He shook Stu's hand. "Alright."

"Alright," Stu said.

Without another word the couple headed back down the corridor through which they'd come. Brooks sat up when the couple left and tried to follow them with his gaze down the darkened hallway.

"Where are they going?" Brooks asked.

"Does it matter?" Jacob said.

Stu wasn't the only one, Jacob saw, who had his filter on. Apparently, Brooks had had enough of arguing. With a shake of his head, he went back to reading.

Good, Jacob thought. Getting better.

He found a desk at the end of the room and sat down. To his right, he had a view out the window. He couldn't see much. Just the bulky silhouette of a hangar, and beyond that, the three long shades of the aerofluyts. Three stories below him, the streets were probably filled with the undead. By now, they should be teeming through every building, every alleyway, searching to alleviate a hunger that could never be assuaged.

Jacob turned away from the window.

He couldn't see the dead from here, and frankly, at the moment, he just didn't care. There was already so much to worry about.

Or, rather, so much to remember.

It was hard to believe that he'd set out less than two months before with eleven other explorers to see what lay beyond the walls of his home in Arbella. He hadn't thought of the expedition much since waking up in the hospital. He'd been more interested in Megan, the hot nurse.

But here in the depths of this building, surrounded by a legion of the undead, with no company but a man he didn't trust and the darkness to hold his hand, his mind turned to the friends he'd lost.

To the friends, he couldn't help but think, that he'd led to the slaughter.

And they'd started out with such high ideals. Back home, they didn't have to deal with issues like whether or not the morphic field generators were killing their brains. Back home, their biggest concern had been the expansionist question. To those who thought long and hard on such issues, it was endlessly complex, but it really boiled down to one simple truth. Arbella had survived the zombie apocalypse. They'd done well for themselves. They'd turned a deserted town into a new home, and there, they'd not only survived, but thrived. They'd walled up the town and turned every available resource toward the maintenance and the prosperity of their community.

Jacob was very proud of that.

He'd lived nearly his entire life in Arbella, and he'd, as much as anyone, been responsible for making his community's success a fact of life.

Only now, thirty years after zombies filled the land, Arbella had become so successful that their walls couldn't contain them anymore. Jacob and quite a few of his friends, nearly all of them of the younger generation, believed that the answer to the problem was expansion. They were living in a Malthusian pressure cooker. It hadn't exploded yet, but it was only a matter of time. The First Generation, of which his mother was a proud member, had already admitted the necessity of expansion. That much was an accepted fact. But the fear was still there. The elders, the First Generation, thought they had it good behind Arbella's walls. They knew, in their hearts, that the walls needed to be pushed farther out into the Zone, that more land needed to be taken under Arbella's wings, but they weren't quite ready to commit.

They invariably came back with some version of the same tired old truism. *Our strategy saved our lives, and it has worked brilliantly since then. Just look at our success. The world out there wants to kill us. No good can come from pushing into that world. You are safe here. You have a good and a happy home here. Outside those walls, you'll find only death.*

Jacob and his friends had argued until they were blue in the face, but the First Generation refused to budge.

At least, right up to the moment that they agreed to let Jacob lead a team of explorers out into the Zone.

"Go see what's out there," Arbella's leaders had told him. "Come back and tell us. Then we'll make a decision."

Things had seemed so bright and shiny at that moment.

They were considerably less so now.

Now, after losing eleven of Arbella's best and brightest to Slavers and zombies, to murderers and thieves, and, in the case of Nick Carroll, his best friend, to Arbella's own Code of justice, he wondered at the price.

And to end up here. In a nation of hypocrites who hated everything he'd been taught to believe.

Worse still was the war he fought with his conscience. It was one thing to believe in the expansionist philosophy, to preach it in the streets and in the Council chambers, but it was quite another thing to lead ten of your closest friends to the slaughter in order to prove it.

He was going to have a hard time living with that.

His thoughts ran that way for hours, beating himself up one moment, thinking of all the ways he was right the next, but it was all just the same pony running around the same track. He got nowhere, and he proved nothing.

But then, shortly before the sun came up, his thoughts were broken by a scream.

He sat up, and realized with a sense of admonishment that he'd let himself drift.

He stared across the lab and saw Brooks sitting in the same place he'd been before, his back against the wall, the tablet resting on his knees. Only now the man was sitting up, his attention focused on the door to the autopsy room behind Jacob.

"What was that?" Brooks said.

"Stay there," Jacob said.

He rose from his chair and kicked it out of the way, the pistol already in his hand. Inside the lab, Chelsea and Kelly were screaming. Jacob tried the door, but it was locked. He hit it with his fists, kicked it.

"Open the door!" he yelled.

One of the women screamed again. Jacob rammed the door with his shoulder, but it wouldn't budge.

"What's going on?" Brooks said from behind him.

"How the fuck should I know?" Jacob said.

He rammed the door again, without success. "Kelly," he said, pounding on the door, "it's locked. What's going on?"

Something inside the lab crashed. He heard metal clattering onto the floor and glass shattering.

"Kelly!"

There was a second crash, more broken glass, and then everything went quiet for a moment.

Jacob hit the door again. "Kelly, open this thing up! It's locked."

The lock clicked. Jacob pushed the door open and ran inside. The lab was a mess. There was broken glass and cups and plastic tubs all over the floor. Chelsea was in a corner of the room, huddled into a ball on the floor, shaking uncontrollably, her face a mask of disbelief and shock, streaked with tears. Kelly was standing in the middle of the room, breathing hard, terrified.

Jacob heard glass snapping over to his right. Miriam was bent over, her head stuck in a glass case. She was thrashing, trying to pull herself loose, spraying blood all over the place, but it was no good. A large piece of glass had pierced her throat, and it held her pinned like a bug in a display case.

"Miriam, no!" Brooks pushed his way around Jacob and ran for the woman's side. He stared at her in horror, his mouth hanging open. "Oh no, Miriam. Oh no!"

Miriam's corpse continued to thrash. She grunted and snarled, even as her throat filled with blood.

Brooks backed away, his hand over his mouth. "Oh, baby, no."

Suddenly Miriam turned her head toward Brooks.

The movement was enough to shift her weight on the glass shard that held her pinned and it snapped. She pulled herself from the cabinet and took a few halting steps toward Brooks.

"Oh, baby," Brooks said, shaking his head as he backed away. "Baby, no."

Miriam opened her mouth and a small river of blood seeped out. Her clothes were soaked through with her blood, the white of the blouse she wore only visible on the sleeves. She looked around her, then stretched her hands toward Brooks and went after him.

Jacob reacted the only way he could. He shoved her down so that she was bent over one of the autopsy tables, put the muzzle of his pistol on the back of her head, and fired.

From the corner, Chelsea let out a horrible scream.

Brooks looked very close to throwing up, and when Miriam's body slid off the table and collapsed on the floor, he did.

A stunned silence settled over the group.

Kelly moved to Jacob's side.

"What happened?" he finally asked.

"I don't know," Kelly said. "We were asleep. I woke up to Chelsea screaming. Miriam was on top of her, trying to claw through her blankets."

"She'd already turned?"

Kelly nodded.

Jacob tried to process what he was seeing. How could the woman have died? Was she injured in the crash? He hadn't thought so, and thinking back over their run through the city, and again through the tunnels, he hadn't seen any signs that she was hurt.

"Did she say anything? Complain of any pain?"

Kelly shook her head.

Jacob looked over at Chelsea, but the girl looked unreachable. The grief and shock and pain on her face were frightening to behold.

On the opposite side of the room, Brooks was nearly doubled over, one hand on his knee, the other wiping away the vomit from his lips. Jacob wasn't quite sure what to make of him anymore.

Still lost for answers, Jacob looked back down at the corpse of Dr. Miriam Sayer. From the mouth up, there was nothing left of her head.

But then Jacob noticed something.

He knelt down next to the corpse and cupped her chin in his hand.

"Don't you touch her!" Chelsea screamed.

"I'm sorry, Chelsea, I have to."

He turned what was left of her head to one side, then pushed it back the other way. Finally, he tilted the chin up.

"What are you doing?" Brooks said.

Jacob stood up. "Look at that."

Brooks looked like that was the last thing he wanted to do, but he stepped forward and squinted at Miriam Sayer's neck. "What in the world is that? Is that a bruise?"

"Yep," Jacob said. He glanced again at the bruise. The basic pattern was familiar. He'd seen them before in family violence cases back in Arbella, when a drunk husband would choke his wife. He recognized the fingertip marks on the left side of Miriam's throat, meaning whoever had done it was probably right-handed, though the index and middle finger marks showed odd patterns on them, like the murderer had been holding something in his hands when he choked her.

"I don't understand," Chelsea said. "What bruise?"

"On her neck," Jacob said. "Chelsea, somebody killed her."

CHAPTER 19

Chelsea stood and crossed the room to her aunt's corpse on wobbly legs. She stopped a few feet from the body and looked down like a woman who was standing on the edge of a very high cliff.

Then her face seemed to harden.

She looked at Brooks, and the eyes that had been blurry and red with tears now glowed with hatred. "You did this," she said. "You did this!"

"No," Brooks said.

But it was too late. Chelsea ran at him, slashing at his face with her fingernails, kicking him with everything she had. "Liar!" she screamed. "You fucking liar!"

Brooks had been taken off guard, or perhaps he was still in shock from Miriam's death. He tried to fight the girl off, but she raged like a wildcat on his face.

Finally, Jacob intervened. He grabbed Chelsea by the arm, but she slipped out of his hands. He went at her again, this time hooking his arms under her arms and clasping his hands together behind her neck. He pulled it back and fell into one of the autopsy tables. It served as a support for him, and he held her there, waiting for some of the fight to ebb out of her.

When at last she stopped screaming he tried talking to her. "Chelsea, just stop. Stop, okay? Let me figure this out."

"He murdered her," Chelsea said. "I don't understand it. I was sleeping right next to her."

"I'm gonna let you go," he said. "But I need you to let me figure this out. Attacking him isn't going to solve anything."

The girl stopped struggling.

"We good?"

"Yes," she said.

Slowly, he let her go.

Brooks stood on his side of the room, watching the girl warily while he rubbed his scratched-up wrists and cheeks. He was bleeding in several places, including a nasty cut near his left eye.

Jacob walked over to the man. "Show me your hands."

"Another baseless accusation, Jacob?"

"Just show me your damn hands."

"I knew her better than any of you," he said. He nodded at Chelsea. "Even you. I didn't kill her. I would never harm her."

"Show me your hands," Jacob said. "Now."

Brooks turned a *fuck you* stare at him, but held out his hands. "Happy now?"

"Turn them over, asshole. I want to see your fingertips."

Brooks flipped his hands over. "Are we done now?" he asked.

"Yeah, we're done."

Jacob turned away. He looked around the room. Whoever had killed Miriam had locked the door leading to where Jacob and Brooks had been, which meant that he must have left through one of the two back doors. One of the doors had a stack of boxes in front of it, so it probably wasn't that one. He went to the third door and looked at the knob. No fingerprints that he could see, just smudges. That wouldn't be any help.

"Wait a minute," Chelsea said. "What about him?"

Jacob turned back to her and sighed. "He didn't do it."

"Oh good, at last," Brooks said. "The cop gets one right."

"Yes, he did!" Chelsea shouted.

"No, he didn't. I didn't think he did. I was out there with him the whole time you were in here. I would have noticed if he'd slipped off. He didn't."

"Then why go through the charade of looking at my hands?" Brooks said. "Was that just the cop pushing his weight around?"

"No, that was me not trusting you. I think you're a lying sack of shit, Lester Brooks, and I think you're guilty as sin for sending those men after us." He gestured at Miriam's corpse. "But this you didn't do."

He pulled his pistol again and walked toward the door the killer had gone out.

"Where are you going?" Kelly said.

"Whoever did this went this way. I'm gonna see what I can find."

With that he stepped through the door and into a large, tiled hallway. To his left was a workstation, a large, neat desk like the kind he'd seen in hospitals while in the Zone with the salvage teams years ago. To his right, the hallway branched off in several directions.

The guy could have gone down any one of the halls, but something in Jacob's gut told him to check the large room at the end of the hall.

He made it about halfway down the hall before he stopped.

The hairs at the back of his neck were tingling.

He stood still and listened.

A moment later, he heard feet scraping along the tiled floor. He raised his weapon and walked slowly forward. As he neared the mouth of the hallway, he saw a large, round room. He was on the second story. A wide balcony wrapped all the way around the round room, looking down on a common area below. Jacob went to the right side of the hallway, put his back against the wall, and slowly advanced toward the end of the hallway, trying to maximize what he could see of the balcony.

Sure enough, two gray-looking corpses were trudging along near the railing, headed his way. Behind them, six more were climbing the stairs.

Damn it, he thought. That could only mean one thing. Whoever had killed Miriam had also opened the barricades that kept their shelter safe.

Well, it wasn't safe anymore.

He ran back down the hallway as quietly as he could. Once back inside the lab with the others, he brought them up to speed. "We need to get out of here," he said.

"And go where, exactly?" Brooks said.

"I don't know. Anywhere but here. They're about to come through that door."

"We can't leave this building," Brooks said.

Jacob raised an eyebrow at him. "Did you not hear what I just said? The defenses have been compromised. You remember the one hundred million zombies all around us? Well, they're about to find their way in here."

"The extraction team is meeting us here. If we're not here, they won't stay. We'll die here."

"We'll die if we stay here."

"Not if we go to the roof."

Jacob thought about that for a moment. "No," he said. "That won't work, either. You said the extraction team was forty-eight hours away at the earliest, right?"

Brooks nodded.

"That's two days on the roof in the El Paso summer heat with no water and no food. And if the exposure doesn't kill us, the zombies surely will when they bust through the roof access door. No thanks. The roof is a death trap."

"I'm not going out there."

"Fine," Jacob said. "I've told you already. You're not a hostage. If you want to go off on your own, you're welcome to it."

"That won't work, either, and you know it. We have to stay together."

"Suit yourself." He pointed to Chelsea. "Would you please lock that door? That'll buy us some time. I think we need to go back that way," he said to Kelly, indicating the door Miriam's killer had locked on them.

"Why that way?"

"There's a passageway out there that should lead to a side door. The zombies don't know we're in here, so we might have a chance of slipping away unseen. And besides, that'll put us on the west side of the building. We'll be able to run to the buildings south of here or head toward the aerofluyts, depending on which way looks easiest."

Chelsea had gone to the door while Jacob was lay-ing out their plan. Out of the corner of his eye, he saw her start to close the door, when a zombie hit it from the other side. The door flew back in the girl's face, and she let out a startled scream. An arm came through the door as the zombie uttered its feeding moan.

Jacob darted forward and pulled Chelsea out of the way. "Get back!" he said.

The zombie stumbled through the door. It was a herd zombie, gray from its desiccated and cadaverous face down to its feet, where the skin had all but worn away, leaving nothing but bone that was naked and cracked. Jacob could hardly tell if the thing had once been a man or a woman. Decay had taken it long beyond that point.

But as it stumbled into the room, it carried with it an unmistakable stench of decay. The smell was so overpowering it seemed to fill the room, and it pushed Jacob away like a living thing, with a power all its own. He fought back the urge to wretch. Instead he backed up, pushed Chelsea out of the way, and put a compressed-air round in the center of the thing's head.

There were two more, just as rotted away, just as sexless, as the first. He dropped them both, then stepped into the hallway.

A woman in the remnants of a dress moaned and raised her hands to clutch at him, even though she was a good twenty feet away.

Jacob closed the distance quickly and put her down.

Beyond her, the large open room at the end of the hallway teemed with movement. The zombies had found their way inside.

He glanced down at the weapon in his hands and was surprised to see he had only four rounds left.

"Damn it," he muttered.

Though he was on fire inside, he forced himself to hold it together. He wanted to sprint for the door, but he knew the others would key off the way he behaved, so he forced himself to walk back to the room. Chelsea had come to the door to see what was going on. He put a hand on her shoulder and said, "Back inside, okay?"

He closed and locked the door.

"We need to get moving," he said. He looked over at Brooks. "How many magazines do you have left?"

"Six, I think."

"Okay, let me have them. I'm down to four rounds."

Brooks hesitated.

It was long enough to get Jacob's attention.

"Hand 'em over," Jacob said.

"No, you give me the gun."

"Brooks, I'm not playing with you."

"Nor I with you. The gun is no good without the ammunition, so turn it over."

"I will not negotiate when it comes to my survival," Jacob said. "Give me the fucking ammunition right now."

"Or you'll—"

Jacob threw a roundhouse to the man's chin before he could finish his sentence. Brooks didn't go down, but he fell back in sudden terror. "What's wrong with you?" Brooks said. "Is this how cops force other people to do what they want?"

"No," Jacob said. "This is how men survive."

He threw another roundhouse at Brooks, catching him under the chin. But this time he didn't stop. He moved in close and threw two sharp jabs with his right, causing Brooks to fall over onto his back. Jacob jumped onto the man's chest and started hammering blows to the man's face. As hard as he could. As fast as he could.

Brooks grabbed Jacob's arm, but it was an impotent gesture, and when Jacob felt the man's grip go slack, he leaned back, grabbed hold of Brooks's gray hair, and tilted his head back.

Brooks stared up at him through eyes filled with blood. His lips looked like smashed fruit. He was covered in blood.

"I told you not to fuck with my survival," Jacob said.

Then he slammed his elbow down on the bridge of Brooks's nose. The bones broke with a horrible *crack*, and Brooks went limp. Jacob fished through the man's pocket and came away with six magazines. About three hundred and eighty rounds to work with. Not nearly enough, but he'd make it work. He always did.

"Alright, come on," he said, gently, but firmly, slapping Brooks's face. "Come on, get up."

Brooks came to, blinking his eyes.

When he realized it was Jacob still standing over him, he recoiled.

"Don't worry," Jacob said. "I got what I needed. Now get up, we need to get out of here."

CHAPTER 20

As a teenager, Jacob had been picked for the salvage teams. Many his age had applied, though few got in. Those who made it onto the teams were said to be the best, which he'd found funny, because the selection process hadn't been all that hard. The physical fitness tests were supposed to be rigorous, but Jacob could run all day long, and sit-ups and push-ups were a piece of cake. The intelligence tests, which Jacob had gone into thinking there was no way in hell he'd even come close to passing, at least not without Kelly's answer sheet to cheat off of, had been surprisingly easy.

They wanted people who could fix things.

People who could take one thing that was broken, and make something new of it.

He'd breezed right through it.

It was considered quite an honor to be picked for the teams. Nobody else got to go outside the walls. Nobody else learned about the technology of the Old World like those picked for the teams. It had made him a star among his friends.

Not even Nick, Nick the badass who had once whipped his ass in a fight, had made the final list.

And meanwhile, his knowledge of zombie behavior grew by leaps and bounds.

Zombie behavior, his instructors had said, was consistent and predictable. They could be fast or slow, strong or barely able to stay upright, ravenous and relentless or so weak they could only moan from the shadows of some crumbling doorway.

It didn't matter.

Their behavior was always the same, as constant as a running river.

A zombie will attack if prey is present. A zombie will not ever fail to attack. A zombie will attack, regardless of the odds against it, and it will continue to attack until it is physically unable to move.

A zombie will not stop, and it will not show mercy.

A zombie won't recognize you, because the person who used to live in that shell doesn't live there anymore.

They have no strategy, no purpose, no ultimate goal. They exist only to feed. And you are the food. They are a force of nature not made by nature, and that internal conflict is the only thing that drives them. They don't sleep. They don't rest. They don't ever stop. They will explore every nook, every cranny, to feed their need. If you hide, they will eventually find you, because they search all day, every day, without stop.

They don't rely on your stupidity, but on your single careless moment.

The zombie lives its undead life for the moment you

get too tired, for the moment you let your guard down, for the moment you need to sleep.

The odds sounded steep indeed, but his instructors had taught him a few things, and as he looked out the window over the streets of El Paso and the wretched, undead things that massed there, he felt like he could do this.

Perhaps there were a hundred million zombies out there, but at this spot, he saw fewer than a hundred, and those groping impotently as they tried to rejoin the main body of the herd.

That was another element of zombie behavior. They sought, constantly sought, the company of other zombies. A zombie by itself usually didn't make it long. Something happened, some accident, some random thing that inevitably caused their second death.

But zombies in a herd, they could stay intact for as long as the CDHLs saturated their cell structure and prevented decay.

Eight to ten years in some cases.

The zombie he'd faced upstairs in the lab, the one he couldn't even decide if it had once been male or female, was a good example. It might have been six to eight years old, maybe even older.

And the zombies in the streets outside were no exception. They looked uniformly gray and desiccated, rotten to the point they could barely stand up, much less give chase. Even at a glance, he could see a course through their numbers. He hadn't thought of Stu and Juliette since they'd left earlier that morning, because, truthfully, he hadn't given them much of a chance, but looking at the street now, he wondered if maybe they could have made it after all.

"Jacob?"

It was Kelly.

And he recognized that worried tone.

Smart as she was, she'd no doubt overthought every possible angle of their escape. That was the difference between them. She reasoned. She considered. She thought of every option, and wondered over each detail like a mother worrying over a child. He, on the other hand, saw only possibilities, and made the decision to take the leap.

He looked at the group staggered behind him. Kelly, right at his shoulder, right where he knew she'd be. Chelsea, her face still stained with emotion, right behind her. Kelly he wasn't worried about, but Chelsea was something else. Since seeing her aunt zombified and then blasted into muck on the wall, she'd retreated inward. Jacob couldn't really blame her, of course. She'd already lost her parents, and her older brother, and her lover, and now her aunt. She'd had so much taken from her, and now she was all alone in a world that wanted her run up on charges while running her father's reputation through the mud. And, on top of that, she was only seventeen. That was a lot of load to carry for such young shoulders.

But it couldn't really be helped, either. They were all up to their chins in troubles. He just hoped that the girl would be able to hold it all together long enough for them to get out of El Paso. From there, well, from there they'd figure it out. Maybe they could bring her back to Arbella. Everybody there was an orphan, of one form or another.

Farther on behind Chelsea, lurking in the shadows, was a wounded and wary Lester Brooks. Why the man had decided to come with them Jacob didn't know, and frankly he didn't care. Few things mattered to Jacob more than personal integrity, and from where he stood, Brooks was utterly lacking on that front.

"Okay," he said. "There's a building over by the main hangars, due north of here. Can you see it? It's right through there."

Kelly followed the line of his finger toward a squat cube of a building, five stories high.

"That one there?"

"Yes."

"That's our target. If we need to, we'll veer off to one of the buildings over in that direction, but that building is where I want us to end up."

"Why?"

"Look at it. See the fire escape? It's one of the only ones around that still has that. That means it's an older building. It'll have the same defenses as the rest of these buildings, I'm guessing, but that fire escape gives us a way to get in without compromising those ground defenses."

Kelly nodded, but was clearly out of her element. "Okay, I trust you," she said.

"Alright."

Jacob went down the stairs and pushed the door open. He counted sixteen zombies within what he considered the danger zone, close enough that they could attack, if they were strong enough.

None did, though. The few that spotted them twisted their broken bodies toward the group, and a few even raised their hands to clutch at Jacob and the others, but most were so weak they couldn't even utter the feeding moan that attracted the rest of the herd.

As they rounded a corner, a zombie fell out of a doorway and landed with its arms on Chelsea's shoulders. She screamed, twisted away from the thing, and broke into a run.

"Chelsea, no!" Jacob said.

He put the zombie down with a shot to the back of its head and ran the young girl down. When he caught her, he was forced to hold her tightly. She thrashed and whined as she tried to break his grip.

"Don't run," he whispered. "Not yet. That's the secret. Go too fast and they'll zero in on you. We walk until we have to run."

"Let go of me. I can't take it anymore. That moaning. Oh God, make them stop."

She felt like she was about to run again.

"I know it's scary," he said. "Please. Just don't run. Fight the fear."

She was tense, her body like a spring under pressure, but at last she nodded.

"You can do this," he said. "Just don't run. At least not until I say so."

"Okay."

"Good girl."

He looked back at Kelly and Brooks and nodded. Kelly nodded back. Brooks didn't nod. He looked like he was still waiting to figure out another way to handle the situation at hand. Jacob would have to watch him.

Dawn was just beginning to color the eastern sky, and it shed an orange glow over the streets of the city. From the window, Jacob had seen a handful of decrepit zombies slogging their way toward the rest of the herd, but now that dawn had broken, he saw hundreds more in the shadows. He'd seen something like it happen once, years ago, while he and Kelly were sleeping on the banks of the Mississippi. He'd woken just before first light. A short field of grass had separated them from the riverbank. In the gray light that seeped into the world just before dawn, that field of grass had looked completely empty. But as the sun rose, he watched the field fill with light, and he was surprised to see a herd of deer there. They'd been there all along, just unseen. It was scary that the same thing could happen with zombies. And scarier still that he hadn't realized it before now.

Jacob took a look around, wondering which way to lead his little party.

"I want to get out of here right now," Chelsea said.

"She's right, Jacob," Kelly said. "I think we're starting to attract some attention."

"Yeah, I agree." He pointed to a small two-story office building. "There aren't as many coming around the left side of that building. Let's skirt it on that side."

He started them forward. A few of the zombies closest to them lumbered their way, and Jacob got ready to fire when they came in range. But just as they were about to reach the building, several of the zombies twisted around at a change in the herd's moaning and moved in a different direction.

"Where are they going?" Kelly said.

"I don't know. Let's just keep going."

"No, Jacob, wait! Look there!"

Jacob caught movement between the buildings. A figure was crossing their line of travel at a measured trot, gunning down the zombies that got too close to him. Between the low light and his failing eyes, Jacob wasn't sure who it was, but it looked like Jordan Anson.

Anson saw them a moment later. He raised his weapon instinctively, then lowered it, clearly surprised to see other living people out here.

He motioned for them to meet him on the far side of the building.

When they finally caught up with him, Jacob was taken aback. Anson looked like he'd been through hell. His chest and arms were spattered with gore and parts of his armor were torn. Several metal panels hung from frayed Kevlar. His hair was wet with sweat, his face streaked with dirt and more sweat. He'd gotten his lip busted somewhere along the way. But even through the grime, Jacob could still read the mistrust on the man's face. He held his weapon high, if not exactly pointing it at Jacob and the group.

Brooks had been bringing up the rear. He was winded, and the air going through his busted nose made a wheezing noise as he breathed. Jordan immediately pulled him aside, gave him a once-over, and then turned on Jacob.

This time there was no doubt as to where he was pointing his weapon.

"What did you do to him?"

"We had a disagreement over who should hold the ammunition."

"So you assaulted him?" Jordan said. "This man is a distinguished member of the High Council."

"Well, I didn't vote for him."

Anson shook his head in disbelief. When he spoke he was so mad he could barely spit the words out. "You . . . you . . . who the hell do you think you are?"

"Enough," Brooks said. "There's no time for this. We need to get to shelter."

"That's a good idea, Junior," Jacob said. "And while you're at it, you should check your six."

"What?"

"Behind you."

Anson twisted around. A zombie was just a few meters behind him, and coming closer, its hands clutching for him. He raised his gun and dropped it with a clean hit right between the eyes. Two more of the desiccated things were working their way into the street, and Anson dropped them both moments later.

Three rounds, three head shots. The man was a squirrely little dickhead, but he was a good shot. Jacob filed that away as something to keep in mind later.

"Jacob," Chelsea said, "can we please leave here?"

All the talking and running had really drawn a crowd. They had zombies coming out of the woodwork now, and all of them had zeroed in on Jacob and the others. Most were slow moving, but he spotted a few making their way toward them with a little more haste.

"Yep," he said. "Doing that now. Let's get moving."

The building with the fire escape was still a good four hundred meters away, and most of that across open ground. They were seeing denser concentrations of zombies, too. To Jacob it looked like the main body of the herd had entered the area, for they were seeing stronger and faster zombies, less decayed. He could tell the men from the women now.

With the faster zombies starting to appear, Jacob had to move around a lot more. He found himself having to sprint from to the head of the group to the rear and back again, over and over, in order to intercept some fast mover that had stepped out of the crowd. He was getting tired fast, and his ribs were starting to burn again.

Brooks and Anson had fallen back a bit. Anson was helping the much older Brooks along, and letting Jacob do most of the running around and shooting.

Jacob couldn't help but wonder if that was deliberate.

He didn't trust Anson any more than he trusted Brooks, Anson maybe even less so, but he was running out of juice and he needed the help.

He ran toward Kelly, set up in a shooter's stance, and dropped yet another fast mover that had gotten too close. Then he grabbed Kelly's arm and guided her back to where Brooks and Anson were slowly making their way along.

"Jacob, what are you doing?" Kelly asked. "Let go of my arm."

"I need to even the odds a little here," he said. "Just trust me, okay?"

As he and Kelly approached, Anson stopped and raised his weapon.

"Let her help him," Jacob said. "I need another gun out here."

"I got him," Anson said. "You're doing fine."

"Jordan, no," Brooks said. He was wheezing with every breath now. "Go and help him. Let her help me."

Anson looked like he wanted very badly to say no. Brooks was the senior man, though, and for however deficient he may have been in other aspects of his character, he still respected the older man's authority. He helped Brooks shift his weight to Kelly without saying another word about it.

"I got him," Kelly said with a nod to Jacob.

"Thanks, Kelly." To Anson, Jacob said, "I'll take point. You bring up the rear?"

"Whatever you say." There was a menace in his tone that gave Jacob pause. He didn't really relish the idea of turning his back on this man.

But there wasn't a lot he could do about it. The herd was pressing in, and one of them had gotten too close to Chelsea. It folded its arms around her and she screamed. She thrashed at it, slapped at it. Jacob couldn't get a shot, though. He couldn't risk hitting her.

And then Chelsea surprised him. Her screams turned to a grunt, and she shoved the zombie to one side. It landed off balance and rocked back on its heels.

"Get off me!" she said, and ran at the dead man and shoved him again, this time sending him sprawling backward into the grass.

Jacob took a step toward the zombie and blew its head off before it could get back up.

"Nice move," he said to Chelsea.

"Just get us out of here," she said.

They crossed the remaining stretch of road with Jacob out in front, constantly scanning to the left and right, picking off zombies as they got too close. He also kept a weather eye on the rear. Kelly was doing okay, struggling under the larger man's weight, but still keeping up. Anson was keeping up, as well, and still protecting the rear like he was supposed to, but not firing nearly as much as Jacob.

Not moving around as much, either.

But they did make it, and though they didn't lose anybody, success had cost an awful lot in terms of ammunition. Of the six magazines he'd taken off of Brooks, he only had one left, and that one was down to about thirty rounds.

By the time they made it to the fire escape, they'd put a bit of distance between them and the herd. The fast movers were still coming on strong, but they'd bought a good forty-five seconds before they'd have to start shooting again.

"Dr. Brooks will go first," Anson said.

He jumped up and grabbed the fire escape ladder, letting his body weight pull it down. Jacob had seen several different types of fire escapes during his time with the salvage teams, and he was hoping this one would be the staircase variety, the kind that could accommodate two people at a time. It was instead a single ladder surrounded by a metal tube. That meant taking turns, one at a time, and of course Anson didn't wait for discussion. He took Brooks from Kelly, shoved her out of the way, and then helped the older man onto the rungs.

When Brooks had climbed up a few rungs, Anson went second, again without waiting for discussion.

For a moment, just for a moment, Jacob thought of walking up behind the younger man and painting the wall with his brains. But he held back. Jacob had a dark side, but not an evil one.

Getting just the two of them onto the ladder seemed to take forever. Jacob kept glancing back and forth between the progress they'd made—he could have sworn Anson was taking his sweet time about it, just to be spiteful—and the advancing herd. Things were too hot there. He had to take action.

"Kelly, you and Chelsea get up there as soon as you can. I'll hold these guys off."

It would probably cost him the rest of his ammunition, but it had to be done. The first zombies rushed in, and Jacob began to pick them off with smooth, measured shots. He couldn't afford to waste anything.

He'd dropped a dozen of them by the time Kelly and Chelsea were far enough up the ladder for him to take his turn. He jammed the weapon into the back of his pants and pulled himself up the ladder. Zombie hands grabbed at his legs before he'd managed to ascend two rungs. He kicked and twisted to free his legs, driving his heel down into bloody and ruined faces with all the energy he had left.

And when that didn't work, he pulled his pistol and started blasting away.

Eight zombies went down before he could lift his legs out of reach. He threw his right hand, still holding the pistol, around the ladder, and with his left reached down and pulled the bottom rungs up. They couldn't climb ladders, at least he'd never seen anything like that, but their weight was considerable, and it took everything he had to finally get the thing into the upright position.

Only then did he allow himself to catch his breath.

He glanced down at the huge crowd that had gathered at the foot of the ladder. Turning, he saw a sea of the undead that stretched all the way to the horizon. El Paso was now carpeted with the dead.

Then he looked up.

Kelly was watching him. She offered a weak smile, and he returned it. But his attention was focused one floor above her, where Anson was climbing through a window.

That right there was going to be a problem.

He just knew it.

CHAPTER 21

Jacob reached the window he'd seen the others go through and stopped just below it. He pulled his weapon and carefully moved to the left side of the ladder, so that he could climb around the window without showing himself to whoever might be standing just inside. He was surprised that Anson hadn't already leaned out the window with his gun in his hand and put a round into the top of Jacob's skull.

Still, smart tactics tended to keep one alive, and Jacob had every intention of staying alive.

He eased around to the edge of the window and positioned himself so that he could go through it in a rush, feetfirst, clearing it as fast as possible.

With a deep breath, he swung inside, pistol at the ready.

He landed in what looked to be a classroom. Or maybe a roll call room. There were rows upon rows of chairs with built-in desks, all of them covered in dust, not used in years. On the walls, he saw pictures of groups of men in strange uniforms and fancy insignia that he guessed were Old World military.

Kelly and Chelsea were standing at one end of the room, waiting for him.

Brooks and Anson were at the other end of the room, talking in a quiet huddle. Both men looked up as he rushed the room, but neither showed any reaction, just went back to their conversation.

Jacob turned to Kelly. "What is this place?"

She answered with a shrug.

"Brooks," he said, calling across the room, "what is this place?"

"I have no idea," Brooks answered. He pushed his glasses up the bridge of his broken nose. "My guess, from the stuff on the walls, is that it was once the training center for the various squadrons assigned here."

Jacob nodded. He crossed to the only doorway leading out of the room and stepped into the hallway. He looked left, looked right, and saw nothing but offices and more rooms like the one he'd just left. He did see some stairs at the end of the hallway to his right, though, and he wondered, if this place really was a training center for military personnel, whether they had a kitchen somewhere. He was so hungry he'd kill for a can of tomato puree.

Hell, even for one of those ketchup packets he used to find on the floor in the ruins of fast food restaurants and gas stations.

"Did you guys look around at all?" he said. "Check the access points?"

Anson ignored him. Brooks glanced at him, shook his head, then went back to listening to Anson. The two men looked like they were discussing resources Jacob couldn't even begin to deal with. While he was watching them, the mood between them seemed to get heated, though they kept their voices at a whisper. Anson took off his gloves and threw them onto one of the desks.

Jacob went to the window he'd just jumped through and looked down. Now that it was daylight, he had a fairly good view of just how badly they were screwed. Zombies as far as he could see, crowding into every corner, searching every doorway.

But what he wanted to see was straight below him.

He watched the zombies pressing against the walls of his building, and noticed a subtle, but unmistakable pancaking of bodies as they pressed against the walls.

That was good, he thought. Very good.

Years ago, one of his instructors in survival school had described this very moment. He was the first one Jacob had ever heard use the term *pancaking* to describe zombie behavior.

"We used to see this a lot on freeways," the man had said. His name was Steve Beckwith. He had a big belly and big red arms and a big gray mustache like a walrus, but he knew his shit about zombies. There was a section of the west wall, back in Arbella, named Beckwith Corner, after the action he took during the First Days to secure the town. He was one of Arbella's heroes. "Imagine you're in a car, and all of a sudden, traffic slows to a crawl in your lane, but nobody else's. What do you guess is going on?"

Silence from the class.

"An accident up ahead, right? Well, most of the time, it was nothing. You'd get to the spot where the accident should have been, and there was nothing there. You ended up accelerating back up to speed wondering what in the hell had happened. But you never found out.

"Well, I'm here to tell you what happened. It's called

pancaking. Traffic will be going along like normal, and then something'll happen that causes somebody to tap their brakes. Some asshole changes lanes in front of him or some lady gets on the on ramp still putting on her makeup or whatever the hell it is. So the guy behind that guy taps his brakes. And the guy behind him, and the guy behind him, and on and on until the initial tap exponentially grows into a full-blown stoppage somewhere down the line. It may be hard for you kids to visualize, seeing as none of you ever drove on Little Rock's freeways in rush hour, but trust me. Pancaking. It happens."

Jacob remembered the way the old man had looked across his class of Arbella's toughest customers, supposedly the best and brightest of Arbella's next generation (though Jacob was still convinced they'd made a terrible mistake by letting *him* in the club), and sighed tiredly.

"Let me put it to you numbskulls this way," Beckwith had said. "Let's say you get trapped on the roof of some building someplace, and you look over the side at this huge herd of zombies trying their hardest to get inside and turn you into a buffet. If you see pancaking, like I just described, bodies stacking up at the wall like that, that means you're okay. The zombies haven't found a way inside.

"But if you see movement toward a choke point, like a door—it'll look like sand moving inside an hourglass—then you know you're fucked. They've found a way inside and they're coming to eat your ass. Is that dumbed-down enough for you jackasses?"

"Yes, sir!" the class had answered in unison.

"Outstanding," Beckwith had said. "Might be hope for you ass cracks yet."

Outstanding, indeed, Jacob thought, looking down at the zombies pancaking against the walls of his building. They might just be okay.

He turned back to the room and tried to take it all in. He'd seen other buildings like this. Multipurpose, he'd heard them called. The wall behind Brooks and Anson was only paper-thin. It was an accordion-style faux wood wall designed to divide the room or enlarge it, depending on the need at hand. He walked over to it, ignored the curious looks he got from Brooks and Anson as he passed them, and opened it up, pressing it into its contracted position along the hallway wall.

"What are you doing?" Anson said.

"Expanding our options. Look at that next wall. It's the same as this one. I think we can open up this entire floor, create one giant room."

"What for?" Anson said. "Just sit down and shut up."

"You haven't secured the downstairs, have you?"

"You know I haven't. But we saw that it's—"

"First rule of dealing with zombies," Jacob said. "If it can go wrong, it will go wrong. You always count on defenses failing."

"These were made by people who knew what they were doing," Anson said. "They won't fail."

"But if they do, the zombies will come up here. To right here."

"Yes, and we'll go upstairs to the next level. And the one after that. And if we need to, all the way to the roof."

"But we can better our odds," Jacob said. "We don't need to just retreat. If we open up all these walls, we can create a floodplain."

"What?" Anson said.

"A floodplain. Zombies behave like water," Jacob

said. "You've seen this, right? They go to the easiest areas, just like water seeks out the lowest point. When they move en masse, they flow like a river, finding the areas of least resistance, moving around buildings like they're rocks in a stream."

Anson waved his hand in the air as if to dismiss the whole thing. "Spare me the Zen Buddhist crap, will you please? Do you mind? We're talking business here."

"Yes, but we can do better. Look, if we open up all these walls, we create one large room. Should a breach occur, and the zombies get in, they'll come here. If we don't have a floodplain, they'll move to the choke point, and that will be whatever pathway we've chosen to get to the next floor above us. All we'll be doing is speeding them up. But if we open up a floodplain, they'll spread out first. They'll explore. That's what they do. If we want to buy ourselves all the extra time we can, we have to play to their nature. And besides, what can it hurt?"

Anson dismissed him with a wave of his hand.

Brooks, though, leaned close to Anson and whispered something to him. The younger man looked angry at first, but then his expression softened, and by the time Brooks was done talking, the younger man was nodding right along with him.

Without explanation to Jacob, the two of them went down the length of the building, opening up walls and creating space. By the time all was said and done, they were on the opposite sides of the building, but still plainly visible from where Jacob and the women stood.

"What do you suppose that was all about?" Kelly said.

"I bet I know," Chelsea said. "They want to be as far away from us as possible so they could talk about how they are going to kill us."

Her tone tripped something in Jacob he didn't like. "Chelsea, come on. Don't you think—"

"Think what? What are you trying to tell me?"

"Chelsea," Kelly said, only without any of the sarcastic, passive-aggressive tone Jacob had used, "we're only trying to say that things have gotten a little more personal than before. They're in this, same as we are. I think they're probably arguing about the extraction they keep talking about. That has to be the most important thing on their minds. Isn't it the most important thing on ours?"

Jacob could see by the look on Kelly's face that she had intended the question purely rhetorically, but to Chelsea it was anything but.

"No," the girl said. "No, it's not. I don't give a fuck if I live or die, Kelly. And don't even for a second try to buddy up to me. You have no idea what life is like. I saw you in that Slaver caravan. I know your husband died defending you. I watched the whole thing. But at least you had somebody. I lived there for seven fucking years, Kelly, and I had nobody. Do you have any idea how many times those motherfuckers raped me? Do you? Do you know how many times my older brother stood by and watched?"

"No," Kelly said, lowering her head.

"Every goddamn night!"

"Chelsea, I . . ."

"You what?" Chelsea said. "What can you possibly say right now? You know what kept me from slashing my wrists every time somebody put a blade in my hand? It was the belief that I'd come home, back here, one day, and that everything would be fine. I wouldn't have my parents, but I'd still be the daughter of Alfred and Suzanne Walker, two of the most distinguished scientists in my entire community. I wouldn't have them to come home to, but I would have a community to come home to. They always said it took a village to raise a child. I wanted that village. I wanted people who welcomed me because they knew the pedigree I bore. They knew I was one of them. But when I finally did come back, I found people coming out of the woodwork to ruin my father's reputation."

Chelsea paused there. When Kelly tried to speak, Chelsea waved her off with a sharp flourish of her hand. "What are you going to say, Kelly? That you get it? That you grok me? You don't. You don't have a fucking clue. How many times have you been raped?"

"What?" Kelly said, totally taken aback.

"You heard me. How many times?"

"Well . . . I've never . . ."

"Great," Chelsea said. "Come back to me when it becomes a nightly occurrence. And then come back to me a second time when you wake from the dream, only to discover that it's happening all over again."

She stared at both of them, challenging either of them to say something, anything.

When neither did, she waved a hand at them and said, "Fine. Fuck you. I'm going to sleep."

Then, without another word, she walked over to a corner of the room, sat down, curled into a ball, and started to cry.

"Jesus," Jacob said.

"Yeah, that's not gonna help," said Kelly.

"I didn't . . . I didn't even . . ."

"I didn't, either," Kelly said. "Nobody would have."

"I've dealt with rape cases before. I've even talked to little girls about the things their uncles or their cousins did, but I haven't ever . . ." Jacob threw up his hands. "What was I supposed to say?"

"I don't know."

She took his hands in hers and looked into his eyes. In that moment, Jacob saw the past—the glorious, unambiguous past—and at once his future, an uncertain desert with only the vaguest promise of life somewhere in the distance.

Unless it was a mirage.

He squeezed her hand. "Kelly, I . . . I've never been very good at this stuff. Talking to her, I felt like I didn't have the first fucking clue about what to do. I feel like I spend most of my life that way."

"Me, too," she said, and managed a chuckle.

He didn't even smile, though. "No, you don't."

"What?"

"You don't feel like you're lost. You're you. You've got all this shit figured out. You're not like the rest of us. You never have been."

"That's not true."

"Isn't it? I watched you growing up. I knew you were special even before you did."

Kelly shook her head in confusion, even though she didn't pull her hands away from his.

"There's no shame in it, Kelly. You've got life figured out. That's a good thing."

"Jacob, that's not true. Don't be cruel."

That surprised him. "Cruel? Kelly, I'm not trying to be . . ."

"I know," she said. She took her hands away from his. "It just feels cruel, because I know it's not true."

"Kelly, I know you. Don't you know that? I know you."

She turned away with a sour look on her face, like he'd gone below the belt.

"And I don't mean *know* you that way. I mean, I know you like we used to talk. I used to spend hours listening to you, Kelly. I know you. I know what's going on in that head of yours, somewhere."

"You do, huh?"

"Yeah, I do."

"Tell me then."

So, she'd laid down the challenge. She wanted to talk, but she wanted him to earn it. Jacob didn't even hesitate. "You used to love me, but now you hate me. You blame me for Barry's death. You do, don't you?"

She said nothing.

"Well? Go on, tell me if it isn't true."

To his great surprise, she said, "It isn't."

Jacob said nothing in reply. He was too stunned.

"I don't hate you, Jacob. I know I said I did, but I didn't mean it."

She waited. "Nothing? That means nothing to you?"

"It does," he said. He reached for something to say, anything, but there was nothing there. "Kelly, I . . ."

"Jacob," she said. "You're a good man."

"Oh God," he said. He knew what that meant. The good man line, the kiss of death. He'd been hoping . . . he hadn't let himself realize it until now, but all along he'd been hoping that the old feelings between them would rekindle.

But, of course, her husband of twelve years was dead now just three months.

He hadn't read *Hamlet* since grade school, and he'd barely understood half of it even then, but he did remember the line about a marriage following hard upon a funeral. The thought of being *that* guy, of being Claudius, disgusted him.

And when it came to Kelly, his mind never tolerated disgust.

She was worth more than that.

But, like usual, it was Kelly who came to the rescue. She grabbed his swollen and bloodied hands in hers and squeezed them to her breast. "Jacob, I don't hate you. I did, but that was only me being crazy. Barry had just died. He'd died defending me. And then everyone else. It was all too much. I had to lash out, and I lashed out at you."

"Kelly, I . . ."

"You don't understand." It wasn't a question. "How can men use that line like a weapon? I'll never get that. You say that, and it puts it all back on me to explain."

Jacob had no idea what she was talking about, but he knew he loved her. He knew his hands in hers felt right. He knew his hands against her breast felt right.

"Jacob, you went to all the parties Barry and I threw, right? You saw all the booze, all the drinking?"

He nodded.

"The two of us," Kelly said, shaking her head, "made the best bathtub gin in the whole town."

"That's true," he said.

"Yeah. It was. I don't know if you ever picked up on it, Jacob, but I was drunk all the time back then. Barry was, too. We were fucking wasted every time we stepped outside of our house. There were mornings I'd wake up and put down a mason jar of gin for breakfast. I've been sober these last few weeks, but believe me, Jacob, it hasn't been by choice. It's been torture."

Jacob listened without really understanding. The cop

in him heard "alcoholic" and put her in a box in one corner of his understanding, but the seventeen-year-old kid in him, the one who saw her as a girl on the verge of womanhood, who had tasted her sweat on her nipples, felt lost.

"Jacob, we fought all the time. I mean *all* the time. Sometimes it got bad."

"You mean he hit you?"

She nodded.

"Oh shit, Kelly. Why didn't you tell me?"

"Because you would have done what, Jacob? Beat the fuck out of him?"

"Probably, yeah."

She shook her head and turned away.

"What?" he said. "You know I would have."

"Yeah, I know, and that's the deal here. Jacob, the thing with you is that you look at every problem you see like it's a nail, and you've got the world's only hammer."

"What? What in the hell does that mean?"

"Jacob, don't yell at me."

"I'm not . . ." He stopped for a second, took a breath, and tried again. "I'm sorry. I didn't mean to yell. It's just, sometimes, I have no idea what you're talking about."

"It's a Mark Twain quote. 'To a man with a hammer, everything looks like a nail.' "

"What is that even supposed to mean?"

"Jacob, it's just an expression."

"Yeah, but what does it mean? What are you saying?"

"I'm not saying anything about you, Jacob. For God's sake, it's not about you. It's about me."

Jacob held up his hands like he was asking for alms. "I'm sorry," he said. "I'm not trying to be stupid. I just don't understand you sometimes. First I'm the bad guy and then it's all about you. Just tell me what I'm supposed to do here and I'll do it."

"Nothing, Jacob. Look, I'm trying to tell you that my marriage was ending. I mean, even before we left Arbella. Barry and I, we were done. Except that neither of us wanted to admit it. I kept telling myself that going on this expedition together was going to be the thing that jump-started us. You know, the thing that put us back on the rails? Instead he got . . . he died. And I was left with all this crap in my head that I can't sort out."

There was more she wanted to say, but she was crying now, and Jacob did the only thing he knew how to do in situations like this. He pulled her close to his chest and hugged her and let her soak his shirt with her tears.

But only for a moment.

He pushed her to arm's length and turned away.

"I'm sorry," she said, and hastily wiped the tears from her cheeks.

"Kelly, hush."

He saw her take her hands away from her face and stare at him indignantly. He pushed past her. His attention was focused on the pair of gloves Jordan Anson had left on the desk where he and Brooks had argued earlier.

He walked over to the table where they lay and took a moment to stare at them.

"Jacob, what is it?"

He didn't acknowledge her. Instead, he scooped up the gloves and headed toward the other side of the room, where Brooks and Anson were talking.

"Jacob, what is it?"

"Proof," he said.

He advanced on the two men. Anson saw him coming halfway across the room and pulled his weapon. He didn't point it at Jacob, but he definitely had it at the ready.

"You killed her," Jacob said to Anson, not even trying to hide his anger. He threw the gloves down on the table between them. "It was you."

"Jacob, please," Brooks said. "Now is not the time."

"Look at the fucking gloves," Jacob said.

Brooks just stared at him.

"Look at them!"

Before Anson could raise his gun, Jacob drew his and pointed it at Anson's face.

Brooks stood over the table, looking at the gloves. They were black Kevlar, badly frayed, like the rest of Anson's outfit. The knuckles were reinforced with armor, as were the backs of the hands and the tops of the fingers. But it was the underside of the fingers that had attracted Jacob's eye, and it looked like Brooks had noticed, too.

The stitching that held the index and middle fingers together had come undone on the right hand. Both fingers had thick cords of stitching across the pads of the fingers, pulled out of place by God knows what.

"What are you talking about?" Anson said.

"Quiet," Brooks said. The younger man turned on him, but Brooks just waved his objections away. He picked up the gloves and turned them over and over in his hands, his eyes tightly focused, but his mind clearly somewhere else.

Anson looked eerily calm about the whole thing. He even lowered his rifle.

"What in the hell is he talking about?" Anson said. "I haven't killed anybody."

"I said, be quiet!" Brooks said.

Without any warning at all, the older man lunged forward and yanked the pistol from Anson's hand.

"Hey!" Anson said. "Les, what are you doing?"

"You killed her, didn't you? Everything he said, it's all true."

The look on Brooks's face was all the proof Jacob needed. He hadn't trusted a word the man had said up to that moment, but he trusted the look of betrayal, of hurt, or confusion, and of rage that the man now wore. That was patently clear. And it said more than the man could ever put into words.

Jacob raised his other hand to the weapon, gripping it tightly in a Weaver's stance. He looked down the length of the barrel at Anson and said, "I've done this twice before. Both times the men in your position chose to close their eyes. It's up to you, though."

Anson didn't even acknowledge him. He turned to Brooks and tried to hold on to the icy calm that he'd mastered so easily up to that point. "What are you doing, Les?" he said. A line of sweat rolled down his cheek. "Answer me! What are you doing? It's me, Les."

Brooks shook his head, clearly at odds with what he was doing.

The gun stayed trained on Anson's head, though; Jacob was glad to see that.

"Why did you do it?" Brooks said. "I loved her. I told you that. She was the whole reason I came here."

Anson said nothing.

Jacob reached out and touched Brooks on the shoulder. With a nod, he waved him back. Then he turned his attention back to Anson. "You sent your men to kill Chelsea Walker. You used your position in the High Council to bury her father's research and possibly doom the rest of your society to a future of senility. You gassed an entire region of this city, killing thousands. And you murdered Miriam Sayer with your bare hands. You, sir, are guilty."

"Go fuck yourself," Anson said. "I haven't done a damn thing wrong."

"My people have a Code. You've read it. I remember you mocking it. But know this: You have been found guilty of the crimes of corruption and murder, and those are crimes that threaten us all. You mocked my Code, but the Code is very clear on what I have to do right now."

Jacob raised the pistol and tightened his grip. When he'd been forced to put Jerry Greider down, he'd been sick to his stomach. When he'd killed Nick, he'd felt only the emptiness that those who have been betrayed can feel. But now, looking down the barrel of his gun, Jacob felt nothing but conviction. Jordan Anson, more than any man he'd ever met, deserved to die.

"Spare me the platitudes," Anson said. "Your Code is for primitives." He turned to Brooks. "And you, what are you doing?"

"Don't," Brooks said.

"Don't what?" Anson snapped back. "What are you doing, old man? You know me. You know what this is. You know what this all about."

"I don't care about the rest of it," Brooks said. "The gas, the deception. I don't care. But I loved her. I loved her!"

"She was collateral damage, my friend," Anson said as he reached under his left arm and pulled his body armor open.

"Stop!" Jacob shouted. He couldn't see Anson's hand, and that raised the hairs on the back of his head.

Anson reached into the folds of his armor and came out with a small silver cylinder about the size of a fountain pen.

"Stop!" Jacob shouted again. "Drop it!"

Anson still refused to look at him. "She was going to ruin us. You know that. What else was I supposed to do?"

Brooks looked like he was still trying to take it all in. He shook his head. "You killed her."

Anson twisted one end of the cylinder in his hand. "Yeah, I'm afraid I did, old friend. But if you want to stay on top, sometimes you have to make the hard choices. Sorry about this."

He tossed the cylinder into the center of the room, then bolted toward the door.

Jacob almost shot him, but it happened so quickly. Anson's distraction had worked. Jacob lost just a moment, less than a second, watching the cylinder fly over his shoulder, and in that moment, Anson ran through the door and headed down the stairs. By the time Jacob realized what was happening, he didn't have a shot.

"Grenade!" Brooks screamed.

For a moment, time stood still around Jacob. His brain registered the danger, but it was still sluggish. He was frozen from the realization that he was standing on top of a bomb, and still he couldn't move. He saw Brooks running to the wall and flattening himself there. He saw the cylinder—the grenade—rolling across the floor. And beyond the grenade, Kelly, looking stricken.

It was the fear on Kelly's face that made him move.

Even before he scooped it up he knew he couldn't throw it through the window glass. It was too lightweight for that. He ran to the window instead and smashed it out with his elbow. He caught a quick glance at the street two stories below him, thick with zombies, and tossed the grenade into their midst.

The device exploded before he had a chance to get back from the window. The concussive blast hit so hard it shook the building and sent Jacob flying. Flat on his back, he blinked, and rolled out of the way just as a section of the ceiling gave way and fell like a mudslide onto the floor.

His head ringing, Jacob climbed to his feet. The room was filled with swirling dust. There was a hole in the wall where the window had been, and the ceiling above it was black from the burn. Down below in the street, he could hear the zombie moans intensifying.

He looked around for Kelly. She'd been knocked to the ground, but she, too, was getting up. Slowly, painfully. She propped herself up on a desk and stayed there, blinking at the floor.

"Are you okay?" he asked her.

"Don't touch me," she said. "I'm kind of dizzy."

He couldn't see Brooks through the clouds of dust hanging in the room, but there was no time to check on him. He had to catch Anson before the man made it out of the building.

Jacob ran out of the room, looked left and then right. There were stairs at either end of the hall, and he couldn't see Anson to tell which way he'd gone. So he did something that had served him well in foot chases in the past. He closed his eyes and tried to remember exactly what had happened as Anson threw the grenade and turned to run.

Left, he thought.

He ran for the metal door that led to the stairwell

and threw it open. It slammed against the wall as he charged through and rounded the first landing.

Anson was standing at the base of the stairs, a pistol in his hand.

Jacob put on the brakes and backed up behind the wall just as Anson started to fire. The *pop, pop, pop* of small arms fire echoed through the stairwell as a small section of the wall next to his head exploded.

Jacob stared at the holes in the wall and thought: *A gun. A real gun. Damn, this is going to suck.*

He backed away from the corner and started to slowly move around it, leading with his gun, revealing a little bit of the stairwell at a time until he could see the base of the stairs.

Anson was gone. The stairs were empty.

Jacob had a choice. He could descend slowly, carefully, watching the opening at the foot of the stairs for some indication of what Anson was doing. The trouble was, that left him in a deadly funnel, a sitting duck as he slowly inched down the stairs. If Anson peeked into the stairwell and saw him framed there, nowhere to hide, nothing to use for cover, he could simply light him up. Throw enough rounds into a small space and you're bound to hit something. That's why they called it fish in a barrel.

Jacob's other choice was to rush headlong down the stairs, be reckless, take the fight to the attacker.

It really wasn't a choice at all.

As he ran down the stairs, he thought of what Kelly had said. The man with a hammer.

But sometimes the problem really was a nail, and it needed a hammer.

He reached the bottom of the stairs and saw Anson just ahead of him. The man turned, startled. He clearly hadn't expected Jacob to rush him. He was standing in the middle of what must have been a break room for the flight squadrons who used to work out of this building. More pictures of men in strange uniforms decorated the walls. Outside the glass doors to Jacob's left was an outdoor kitchen, all rusted now and falling apart. There were couches and chairs in the center of the room, and to his right, a bar filled with dusty bottles.

Jacob took it all in at a glance, but the only thing that really mattered to him was Jordan Anson, turning to face him. Jacob threw his shoulder into the man's chest before he had a chance to fire and drove him back across the room.

The two men crashed into a glass trophy case standing at the far wall amid an explosion of glass. At some point in the charge and tackle, Jacob had lost his gun. He stood and looked for it, but didn't see it.

Anson didn't have his pistol, either.

There were trophies all over the place, though. Jacob scooped up one of them, some sleek-looking plane doing a barrel roll on a heavy wooden base. He swung it at Anson's head, connecting with his chin with a sharp *crack*.

For a moment, Anson seemed to sag into a heap.

Jacob raised the trophy over his head and was about to bring it down hard on Anson's head when the man suddenly shifted from under him. He reached into the folds of his body armor, came up with a combat knife, a mean-looking six-inch blade, and slashed at Jacob.

Jacob backed away, but he wasn't fast enough. The blade caught him across the chest, ripping a gash through his shirt and cutting a deep gouge in his skin. The cut didn't hurt at first, not until he backed away again and had a moment to realize how badly he'd been cut. Then the burning started, and it spread all the way to the bone.

Even though he'd been protected by his Kevlar armor, the back of Anson's neck and arms were dotted with blood and bits of broken glass. He didn't let it slow him down, though. He lashed out at Jacob again, forcing him back to the center of the room, and then crouched before him with the knife held in a fencer's grip, his free hand held back, close to his body, to protect the heart and liver.

The man had clearly been trained to fight with a knife.

There was a couch to his right. Jacob backed up again and skirted around the end of it, kicking at the corner so that the couch skidded between them.

Anson kicked the couch back at him, opening the gap again, and advanced, holding the knife out in front of him the whole time.

It was Anson's first real mistake.

Jacob had backed up against the end of the bar. As Anson advanced, Jacob hooked his foot around the base of the nearest bar stool. He kept his eyes on Anson's shoulders. Even a pro telegraphed their moves through their shoulders, and Anson was no exception. He gathered himself together, tensing, and then lunged.

Jacob was ready for it.

He kicked the bar stool toward Anson. It skidded across the floor and hit the man just below the knee with enough force to trip him up.

Anson's knife hand dipped low. His gaze dipped down. His free hand shot out for balance.

It was the break Jacob needed. He stepped forward and kicked at Anson's knife hand, connecting just below the wrist. The knife went flying and Anson pulled his hand back in surprise, even though the body armor shielded him from any serious injury.

But Anson wasn't out of the fight. He charged Jacob, tackling him to the ground and slamming him into the floor so hard it knocked the wind out of Jacob.

Jacob broke contact with him when they hit the ground and rolled away. Anson came up, scrambling to keep him from getting to his feet.

Jacob slapped at him as he rolled away, but Anson had the jump on him. He was able to kick Jacob's legs out from under him and push him facedown to the floor.

Anson held him there.

Jacob twisted as hard as he could and managed to roll out from under the man's weight. He landed on his knees at the edge of the bar. There was no way he could get to his feet before Anson. All he could do was brace for the impact.

Anson laid into him with his shoulder and sent him flying into the back of the bar. Something above him gave way, and a cascade of bottles rolled down on top of him and all around him, shattering everywhere. Anson had remained silent the entire fight, but he suddenly roared with anger and charged again. He swung at Jacob's face, telegraphing his move with his eyes. It was like he had suddenly lost the control and technique that had defined his fighting until that moment.

Jacob didn't question why. He raised his left leg and caught Anson in the chin as he tried to land his punch.

Anson grunted from the pain and sagged to his knees. Jacob jumped on him, and both men rolled across the broken glass and spilled alcohol, kicking and punching. Anson was fast with his hands, and Jacob took three hard jabs to the face as he rolled off him, but it gave him the opening he needed. Anson's crotch was wide open, and Jacob threw his knee as hard as he could into the man's balls.

Even with the protection of a hard plastic cup, Anson doubled over in pain.

Jacob reached out for the closest thing he could find, a bottle of Jack Daniel's, and smashed it across Anson's face.

The bottle shattered, knocking Anson flat. He lay on his back, arms spread wide to the ceiling, a look of blind confusion on his face.

Jacob found himself holding the neck of the broken bottle. He rolled over and straddled Anson, his knees pinning Anson's arms to the floor.

Anson groaned at him, trying to speak.

"You know what," Jacob said. "Fuck you. I hope this hurts."

He brought the broken end of the bottle down on Anson's face as hard as he could. It got stuck there, and Jacob had to wrench it back and forth to pull it free. And when he finally got it free, he slammed it down again and again and again, spraying blood everywhere.

He drove the broken bottle into the man's face over and over until he could no longer swing his arms. When he was done, there was nothing left but a bloody hole where the man's face had been. Jordan's arms had long since ceased twitching. His body lay motionless, blood oozing into a puddle around his head.

Jacob climbed to his feet, all his bumps and bruises screaming at him.

He staggered around the room until he found Anson's pistol.

A real Colt 1911 A1.

One of the best damn weapons ever made.

Jacob had seen a few of them in his day, but most were tired old warriors, dented and rusted and only shadows of the firearm they had once been.

But not this one.

This one was pristine.

A subdued black barrel. Synthetic grips, not the walnut that most models had. Jacob wrapped his hand around the receiver and felt like a hammer had just been put in his hands.

Then he looked down at Jordan Anson.

And realized he was looking at a nail.

CHAPTER 22

The fighting had drawn a crowd.

Jacob turned away from Jordan's corpse and found himself looking at hundreds of zombies, all of them beating against the glass that made up the outside wall. As they moved against each other, shuffled for position, lanes would occasionally open up between them. When that happened, he could see what had once been a fancy, built-in barbeque grill out on the patio. Looking back at the room he'd just wrecked in his fight with Jordan Anson, he couldn't help but think that the pilots who used to use this area as their rec room must have lived pretty good lives. Must have been fun racking up all these trophies, posing for all these pictures, cooking out on that grill, bellying up to the bar.

God, he had memories of outdoor cookouts.

But that was from another time.

With a heavy sigh, he turned back to Anson's body on the floor and forced himself to come back to the present. He had things to do, responsibilities, people who were counting on him. He knelt next to Anson's body and forced open his body armor. Inside, he found four more of the grenades that Anson had tried to kill him with. He also found three more magazines to go with the Colt 1911 A1 he'd found, and that was fucking sweet. Like Christmas when he was a kid.

The glass cracked behind him. Jacob twisted around, ready to fight if he had to, but the sliding glass doors hadn't given way yet.

They would soon, though. He knew that.

He started toward the stairs and was about to start back up to rejoin the others when he caught movement out of the corner of his eye.

He stopped and watched.

The zombies out beyond the barbeque grill were walking away.

Slowly, in groups of twos and threes, more and more zombies were walking away, all of them headed in the same direction. The only ones who remained were the ones looking right at him.

Curious, Jacob stepped off the stairs and went to the window.

The small section of the herd clustered there went wild, moaning loudly and banging on the glass, but Jacob ignored them. Out beyond the barbeque grill there was a road that led to the hangars. To his right, a good ways off, were the hulking forms of the aerofluyts. In between was a seething sea of faces and twitching bodies.

But he didn't see why the zombies were turning away.

At least not at first.

Then he heard a loud, grinding noise, like an engine straining against a heavy load.

The next instant, one of the armored personnel carriers lumbered into view. It stood nearly three times as high as the tallest zombie in the herd, and its ten massive wheels rolled over the dead like a juggernaut, smashing bodies flat. The zombies rushed to the vehicle and scrambled onto it. Those who couldn't climb on top of it were pulled under and smashed. Though it had to weigh forty-five hundred kilograms easy, the bodies were so thick in places that its engines strained to roll over them.

And then, to Jacob's surprise, the thing stopped.

It rolled over yet another mound of bodies, seemed to pause for a second, rocked in place as though finding its level, and then just stopped.

"What in the hell?" Jacob said.

For a moment, the vehicle, and everything around it, was still. And then the dead climbed their way back onto it and started clawing at the roof access.

"What the hell? Come on, move."

He couldn't see what they were waiting for. It was Stu and Juliette inside that thing; he was sure of that. But they'd stopped a good hundred and fifty meters from the nearest entrance to the building. They weren't anywhere close.

Jacob ran up the stairs, back to the classroom. Dust still swirled in the air. Brooks was sitting in a chair, his face bleeding. Kelly was standing over him, tending to his injuries while Chelsea looked on, her face inscrutable. The girl had been through a lot, and it had filled her with hate. That hate was bleeding away now that she knew the truth about who was responsible for the things that had happened to them, but it hadn't gone away entirely. She still looked on Lester Brooks like he was something nasty she'd stepped in.

Jacob met Kelly's gaze and nodded.

Kelly nodded back.

That was good enough for him. He went to the side window and knocked it out with his elbow. With all the glass gone, he leaned his head out the window. The herd was so packed in he couldn't see the ground. The armored personnel carrier stood out like a rock in a stream. The zombies climbed all over it, but they couldn't find a way in.

And yet the thing still hadn't moved.

"What is it, Jacob?" Kelly asked.

He glanced over his shoulder. She'd left Brooks's side. The older man was holding a rag to the side of his bleeding head, but he looked like he'd be fine. "I think it's Stu and Juliette," he said.

"What? They made it?"

"I'm not sure," he said. "They're still kind of far away."

She joined him at the window. "What are they waiting for?"

"I don't know," he said. "I haven't seen any movement at all. They rolled to a stop there and haven't moved."

"Do you think they're okay?"

He turned and gave her a look. "How in the hell would I know that?"

"Jacob, I don't— Oh my God! What happened to you?"

"I'm fine," he said.

"But all that blood . . ."

"It's not mine," he said. "Most of it, anyway."

"What's going on there?" It was Brooks. He went to the next window and looked out. He blinked at the sunlight, and then frowned as he took in the scene. "Is that the APV Dr. Sayers's assistants went to fetch?"

"I think so, yeah."

"Where are they?"

"Probably still inside the vehicle," Jacob said. "I watched them drive it to that spot and stop. Nothing's happened since."

"You mean, they haven't come out yet?"

"Nope. Just sitting there."

"You mean, you haven't talked to them yet?" He glared at Jacob, then seemed to see him for the first time. "What happened to you? Where's Jordan?"

"Well," said Jacob, pointing to the blood on his clothes, "there's a little of him of here, and here, but most of him is spread out like jelly on toast on the floor downstairs."

Brooks closed his eyes, clearly at war with himself over how to feel about Jordan's death, but when he opened his eyes again, he looked like a man who had resigned himself to eat a shit sandwich. "We have to start talking to them in the APV."

"Yeah, that'd be nice," Jacob said. "How do you propose we do that? Smoke signals?"

"No," Brooks said. "There's a faster way. All the APVs have an onboard radio system that monitors the emergency channel. If their radio is on, they should hear me." He pulled the collar loose on his body armor and worked a microphone up to his throat. "This is Dr. Lester Brooks. I'm looking at an APV approximately one hundred and fifty meters from the Squadron Command Headquarters Building. Is anyone monitoring this side?"

There was a pause, and then Stu's excited voice came over the radio. "Dr. Brooks! This is Dr. Stewart Huffman. My wife and I are here."

"Excellent," said Brooks. "Glad you guys made it."

"Is everyone there okay?" Stu asked. "We saw the explosion."

"There are four of us here," Brooks said. "We're not injured. But we need you to bring the APV closer to the building. You're too far away for us to hook up with you."

"Can't do it, Dr. Brooks. We're on backup solar power right now, and that just ran out. We have to wait for the batteries to recharge before we can go anywhere."

Brooks frowned at that. "What happened to the morphic field generator?"

"My guess is it's functioning normally," Stu said. "The trouble is, somebody removed the power cells."

"Come again?"

"Yes, sir. We spent all of last night going from one aerofluyt to the next. Every single APV has been sabotaged."

Brooks hit a button on his microphone and shook his head in frustration. "Jordan, you crazy bastard. What did you do?"

"What did he do?" Jacob asked. "What's going on?"

Brooks drew a deep breath and collected himself. "The APVs run off of a morphic field generator. It can run for decades, if it needs to, but only if it has a power cell to enable field generation. Apparently Jordan Anson removed those power cells in order to cut off your . . . well, our, escape."

Jacob took a moment to let that sink in. "I just don't see how that is possible," he said. "How would he know to do that?"

"That would be the easy part. Jordan was one of the smartest men I've ever known. It wouldn't surprise me if he anticipated other avenues of escape and blocked those, as well."

"But how?" Jacob asked. "I mean, he had body armor on and everything, but there's no way he could have covered that much ground with all those zombies out there. Not unless there are tunnels leading out to the aerofluyts."

"There aren't," Brooks said. "And I thought this was part of your theory, Jacob. I'm sure he had help. His goon squads, I believe you called them."

"Oh," Jacob said.

"Yeah." Brooks touched his microphone again. "Dr. Huffman, are you still monitoring this side?"

"Yes, sir," came Stu's voice over the speaker on Brooks's microphone. "I'm here."

"How much power do you have?"

"Uh, sir, we're dead in the water out here. We had to charge up the solar cells all morning and that only got us to thirty percent. That was barely enough to get us here."

"Thirty percent was barely enough?"

"Sir, there's a lot of zombies out here. Driving through those crowds drains the power down fast. And they were never meant to power the drive system anyway, just the electrical systems."

Brooks shook his head in frustration. "Okay, so you're at zero now?"

"Basically, yeah," Stu said. "We're charging up again, but we won't have enough to go anywhere for another two hours at least."

"Well, that limits our options considerably," Brooks said. "Okay, I guess you'll just have to continue charging. When you've got enough power to link up with us, you can pull right up to the door for us."

"Yes, sir," Stu said. "I'm guessing, at this rate, we can power up enough to cover that distance in about twenty minutes. After that, though, we'll have to park and recharge for a good long time."

"Acknowledged," Brooks said.

"And so then what?" Kelly asked. "What do we do after the solar cells have recharged the batteries?"

"Well, we could run it until the batteries are depleted, wait for it to charge again, and then repeat. We do that until we clear the herd. The problem is, of course, that we'll only be able to charge in the daytime. That puts some real limits on our ability to cover ground quickly."

"How long would it take to clear the herd doing that?"

"Who knows? A couple of weeks, maybe."

"And there's not another way?"

"Not without that power cell," Brooks said. "The APVs have three separate power systems, but the . . ."

He trailed off, lost in thought.

"Wait a second," he said. He tapped his microphone again. "Dr. Huffman, why didn't you try fast-charging at the couplings aboard the aerofluyts?"

"We did, sir. We tried that, but the power's been cut to the aerofluyts. It was turned off at origination. We couldn't make it over there to see what exactly had happened, but it looks like it was just turned off."

"To all three aerofluyts?"

"Yes, sir," Stu said. "And that's not the worst of it, I'm afraid. When the power went out, all systems shut down, including the security systems. At first, when we realized the power cells were missing, we figured we might be able to take shelter in the aerofluyts, but with the security system down and all the doors open, I'm afraid all three have been overrun."

"Damn," Brooks said. He thanked Stu and disconnected his microphone. "Well," he said to the others, "looks like we've only got the one option now. I guess we wait."

"Uh, guys . . ."

It was Chelsea. Jacob had seen her walk out the door and glance up and down the hallway, but he thought she was merely being curious. He hadn't paid much attention to her because he was so focused on Brooks. But now the look on her face had him worried.

She came into the room, still looking back at the stairs where Jacob had chased Anson.

"Chelsea, what is it?" Jacob said.

"I think we've got trouble."

Jacob pushed his way into the hallway. Downstairs, he could hear glass breaking. It didn't surprise him. He was actually kind of shocked they hadn't forced their way through already. "Okay," he said to Brooks. "Can you call Stu back and tell him we're coming to him right now? Kelly, you and Chelsea ready to make a break for it?"

"What?" Kelly said. "We can't go out there. Jacob, look!"

"I know," he said. "But we don't have any other choice."

Brooks glanced out the window again at the horde gathering in the street. "Jacob, we need to come up with another solution. We'll never make it through that."

"We'll make it," Jacob said. He took the grenades he'd taken off Jordan Anson out of his pocket. "Your buddy had a pretty good stash of weapons on him. I got his pistol, too."

Brooks stared at the metal cylinder, at war again with himself. He shook his head bitterly. "I understand why he would do this."

"Money, right? Once word got out that the technology was bad, he was going to lose everything. Fame and fortune and all that."

"Yeah, something like that. It's just that, I knew him. I thought I did anyway. He believed in the society we'd created. No guns, no cops. Why would he do this?"

"Beats me," Jacob said. "Maybe he was just an asshole."

"He was my friend," Brooks said.

Jacob shrugged. "Your friend was an asshole. Then again, so are you, but you know, whatever."

Jacob pushed him out of the way. He leaned out the window and tried to get a sense for the best way to get to the APV.

From behind him, he heard Chelsea cry out, "Jacob, they're coming."

"Got it," he said.

He put three of the grenades in his pocket and held the other up to see how it worked. The one Jordan had thrown took about five seconds to blow, and Jacob remembered the man twisting the cylinder just one click. The first mark on the barrel was a thin, black line. There were four more black lines arranged around the circumference, each one thicker than the one before it. He figured those indicated increasing longer delays on detonation. Simple enough. He twisted the cylinder all the way to the fattest line, glanced out the window again, and threw the grenade into the crowd.

"Alright," he said. "Time to move. We'll hit those stairs right there and move outside as fast as we can. Stay behind me because I plan on using a few more of these."

Jacob had just stepped into the hall when the grenade

went off. The blast rattled the whole building and nearly knocked him off his feet, but he didn't let it slow him down. He charged for the stairwell and saw two zombies struggling to get back on their feet. He shot the first one with the Colt right above its right ear, and the impact nearly split its rotten head in two.

The second zombie managed to get to its feet, but it was having trouble navigating the stairs. It got turned around and couldn't figure out how to face its meal again. Jacob bum-rushed the dead man, throwing his shoulder in his chest and driving him back toward the sliding glass doors. Two other zombies had already made it through the shattered windows, but Jacob was able to drive the zombie into them, knocking all three to the ground.

To his left, more of the dead were coming through the window. They sliced themselves up on the jagged glass still in the sill, but of course they didn't even register the pain. Jacob shot all three in the head, then waved Kelly and the others through the door. "Come on, hurry!" he said.

Once Brooks made it through, Jacob took his position at the front. Ahead of them, they got a view of just how much destruction the grenade had caused. Jacob saw a field of broken and blasted-apart corpses. Arms and legs were festooned off the sides of the building. Burned and, in most cases, unidentifiable body parts were everywhere. It was hard to walk without tripping over an arm or a leg or somebody's shattered head. But of course the zombies gave them no quarter. Even after the devastating blast, more zombies were already closing in to fill the gap.

Jacob pulled another grenade and tossed it into the crowd ahead.

"Get down!" he shouted.

Everybody hit the ground. Jacob, who had been through this before, knew to cup his hands over his ears and open his mouth to ease the pressure.

It did little good when the bomb went off, though. The shock wave hit him, and after it was over, he couldn't hear a damn thing but a constant ringing. *Get to your feet*, a voice inside his head roared. *Get to your feet!*

He stood up, dizzy as hell and uncertain which way he was facing. All he could see was a rain of black ash in the air. Jacob blinked and pivoted around, trying to get his bearings. He saw the APV up ahead, nothing but body parts all around it, but he didn't see Kelly and the others.

"Kelly!" he screamed. "Kelly!"

He heard groaning behind him. He spun around so quickly he nearly pitched over. Kelly was facedown in the grass, trying to say his name. Chelsea was next to her, and it looked like she was unconscious.

He knelt by Kelly's side. "Where are you hurt?" he asked.

"Jacob, I . . . I can't . . . I can't . . ."

"Shit," he said. He reached down, scooped her up, and put her over his shoulder in a fireman's carry. He did the same with Chelsea and ran for the APV.

The side door was locked tight, so he kicked it with all the strength he had left.

"Stu!" he yelled. "Open the fucking door!"

The next instant the door cracked open and Stu stuck his head out. Stu's mouth fell open at the carnage. "Holy hell," he said.

"Help me with them," Jacob said.

He handed Kelly to him first, and then Chelsea. Stu

and Juliette took the women and led them into the darkness of the APV's belly.

"Where's Brooks?" Stu asked.

"I don't know. I'm going to find him. You got them?"

"We got this."

Jacob stepped away from the APV. The black ash from a thousand burned bodies still hung in the air. The smell of burning flesh was overpowering. He pushed through it, though, and worked his way back to where they'd been standing when the grenade went off.

He found Brooks crumpled against a wall.

"Brooks," Jacob said, "can you hear me?"

The older man opened his eyes. They were yellowed and bloodshot. His milk and coffee complexion was discolored from the ash. It was all in his white hair, on his teeth, hanging from his eyelashes.

"I can't move," he said. "It's my legs. I can't feel them."

"Yeah," Jacob said. "I've been there before. Come on, I'll help you up."

"No, Jacob. I mean it. Something's wrong. I think my back might be broken."

"Okay," Jacob said. "No worries. I'll carry you."

Jacob picked him up as gently as he could, trying hard to keep his back in the exact same position it had been on the ground. He had probably eight meters to go, which wouldn't have been a problem, except that the dead were already marching toward the disturbance.

"Gotta hurry," Jacob said. "Sorry if this hurts."

He took off in a run, dodging the dead whenever they got too close. Brooks screamed from the pain, but

Jacob didn't dare stop running, not with skeletal zombies falling on his shoulders, clutching at his hair.

"Hang in there," he said to Brooks. "Just hang on."

There was a pile of debris in front of him—hulking chunks of concrete shot through with twisted rebar. Zombies were coming around on either side. He turned, looking for a way to end-run around them, but he was blocked there, too.

"Sorry to do this to you, Brooks," Jacob said.

He heaved the man up and over his left shoulder, freeing up his gun hand. Even with Brooks screaming in his ear, Jacob took the time to chart his course. Rushed shooting was bad shooting, and he only had the one chance to get this right.

There were two fast-moving zombies coming around the right side of the debris pile. On the left were four zombies, all slow movers, barely shambling along. He could take out the four pretty easily. He might even be able to simply move around them. But that would leave the fast movers at his back, and that was a variable he wasn't prepared to allow.

He turned to his right, sighted the Colt's front sights on the leading zombie, and fired.

God, he loved the Colt!

The zombie nearly did a backflip when it was hit in the face with the forty-five-caliber round. The zombie behind it bounded over the corpse, only to get a second round square in the forehead. Both zombies dropped to the ground, going nowhere, dead for real this time.

Jacob saw the gap they left and ran for it.

Stu was at the open door, waving him on.

"I think his back is broken," Jacob said.

"Oh shit," Stu said. Whether from the pain or from

something else, Jacob wasn't sure, but the man had passed out. Stu slapped his face, but Brooks was unresponsive. "Does he have a pulse?" He put his fingers up to Brooks's neck, but Jacob could tell the man was pressing too hard. "I can't feel a pulse. We need to do CPR."

Stu put his hands on Brooks's neck, like he was choking him.

"No!" Jacob said, and moved his hands down to the base of Brooks's sternum. "It's down here, two fingers up from the base of the sternum."

Stu moved his hands down where Jacob pointed, but Jacob didn't let him continue.

"Stand by, let me check for a pulse."

"He doesn't have a pulse. I already checked."

"Yes, he does!" Jacob said. "I can feel it. You don't need the CPR if he's got a pulse. Just get him inside. I'll cover you."

One thing Jacob could say about Stu. The man took direction well. He called to Juliette to help him. Together, they started pulling Brooks into the APV.

Jacob spun around to face the horde that had been gathering at his back.

There were four right in front of him. He pulled the trigger on the first one, dropped him, and then realized that the slide had locked back in the empty position. The Colt was a masterpiece of the armor's art, but it only carried seven bullets, and he'd just reached the end of that line.

"Need you to hurry it up there, Stu," he said.

"Almost there."

Jacob ejected the spent magazine and slapped in a new one. He quickly dispatched the other zombies, but that just left room for a hundred more right behind them.

"Stu?"

"Clear!" the man said. "Get in here!"

Jacob didn't need to be told twice. He ran for the door and jumped through just as the zombies were putting their hands on him.

He landed at Kelly's feet.

Her face was covered in ash and she had that two-thousand-yard stare, but he saw her eyes focus on his.

"Hey," he said. "How you doing?"

At first she didn't react, but slowly, a smile lit the corners of her mouth.

Chapter 23

Like most of the citizens of Arbella, Jacob had received basic emergency medical training. He could do the easy stuff, like CPR, burns and cuts, heatstroke, and snake bites. He could even set a broken bone, if he had to. Not well, but he could do it. So he sat Kelly and Chelsea down and gave them both a casual once-over. Both were complaining of a loud ringing in their ears, and Kelly said she thought she had something caught in her eye, but neither woman was seriously hurt. Just covered in dirt from head to toe.

Brooks was a harder case. He was drifting in and out of consciousness, no doubt from the pain. He had some nasty-looking cuts on his face and bits of broken glass in his hair, and he was wheezing through the broken nose Jacob had given him earlier. Stu and Juliette had him on one of the medical couches in the back of the transport. Jacob was familiar with some of the medical scanners they were using on Brooks from his time in the hospital back in Temple, but he had no idea what the blinking lights and fluctuating graphs meant. He waited for Stu and Juliette to finish whatever they were doing.

Finally, Juliette pointed to a green and grainy image on a computer screen that sort of looked like an X-ray of Brooks's lower spine. "See, right there?" she said to Stu.

He squinted at the image. "Yeah, I see it. Okay."

"What is it?" Jacob asked.

"Well, the good news is his back isn't broken. Looks like he might have torn some muscles and herniated a disc or two, but it's definitely not broken."

"That's good, right?"

"Well, yeah," Stu said. "Trouble is, he's going to be in some serious pain for a long while. I don't know if you've ever had a herniated disc before, but in case you haven't, trust me, it hurts like hell. I think we can pretty much guarantee that he won't be able to walk until we get him some real medical treatment."

"Can you give anything to help with the pain?"

"That's our other problem," Stu said. "No supplies."

"What do you mean?"

"I mean they were getting ready to put these APVs out of service. They were in the process of stripping them. This was the only one that they hadn't started tearing the guts out of yet. But they've already off-loaded all the medical supplies."

Jacob nodded. "What about the other stuff?"

"What other stuff?"

"The food and water?"

Stu and Juliette traded a horrified look. "Oh God," Juliette said. "He's right. There's no food in here."

"Nothing at all?" Jacob asked.

"There's water," Stu said. "The APV has built-in

condensers that make drinking water out of the water vapor in the air. We won't die of thirst, but we don't have any food. The trouble is, the condensers, like the air-conditioning and the navigation system and about a thousand other onboard systems, usually rely on the solar cells for the electricity they run on. Now that we're using that electricity to operate the drivetrain, as well, we'll be lucky to get an hour of travel time a day. And, actually, it'll probably be closer to thirty minutes. We'll have to charge the vehicle during the day, and run as far as we can after sunset. But the whole time we're charging, our subsystems will be using the cells. We'll never be able to reach a full charge that way."

"Why don't we just turn the subsystems off?"

"We can do that, no problem. But, like I said, we have literally thousands of subsystems on this vehicle that don't draw that much power from the cells, like maybe five percent."

"If that," Juliette said.

Stu nodded. "True. The big draw is the air-conditioning. That's probably thirty percent of our power draw right there."

"Do we need that?"

"It gets up to a hundred and fifteen degrees here in El Paso during the day," Stu said. "Imagine being inside this tin can in that kind of heat with no air-conditioning. We'd cook ourselves."

"What about turning it off at night, while we're running?"

"Might buy us some extra driving time," Stu said. "Not much."

Juliette tapped her fingertips and muttered to herself, like she was doing math in her head. "About twenty-one minutes each day," she said. "Assuming the system continues to work at optimal efficiency."

"Right," Stu said. "I think we could expect that efficiency to taper off with time, though. The APV was never meant to run like we're running it. We're putting a huge amount of stress on the system."

"Okay," Jacob said. He held up a hand between them. "That's enough. Miriam was right: You guys give me a headache."

He looked down at Lester Brooks, who was groaning quietly through clenched teeth. The man was still unconscious, though obviously hurting.

Kelly and Chelsea were okay, but he wondered how much longer everybody would be able to hold it together, especially with no food. Seeing the young girl lean against Kelly, and Kelly putting her arm over the girl's shoulder, convinced him they needed another way.

"What other options do we have?" Jacob asked Stu and Juliette.

"What do you mean?" Stu said. "This is it."

"There are always options," Jacob said.

"Not that I can see," Stu said. "What are you going to do, go back out there? You'd be torn to shreds in seconds."

"That's true."

"What if we drive this thing over to the hangar, turn on the power, and then head back over to the charging stations aboard the aerofluyts?"

"That's a possibility," Stu said. "It would at least save us a few days."

"Well, yeah. We'd have to drive over to the hangar, which will take probably about thirty minutes. That's how long it took us to get from the *Einstein* to here.

That'll use up all the charge we've got. Then somebody will have to go outside to turn on the power. Assuming they make it through that, we'll have to wait overnight, then spend most of the next day charging up again, then make the drive to the *Einstein*, where we can dock with one of the rapid charging couplers. Fully charged, we should have about two and a half days of power to get where we're going."

"But that won't be enough to get away from the herd."

"No, it won't. And after that, we'll be back to the food question again. I estimate we have a week's worth of days with no food, no matter what we do."

"So we're screwed no matter what we do."

"Pretty much," Stu said.

Frustrated, Jacob looked away. There was a short set of stairs off to his left that led down to the lower level, into the belly of the APV.

"Unless . . ."

He went down the stairs. Stu watched him go, then glanced at Juliette, shrugged his shoulders, and followed Jacob.

At the base of the stairs, Jacob found a series of three alcoves. Inside each one was a battle suit. Each suit was scuffed up and stained from numerous previous EVAs. They'd all seen plenty of action, that much was obvious, but they all looked sturdy enough.

"What about these?"

Stu's eyebrows went up. "I don't know. What are you thinking?"

"I'm thinking I can shave a day or two off our time," Jacob said. "What if I put one of these on, head to the hangar, and turn the power on? Meanwhile, you guys head to the *Einstein*. I'll turn the power on and meet you there."

Stu cupped his chin in his hand and turned slightly toward Juliette. "Four days without food is a lot better than seven."

"Definitely," she said.

"It won't be easy," Stu said. "The suits are amazing, but they're not indestructible. If they pile on you, they can work their way through the suit in no time."

"So, you're saying, don't get killed," Jacob said. "I got it."

"Well, okay."

Stu looked to Juliette and she shrugged. "It's worth a shot," she said.

"Okay," Stu said. "I agree. Let's hook up."

CHAPTER 24

Stu threw a lever and the suit slid out on rails and slowly rotated around. It was split down the back, with buckles on either side of the seam.

"There's really no easy way to get in," Stu said. "Some go the headfirst route, others go feetfirst. It's your choice."

"Which way do you go?"

"Feetfirst. That way you can point your toes and see where you're putting them."

"Makes sense."

Jacob put a hand on the suit's shoulder and slid his right foot down the suit's pant leg.

"Use the bar," Stu said.

"What?"

Stu patted the metal bar that ran behind the helmet. "It's meant as an assist so you can put both feet down there at the same time. It's easier if you just jump in that way."

"Ah." Jacob grabbed hold of the bar, and, sure enough,

he was able to point his toes down the pant legs and slide right in. "Cool," he said.

"Jacob, I'm not sure about this." It was Kelly. She and Chelsea had gone to the top of the stairs to watch him suit up. "Is this really the best thing we can do?"

"Kelly, I don't want to go a week without food. Do you?"

She crossed her arms over her chest. "I just think this is . . . Jacob, this is crazy."

"Hey," he said. "It's me."

"I know. That's what scares me."

For a moment, his smile wavered. He wanted to say, "Yeah, me, too." Instead, something from deep inside him spoke up. "Kiss me," he said.

"What?"

He couldn't believe he'd said it, either, but it was out there now. "You heard me. Last chance forever."

She didn't smile, but she grabbed hold of the balance bar above him and leaned in for a kiss. He felt her lips touch his, and he suddenly knew what he wanted. Her lips tasted like ash, but she tasted so good. He grabbed her hair and kissed her hard, so roughly it made her gasp. For a moment, she seemed on the verge of pulling back, but then she softened to his kiss.

When he released her, she slowly stood back up and opened her eyes. She was still chalky white from all the ash, but she looked different.

"I'll come back," he said. "I promise."

She nodded. "I'll see you at the *Einstein*."

"You can count on it." He glanced over at Stu. "Okay, what's next?"

"Arch your back. Put your arms through the holes first, then your head through there, at the back of the shoulders. We'll buckle you up once you're inside."

Jacob did as Stu told him. He slid into the armholes and let his fingers sort themselves out into the finger holes on the gloves. That done, he worked his head up into the helmet and twisted and twitched until he felt comfortably seated.

"Good?" Stu asked. His voice sounded tinny and far away.

"Yeah," Jacob said, almost yelling it. "Seal me up."

He'd had to keep his shoulders loose to reach the fingertips of the gloves while the back of the suit was open, but as soon as Stu and Juliette closed it up, he felt everything tighten up around him.

Looking out the faceplate was strange. From the outside, it had a shiny copper color, but it was as clear as window glass from the inside.

Then Stu got in front of him and waved in his face. "There's a red button in front of your chin. Lean forward and tap that with your chin."

Jacob did, and the suit lit up instantly. Digital displays lit up all over the inside of the faceplate. "Whoa!" he said.

"Pretty cool, right?" It took Jacob a second to realize it, but Stu was speaking in a normal voice again, no yelling.

"I can hear you now," Jacob said.

"Yep, I can hear you, too. See those displays in there? Those are suit diagnostics, your basic health screen, and I think this model has sensors to indicate movement in your area."

"Not this model," Juliette said. "This is one of the A2000s. Sensors weren't integrated until the A2400 series."

"Oh, right," Stu said. "Sorry, no sensors. No weapons, either."

"No weapons? Are you kidding?"

"Unfortunately not. But these early suits had a few tricks of their own. See that nozzle on top of your right wrist?"

Jacob raised his right arm, and was surprised as the mechanical assist kicked in.

"Yeah, that'll take a bit to get used to," Stu said. "The suit will amplify any movement you make. That's why you don't need weapons, really. When you get too close to a zombie just hit them. The mechanical assist will give you enough power to probably knock their heads off."

Jacob nodded, a futile gesture as they couldn't see him inside the helmet. "You were saying about this nozzle."

"Oh yeah. These early suits were developed as riot control gear. That nozzle fires a foam that hardens on contact. Spray it at a zombie's legs and it'll be like you threw a lasso at them. Just go easy on it, though. I don't think it carries very much."

"Right," Jacob said. "So, am I ready to go?"

"Yep, let me check something real quick." He ran to the top of the stairs and did something with one of the computers. "Okay," he called down. "Got it. The suit transmits all your vital signs here, and I've just locked your mic open. We'll be able to monitor your life signs continuously, and if you need anything, all you have to do is speak. We're listening."

"Alright, get me out of this cradle so I can go."

Stu hit another lever and it dropped Jacob to the deck. "That way," he said, and pointed Jacob to a large side panel in the wall. "I'll drop the door, but there's going to be zombies all over the place. Get through the door as soon as you can so we can close it back up."

"Got it."

"Jacob," Kelly said. He turned awkwardly in her direction. "You be careful."

She rose up on her toes and kissed the faceplate.

"I will," he said.

"You ready?" Stu said.

Jacob raised his fists and shook them.

"Okay, here goes."

The side panel heaved open. Sunlight flooded into the darkened hold of the APV, but Jacob's faceplate adjusted to the glare and made it so he didn't even have to squint. "Nice," he muttered. But he had to get right back on the clock because as soon as the door tilted far enough to create an opening, arms started reaching through the cracks on either side.

"Hit them hard and see if you can push them back," Stu said.

The next instant, that's exactly what Jacob did. The door tilted all the way open and he rushed the crowd waiting there. With his arms spread wide he scooped up four on each side and heaved them forward, even as he ran over another one.

"Close it," he said.

The door rose back into place quickly, but not before a zombie managed to wedge itself into the crack. Jacob circled back around, his movements stiff and awkward, yet he could feel the tremendous force tied up in every step, every swing of his arms. He grabbed the zombie by its hair and pulled back and down. He'd only intended to pull the thing out of the way of the door, but the mechanical assist snapped the thing's neck. The body fell out of the way, mouth opening and closing as its white eyes locked on Jacob, the head bent all the way back.

"Damn," Jacob said.

He turned toward the main hangar installation and started walking.

Right away a crowd of zombies gathered around him. Pushing the crowd back from the door had given him a false sense of security, and he reached his arms out to do it again.

It was a mistake, and he knew it right away.

His suit was incredibly powerful, but they were many, and their combined weight pushed him back against the hull of the APV so hard and so suddenly that it knocked the wind out of him.

They clawed at his faceplate and pulled at his armor, but they couldn't penetrate. He rooted his legs and found the mechanical assist there enough to make sure he didn't fall to the ground.

"Push them out of the way one at a time," Stu said. "That's the suit's advantage."

"Got it," Jacob said.

He stopped trying to swing his arms like clubs, and instead stuck his gloved hand in the mouth of the nearest zombie and ripped its face in two. Then he shoved that one to the side and started grabbing more zombies. Stu was right. When he focused on them one at a time, the zombies went flying around like birds.

Soon, he was moving again.

The surrounding herd was starting to notice him, and more and more zombies veered his way, but that was okay. He developed a rhythm. As soon as one got too close, he'd grab it, any part of it, and pull down as hard as he could. A few tries and he started to get the hang of bringing the whole zombie down without severing the thing's limbs, but even with practice that still happened. A few of the zombies were so badly decayed it couldn't be helped.

And so he plodded onward, pulling down any zombie that got too close, a juggernaut in the land of the dead.

CHAPTER 25

Jacob hadn't been able to see much except the roofline of the main hangar from the Squadron Training Center Building. But now that he was less than a hundred meters away, he could see all of it. It was really just a big empty barn, open on one side, large enough to house the giant Airbuses of the Old World's military. There was a smaller building off to the right side of it, but it looked like a rusting hulk. He could see leaning walls of corrugated tin forming wide corridors through the open ground floor of the building, but the whole thing looked shoddy and in ill repair.

He turned to the right and saw three aerofluyts in the distance. They were huge and graceful, like skyscrapers turned on their side, and it was hard to believe that something so majestic could be made impotent by a power source so grungy-looking.

It didn't help that there were zombies crawling all over everything.

"This place is a wreck," he said.

"Budget cuts," Stu answered back. "I'll be sure and tell Councilman Brooks when he comes to what you think of our accommodations."

"Yeah," Jacob said. "You do that."

"How you doing?"

A zombie got too close and Jacob grabbed the dead woman's face like he was palming a basketball and threw her to the ground, breaking her back. She lay doubled over, hands groping in the air for a piece of him.

Jacob took a few steps away from her, just so he didn't have to watch.

"I'm doing alright," he said. "No complaints. Now, tell me what I'm looking for."

"Okay, there should be a smaller building to one side of the hangar. Do you see that?"

"The one that looks like it's about to fall over?"

"That's the one," Stu said. "Now, the main floor of that building is made up of mostly access corridors for stuff that needs to go out to aerofluyt yards. There are stairs at different points on the ground floor. You'll need to take any one of them up to the fourth floor. That's the very top. That's where you'll find the flight controller's crow's nest. The main control switch for the entire flight line is there. Get there and I'll walk you through the process to reengage the flight line's power supply."

"Roger that," Jacob said.

He walked toward the hangar, slamming zombies out of the way as he plodded forward. When he reached the base of the building, he found himself facing half a dozen different corridors. There were no signs, no indications of which way to go.

"Shit," he said.

"What is it?" Stu said. He sounded worried.

"Nothing's wrong," Jacob answered. "But this is going to take some time."

There were zombies in every corridor, so it wasn't a matter of choosing the path of least resistance. It was all going to be difficult. Instead, he thought back to what Stu had said, that all these corridors were meant as access points to various parts of the flight line. The building above him seemed cobbled together through simple expediency, with little to no attention whatsoever given to aesthetics. And if the main point of the building was to give the flight line commander a clear view of the flight line, it stood to reason there would be a stairwell on the side of the building that faced the aerofluyts, so that the flight line commander could get to his post as quickly as possible.

So Jacob walked around the perimeter of the building until he came to the flight line side, and sure enough, there was a rickety-looking metal staircase leading up to the fourth floor.

For a moment, Jacob wondered if it could hold his weight. It looked awfully flimsy. But he really didn't have any other choice, and he knew it. Though he hated heights, he was going to have to climb.

As he was thinking, he felt hands fall on his back. He'd really almost stopped caring about the zombies, because even when they managed to grab him, like this one had, the suit allowed him to throw them off with ease. And, of course, he didn't have to worry about them clawing their way through the armor.

He handled this zombie the same way he'd handled the many others that had put their hands on him. He spun around sharply, so suddenly that the zombie didn't have a chance to let go, and sent the thing sprawling in the dirt. This zombie was no exception. Jacob turned quickly, and the thing tumbled into the wall, landing in a rumpled pile of twisted arms and legs against the base of the wall.

Jacob was about to turn back to the unpleasant task of climbing the decayed staircase when he stopped.

Something was glittering in the sunlight about sixty meters away, on the back side of the hangar, though what exactly it was he couldn't say because most of it was hidden from view by a small shed. He advanced on the shed, stopping every few meters to scan his surroundings. North of the hangar, out beyond the shed, there was nothing but open desert.

Desert and zombies as far as the eye could see.

But as he rounded the corner of the shed, he saw one of the oddest things he'd ever laid eyes on. "What the hell?"

"What is it?" Stu said.

"I don't know. Looks like the cars we saw all over Galveston."

"What?"

"Temple, I mean."

"Yeah, I know. What kind of vehicle? Do you mean an electric car?"

"I guess. Doesn't exactly look like the cars I saw back in Temple. Looks more like a miniature version of the APV you guys are in. Looks like it has a little two-wheeled trailer behind it, too."

"Jacob, I . . ."

"Stand by," Jacob said. "Let me check this thing out."

He walked around the vehicle, taking note of all the dents and bloodstains and bits of scalp and bone stuck in its edges. All the damage looked fresh; no rust; nothing wiped away. Jacob went back to the trailer and tried to work the handle. It wouldn't budge, so, figuring it was locked, he used the suit's mechanically assisted strength to pull the lid off the thing.

"Whoa!" he said.

"What is it?" Stu asked. "Come on, Jacob, talk to me. Tell me what you're looking at."

"Those power cells you were telling me about, what do they look like?"

"Power cells? For the APVs?"

"Yeah."

"They're about a third of meter long, maybe about as big around as your thigh."

"Are the ends bright red, and maybe look like they're wet?"

"Yes!" Stu said.

Jacob looked at the stash of twelve cylinders in front of him and thought they looked an awful lot like the capsules he remembered seeing in the tubes at the ruins of drive-through banks back in his salvage team days. Each one was mounted in a special cradle with a switch labeled LOCK/RELEASE next to each one.

Jacob hit one of the release buttons and the metal arms that held one of the cells in its cradle sighed open.

He picked it up, but even with the mechanical assists of his suit, the cell felt incredibly heavy. He turned it over and tried to read the yellow label on the outside of the thing, but the letters were too small.

"So I think I found those cells," he said.

There was a long silence on the other end before Stu finally answered. "Jacob," he said.

"Yeah?"

"Listen—avoid handling those things, okay? They are highly explosive."

"Uh, like how explosive?"

"One of those things will level a good part of this base. Probably half of the city."

"So, don't pick it up?"

"No. Don't do that."

"Okay. Uh, what if I already did?"

"You have . . . you have one of the cells?"

"Yeah."

"Shit," said Stu. "Okay, um, okay. Just stay there. We will come to you, okay?"

"How long's that gonna take? I thought you were going to need all day to charge."

"Yeah, damn it. Jacob, I don't know what to tell you. You're basically holding the equivalent of an atomic bomb in your hands. If that thing gets punctured . . . you'd need to be underground to survive the blast."

"Okay, so don't puncture it. Got it."

"Listen, it's going to take us a full day at least to get to you. Can you secure that thing back where you found it? Maybe we can come to you."

"Okay, I'll try."

Jacob turned the cell in the same direction he remembered it being when he pulled it out of the case and was about to lower it back down when he saw a group of zombies staggering across through the tall grass, their hands up in the familiar groping gesture of zombies reaching for a meal.

They only did that when a living person was present.

Jacob looked down and realized that he'd missed the big white elephant in the room. If this car was here, if the power cells were here, it had to be because Jordan Anson's henchmen were still here.

And the zombies were, as usual, a good indication of where they were.

"Stand by," Jacob said into his mic. "I may need to come up with another solution."

"What?" Stu said. "Jacob, talk to me. What's going on?"

But Jacob said nothing. He moved as quickly as the suit would allow, each foot feeling incredibly heavy, yet striking the earth with terrible power. This was what Frankenstein's creature must have felt with each step, Jacob thought. Such force, such ponderous, yet controlled force.

He made his way around the side of the flight line commander's building, toward the buildings south of the hangar, when he heard the sound of fully automatic gunfire.

He'd fired many such weapons himself. He knew the sound. And he knew the range such weapons had. Turning and looking back, he saw a large cluster of zombies closing in on the far side of the building, exactly where he'd been. He hadn't made it that far, maybe fifty or sixty meters. He still had five hundred meters to go at least before he reached the Squadron Training Center Building, where he and the others had taken shelter before. And the other structures were even farther away than that.

He saw the next few moments play out in slow motion in his mind. Anson had no doubt hired whoever was shooting those weapons. That meant they were pros. Mercenaries. They would return to their vehicle and see that it had been broken into. They would figure, rightly, that Jacob or one of the others was here, and that they had taken one of the power cells. They would figure that same person would make a break for it, and they knew that the APV was back around the Squadron Training Center. They would logically turn south toward that building and, because the suit compromised speed for power, they'd see Jacob plodding along out in the middle of nowhere, no cover, no place to hide. And, of course, their weapons would have no trouble taking him down at that distance. He really would be a sitting duck.

He heard the clatter of gunfire once again and knew what he had to do. He had to get to cover, and the only cover anywhere around here was back in the direction from which he'd come.

There was a shallow drainage ditch not far from him. He put the power cell down in it, and then ran for the hangar.

Or, rather, he tried to run. The suit wouldn't let him. The best he could manage was a hurried walk, each step pounding the earth with a mechanical-sounding *clank clank clank.*

By the time he reached the hangar, there were zombies everywhere.

Jacob knocked one down as he made his way to the structure. There were more up ahead, but they turned away from Jacob and started down one of the corridors. They were met with gunfire.

And then, just as Jacob reached the edge of the flight line commander's building, he saw two figures in black battle suits emerge from one of the corridors. Jacob realized in an instant that he was outgunned. Both figures had large rotary mini guns mounted on their arms, and while they still moved with the same plodding motion he managed in his suit, they were noticeably faster.

They saw him at the same time he saw them. One of the figures raised his mini gun and began to fire just as Jacob ducked into one of the corridors.

Jacob wasn't fast enough, though. A round caught the shoulder of his suit and penetrated the armor. He felt the round bite into his arm as he spun out of the way, but the damage was done. Jacob fell back against one of the corrugated tin walls and knew that the left arm of his suit was filling up with blood.

"Oh shit oh shit oh shit!" he said.

"Jacob!" It was Stu's voice, frantic with alarm. "What is it? Talk to me. I'm showing your suit's been ruptured. Pulse is climbing."

"Radio silence," Jacob said through clenched teeth. "Be quiet for a bit."

Jacob tried to move his left arm, but the gunshot wound had penetrated deep. Jacob could feel the suit closing around the wound, forming a tourniquet and cutting off the pain. He couldn't move his arm.

He groaned to himself, and then made his way down the corridor.

He reached a crossroads. A zombie was standing in the corridor to his left, uncertain of where to go. The way in front of him and to his right was wide open. He could go right, he figured, and end up underneath the rickety staircase that led up to the crow's nest, but he'd have nowhere to go from there.

No, he had to take the fight to the enemy.

He had no weapons, and he couldn't move his left arm, but he had to attack. He knew no other way.

He turned left, toward the zombie.

Jacob figured the only reason it couldn't figure out which way to go was because it had multiple targets to choose from. He could have crushed the zombie with a single blow, but instead he grabbed it by the gray remnant of its shirt and pushed it toward the next intersection.

One of the men in the black battle suits was standing there, trying to decide which way to go. Jacob pushed the zombie into the man and moved to the other side of the corridor, so he could get his right hand into the fight.

The man in the black battle suit knocked the zombie into the wall with a hard swipe of its hand. He watched the zombie crash into the wall and fall to the ground, and that was the break Jacob was looking for. He had no weapons, but he did have the foam spray that Stu had told him about. He raised his right arm and squeezed his ring and pinkie fingers into his palm, activating the foam. It jetted out like water from a fire hose. He could barely believe how much of it there was. It hit the man in the suit and immediately started to harden, locking his gun to his hip like he'd been caught in amber.

The man twitched and twisted like a zombie, but he couldn't break the foam's hold.

The second battle-suited man entered the intersection a moment later. Like his partner, he was armed with a mini gun on his arm. He turned it toward Jacob and began to fire just as Jacob hustled for the next intersection.

Jacob reached the corner and threw himself to the ground.

The suit was incredibly bulky, not at all meant for

ground fighting, but the dive got him out of the way of the bullets. They laced up the metal wall behind him, chewing the tin to bits.

Jacob ended up on his belly, just around the corner. He struggled like a bug to roll over, fighting to get to his feet.

He finally had to put his right hand on the ground and drag his knees forward to find his balance, but eventually he managed to get his legs under him and rock his weight back to the point he could stand up again.

His attention immediately turned to the second battle-suited figure. Jacob sensed the man would press his advantage. If the roles were reversed, that's what he would do. Jacob decided not to run. He knew if he was going to survive he'd have to take the fight to the attacker, so he moved to the corner and waited for the man to show himself.

Even though he was wearing one of the oldest models of the battle suit, Jacob had already sensed the confidence the suit gave the wearer. The second mercenary would no doubt recognize how old Jacob's suit was, and figure he had the advantage.

Jacob was counting on that.

He waited just around the corner for the man to present himself. As soon as he did, Jacob lunged forward. He hooked his right arm under the man's outstretched weapon arm, hooked it over, and wrenched down. He wasn't sure whether he broke the man's arm or not, but even through the suit he could sense the man's alarm and pain.

Jacob didn't give him time to get back on his feet. He stepped in front of the man, who was still on his back, struggling to get back on his feet, and used the last of the foam to hose down the man's faceplate.

The man was struggling frantically to scrape it off as Jacob turned away.

He lumbered down the corridor until he found a way out. He saw the aerofluyts off in the distance and that helped to orient him. He turned right. He also saw that the other eleven power cells were still back in the trailer he'd ransacked. They were maybe forty meters away.

Time for a decision, he told himself.

He could try to make a run for it, though that would no doubt leave him just as out of luck as before. The men in the black battle suits were professionals. They would break the bonds the foam had put them in, and they'd come after him with real guns. It would only be a few seconds before they found their way out of the corridors and filled him with gunfire. He'd be dead in minutes.

But he wasn't out of options. Jacob believed that to his core. As long as he was on his feet, he had options. He had choices to make.

He looked around.

Off to his right lay the city of El Paso. Stu and the others were working their way up from that direction. It would only be a matter of time before they made it to the *Einstein*.

Off to his left was basically nothing but desert. He had the hangar, and the flight line commanders' station, but little else.

And then he stopped.

That wasn't exactly true, was it? He had the car the two mercenaries in the battle suits had driven in on.

And their trailer was loaded down with the most dangerous explosive on the planet, wasn't it?

The answer to that question made up Jacob's mind. He raced forward and grabbed the first zombie he found, a woman of about twenty, wearing the remnants of a lacy top and a short miniskirt.

He couldn't move his left arm, but he did manage to throw his shoulder into the dead woman's back and press her face-first into a nearby wall. Holding her with the help of the suit, he removed the two remaining grenades he'd taken from Jordan Anson, stuck them into the crook of his dead left arm, and twisted the top of the cylinder all the way to the end.

Jacob wasn't positive, but he was guessing that was a minute.

The grenades set, he shoved them down into her underwear and pushed her toward the car.

Much to Jacob's satisfaction, the zombie behaved exactly as she was supposed to do. She plodded forward without any sense of direction, without any objective other than to eat the living.

That meant he wasn't safe here. He turned and ran as fast as the suit would let him for the culvert he'd seeded with the power cell just a little while earlier.

Zombies clustered around him, but Jacob didn't worry about it. The ones he could knock down, he did. The ones he couldn't avoid, he just ran over. They'd all be erased from the planet in less than a minute anyway.

He ran through a corridor until he emerged on the empty plain south of the hangar. From there he ran due south, looking for the drainage ditch where he'd hidden the power cell.

He found it just seconds later. Turning, he was surprised to see that he'd covered so much ground in such a short period of time. Even still, he barely had time to jump into the ditch and press himself into the pipe in its base.

A moment later, the zombie carrying the grenades detonated.

And right after that, the real explosion went off.

CHAPTER 26

"Jacob!"

He opened his eyes. Tried to anyway. He blacked out again.

"Jacob, come on, answer me, baby. Come on, please."

He stirred once more, and managed a groan.

"Jacob? Is that you? Come on, Jacob, it's Kelly. Speak to me. Let me know you're okay."

"Can't move," he managed to say.

"Jacob, where are you? We'll come get you."

"In a ditch," he said. "Inside a pipe. South of the . . . south of the hangar."

"Okay, baby, you hold on. We are on the way."

The grenades he'd detonated outside the Squadron Training Center had left his ears ringing, but that was nothing compared to the tornado alert siren that was currently blaring in his ears. He had barely heard Kelly, even though he had little doubt they'd cranked the gain up on his headset all the way. He blinked until his vision came back into focus. Or at least as close as it was going to get. He was still seeing double, and everything seemed to be floating around him. He focused on the medical diagnostic report screen at the bottom left corner of his faceplate. Blood pressure was 131/84. Pulse was 74. Breathing rate was normal. Temperature was 99.4. So he was fine.

Except that he felt like shit.

He might have blacked out again. He wasn't sure. But he did finally come around sometime later when he felt hands on his boots, tugging him out of the pipe.

He was too shell-shocked to resist, or even to call out. They tugged on his legs and, gradually, he started to slide into the daylight. They rolled him over and faces hovered above him, but he couldn't see them through all the cracks in the faceplate.

Instead he felt himself slipping back into unconsciousness, and as he did, memories floated up to the surface of his mind like soap bubbles. He remembered Kelly at sixteen, giggling at his lame-ass jokes. He remembered the first time she got drunk and tried to sing but only managed to sound like somebody was strangling a cat. And the sight of her in a black bikini, sitting on a wooden rail above the dunking booth at the Arbella Summer Harvest Fair. He'd nearly thrown his arm out just to get a glimpse of her coming out of that water barrel all soaking wet. She'd taunted him the entire time, too, knowing exactly what he was there for.

While his mind was doping him with memory, Kelly and Stu had flipped him over and started working the buckles loose on his suit. When they cracked it open, he was hit with a wall of heat and the stench of a burning city.

"What . . . ?" he said, as they pulled him out.

He separated from the suit, and though they tried to

hold him, he fell onto a black carpet of burned grass. It crunched against his cheek and stained his hands with ash.

"Let's get him up," Kelly said.

They raised him to his feet and Jacob felt such a head rush that he nearly vomited.

And then he looked around at what was left of the city and nearly vomited again.

The land was scorched all around him. The Squadron Training Center was fully engulfed in flame. The bricks of its face glowed red. Its windows were bright orange with fire. Everywhere he turned, he saw the charred bodies of zombies. Thousands and thousands of them. Columns of smoke rose from the ground. The hangar where he'd fought the two mercenaries in battle suits wasn't even there anymore. And farther away, the two nearest aerofluyts were also fully engulfed in flames.

"Did I do all that?" Jacob said.

"Yeah, baby," said Kelly, laughing despite her tears. "Yeah, you did."

"They're not gonna bill me for that, are they?"

"Just shut up, Jacob. God, you had me so worried. The explosion nearly flipped the APV. I thought for sure you were dead."

"Hey," he said. "It's me. I did get shot, though. God, I could use a nap."

They carried him across the scorched desert and set him up on the medical couch next to Brooks. The man had regained consciousness. He was clearly in a lot of pain, but he seemed alert and dealing with it.

"Was that you?" he asked Jacob.

"Afraid so. I just destroyed a lot of your expensive toys, I think."

Brooks tried to laugh, but it turned into a grimace of pain.

"You alright?" Jacob asked.

"No," Brooks said. "Well, better than you, but no."

Kelly appeared at his side. Her cheek was bruised and there was still ash in her hair and on her eyelashes, but she was smiling. "All your vital signs look good," she said. "I can't believe you do the things you do."

"Yeah, well, you know. All in a day's work, right?"

Beside her, Stu laughed. To Kelly, he said, "Your boyfriend is a tank. Four broken ribs, a concussion, multiple gunshot wounds. Good grief." He looked Jacob square in the face. "By any rights, you should be dead."

Jacob coughed in response.

"What were you thinking?" Kelly said.

"Just wanted to get out of life alive," he said. He found Stu hovering over a computer. "Did you get the power cell I found?"

"Yeah, I got it. It's installed and charging up now. We should be at full power in less than twenty minutes."

Jacob nodded to himself. "That's good. Alright." He put a hand on Kelly's arm. She glanced at it, but didn't make a move to push him away.

Instead, she kept her fingers on his forehead and even brushed the hair away from his sweat-stained face. "You are so stupid," she said.

"Yeah, but you heard him, right? He called me your boyfriend."

She laughed. "How about we take that one step at a time, okay?"

From behind Kelly, someone shrieked in frustration.

"Who was that?" Jacob asked.

"Chelsea," Kelly said, her expression turning serious.

"What is wrong with you people?" Chelsea said, storming into the small circle of light around the medical couches. "Seriously. You're making jokes. The whole reason I came here was to clear my father's name. Now the notebooks are gone. I have nothing left to prove his innocence. Nothing. All of this. All of this was for nothing."

She stood there looking at them, daring them to say something.

No one did. Kelly reached down and squeezed Jacob's hand, but it wasn't the action of a lover. He seemed to sense that without the words. He knew Kelly better than anyone, and he knew her heart was breaking for the girl.

Stu and Juliette had suffered, too. They'd lost their boss, and a beloved friend. And this girl, she was the last surviving member of the Walker family. To see her in such pain, in such rage, was, in a way, to relive the death of their friend and mentor.

Brooks, once again, was the cypher. Jacob gave Kelly's hand another squeeze, then turned his head to look at the older man. Brooks had turned his head to find Chelsea out beyond the circle of light, but the pain was obviously flaring up again.

He called out to her, "Chelsea, I read your father's research."

Silence.

"Chelsea?" Brooks said.

The next instant, the girl was at his side, jabbing a finger in his face. "Don't you dare even speak his name, you son of a bitch. You have no right, no right at all! I hope you fucking die on that couch, you bastard. I hope you suffer for the things you did."

Brooks climbed painfully up on his elbows. The action forced him to wince and close his eyes. When he opened them, tears ran down his face from the pain.

Stu rushed to the man's side. "Hey, hey," he said. "Go easy, Dr. Brooks."

"Step out of the way," he said. "I'm fine. Chelsea, will you please come back here? Please, child."

She came back to the side of the bed. From where he lay, Jacob could see her face, and he was pretty sure he'd never seen such naked hatred before. Not even during their time among the Slavers.

"I did try to put the blame for the wreck of the *Darwin* on your father, child, you're right about that."

Chelsea looked like she was about to claw his eyes out.

"Please," he said. "Hear me out. I did do that, and for that error in judgment, I am deeply sorry. I did a disservice to your family based on my scientific prejudice and my personal greed. I was wrong, and I will make that right."

"What are you saying?" Chelsea asked.

"Your aunt never got a chance to tell you about us, did she?"

"What about you?"

Brooks winced again at his pain, but pushed on. "Chelsea, after your father started talking up the Triune Movement, your aunt and I found ourselves constantly showing up at the same functions, the same conventions, giving talks at the same dinners, always saying the same things against your father. I can't tell you how many nights we sat over dinner together, talking about the crazy things your father was saying, and all the while growing closer. Chelsea, I loved your aunt. And I think she loved me. We just couldn't make the long distance thing work, what with her here and me in Temple. It was hard, and eventually, it just got too hard to work."

Chelsea stared down at him with contempt still plain on her face. For a moment, Jacob thought she might actually spit on him.

"Please," Brooks said, still fighting through his pain. "This is important. Do you remember when Jordan Anson asked me to get your father's notebooks?"

The girl nodded.

"When I did, I noticed that she'd been copying them into her data bank. It was stored in her personal account, but I thought I knew what her password would be—and I was right." He smiled at the memory of that, or perhaps of his memory of how the password came to be. He winced again, and then said, "I have all the notebooks on my tablet over there. Everything."

Chelsea turned to the table behind her and picked up the tablet Jacob had seen him reading earlier.

"It's all there," Brooks said again. "Everything your father wrote. I've read it."

"And you're locking it away as evidence, right?"

"It is evidence," Brooks said. "It's evidence the world needs to see."

"What?" Chelsea said.

"When we get back to Temple, I'm going to make sure the world knows what your father had to say. I still don't buy it all, not all of it, but if Miriam thought enough of it to give it a fair shake . . . well, that's good enough for me."

"That'll ruin your reputation," Stu said.

"Probably get me kicked off the Council, too. Might even be enough for the board of directors at my company to vote me out. We'll see."

Chelsea said nothing to that. She hung her head and went forward to the seating area. She sat down with her back to Jacob and the others and started to cry. In the stillness of the darkened hold, he could hear her sobbing.

A moment later, all the lights came on. The air-conditioning started up, blowing waves of cool air over Jacob's sweaty face.

"Looks like we're back in business," Stu said. "You feel well enough to come up front with me?"

"Yeah," Jacob said. "I think so. Kelly, can you help me?"

He sat up and dropped his feet over the edge of the med couch. He rested an arm on Kelly's shoulder and slid off the edge.

"Jacob, I'm not sure about this. You should stay in bed."

"I'm fine," he said. "Stu there said all my vitals showed normal."

"Your blood pressure's a little high, but other than that, yeah, you're okay."

"See?" Jacob said to Kelly. He flashed a smile at her. "I'm good."

They went up front to the cockpit. Stu slid into the driver's seat, and Juliette took the spot next to him. Jacob looked out the windshield at a scorched wasteland. Most of the fires in the buildings had gone out, leaving only blackened skeletons without roofs and windows.

"What do you think the damage is?" Jacob asked. "You think anybody was topside for this?"

"Doubtful," Stu said. "The entire city had already gotten the order to head down below into the safe zones.

If they were above ground, they were doing it contrary to orders."

"What about the herd?" Already he could see figures coated in ash, slogging their way through the burned-out wreckage that had been the air base and most of northern El Paso. There weren't many, but he could see more off to the east.

"I'd say you wiped out about half of one percent of the herd," Stu said. "We're gonna see a whole lot more before this is all over."

"So what's the plan?"

"I was thinking we head to Temple. See if the good doctor back there is true to his word."

"I thought you said we didn't have any food."

"We don't, but now that we've got the power cell fueling us, we can do this trip in less than a day."

Jacob turned to Kelly. "What do you think? You game?"

She put her hand on top of his and stroked the back of his knuckles with her thumb. It was an old gesture he'd forgotten about, though the memory came back to him immediately. She looked right into his eyes. "Let's do it."

He smiled, then gave Stu a pat on the shoulder. "You heard the lady. Let's do it."

"You got it."

Stu pushed the throttle level, and the vehicle lurched forward into a brave new world.